AND DON'T MISS THESE EXCITING
TIME PASSAGES ROMANCES NOW
AVAILABLE FROM JOVE!

*W*AITING
FOR
*Y*ESTERDAY

Jenny Lykins

JOVE BOOKS, NEW YORK

WAITING FOR YESTERDAY

A Jove Book / published by arrangement with
the author

PRINTING HISTORY
Jove edition / August 1997

The Putnam Berkley World Wide Web site address is
http://www.berkley.com

ISBN: 0-515-12129-0

A JOVE BOOK®
Jove Books are published by The Berkley Publishing Group,
200 Madison Avenue, New York, New York 10016.
JOVE and the "J" design are trademarks
belonging to Jove Publications, Inc.

PRINTED IN THE UNITED STATES OF AMERICA

10 9 8 7 6 5 4 3 2 1

For

Linda Massie Hay
My sister, my friend

WAITING
FOR
YESTERDAY

Prologue

"WES HAS GONE to fetch the doctor, Elizabeth. Are the pains coming closer together?"

Chase Alston knew before asking. The pains were far too close. Even as he asked, a fine sheen of sweat appeared on his wife's face, dampening the few dark hairs that had somehow managed to escape the tight knot that perpetually sat on the crown of her head. Her lips tightened into a hard line as the pain increased, and the color drained from her face, but not so much as a whimper escaped into the quiet, chilly room.

Wes would never be able to fetch the doctor in time to deliver the baby. Chase would have to deliver it himself. How ironic.

"May I have a sip of water, Chase?" His wife's voice, though strained with pain, still held that ever-meek tone he'd learned to hate.

Color returned to Elizabeth's face as the labor pain

subsided. Chase rose from his seat by the fire and made his way to the kitchen without a backward glance. He jerked the pump handle three times, snatched a glass from the sideboard, then shoved it under the spewing water. He stared out the frosted window, past his dark reflection and into the inky blackness. He wouldn't allow his jumbled thoughts to focus. He wouldn't think about delivering a baby—*this* baby. He would raise it, he'd be a good father to it, he'd love it as best he could. But, dear God, don't ask him to deliver it.

It wasn't until the icy water poured over his hand that he snapped back to attention.

When he returned to the parlor he found his wife grimacing, in the throes of another labor pain. Watching her face silently contort, watching her huge belly contract into a tight, hard ball, he could almost feel his heart soften toward her, could almost want to touch her.

Almost.

When her body again relaxed against the pillows, he gave her the glass of water. She took a tiny sip and looked up at him.

"Thank you," she said breathlessly.

He ignored her gratitude. It was the last thing he wanted.

"The doctor won't get here in time. Hopefully Wes will stop at the Parkers' long enough to send Alice here." He threw another log on the fire, partly to vent his frustration, partly in an effort to warm the room. Since the bedroom had no fireplace, he had set up the bed in the parlor for Elizabeth's lying-in.

"Everything you'll need," she gasped with the onset of another pain, "is on the chair in our room."

Of course she would have everything prepared. He marched the few steps to the bedroom and instantly found the neat stack of linens, tiny blankets, a tiny gown, twine, a knife. Everything perfectly laid out. Perfectly embroidered, perfectly folded, perfectly stacked, all by his perfect wife.

Perfect.

He grabbed the pile of necessities and returned to the parlor, laying things out as he might need them, forcing his mind not to think. Then the tiniest hint of a moan grabbed his attention.

She had to be in unbearable pain to have allowed the low moan to escape. His wife never gave in to pain. In the time they'd been married he had never once heard her complain. Not even the time she'd sliced her hand wide open on that canning jar. Not even when it got infected.

He turned up the wick in the kerosene lamp and studied her face. She didn't look good. The lack of color in her face couldn't bode well. Dark circles smudged the pale skin beneath her eyes and he knew he needed to check her, but he had no idea what to look for.

He'd delivered his share of colts and calves before, even a lamb or two. There'd been one delivery where he'd had to pull a colt out of its mother because it was coming feet first and the mare was dying. He knew the head should come first.

"Elizabeth"—he forced a tone more gentle than any he'd used since their wedding night—"do you know if this is normal?"

She rode out the rest of the pain, lips pressed in a firm, white line, beads of sweat dotting her forehead and upper lip. When the rock-hard, pointed bulge of her stomach finally rounded out, she gasped for breath and shook her head no.

"No? Do you mean you don't know or it's not normal?"

But he was talking to himself. Elizabeth had fainted.

From what he could tell, she was better off unconscious. But he was worried now. This couldn't be a normal labor.

Damn her! If she'd only told him when the pains had begun this morning, he could have sent for the doctor in plenty of time. But she'd kept that minor detail to herself, cleaning an already sanitary house until she could no longer stand. And now she was left with no one to deliver this baby except a husband who hadn't laid a hand on her since their wedding night.

Chase paced a few steps in the spotless parlor, then stopped to study her face again. She looked even paler than before, if that was possible. Still unconscious, she almost seemed to be sleeping. Now would be the best time to check her, when he wouldn't offend her . . . delicate sensibilities. For the life of him, he didn't know why he should care.

He pulled back the covers and lifted her heavy flannel gown. For a moment he stood stock-still and gaped at the first pregnant belly he'd ever seen.

He hadn't let himself imagine what her stomach might look like. He hadn't wanted to know. The large bulge forever covered by layers of cotton or wool looked nothing like this huge ivory mound with the skin stretched so painfully taut. As he watched, the bulge changed shape, coming to a point, signaling the onset of another contraction. He lowered the gown, not certain if Elizabeth would rouse from her faint.

She came to with a great gasp for air, her fists wadding the bedsheets into twisted knots. She held her breath, her body absolutely motionless, until, finally, her stomach once again softened.

"Elizabeth." Chase dipped a cloth in a bowl of cool water, wrung it out, then wiped the beads of sweat from her face. "I have to check you. I need to see what's wrong."

Panic filled her soft gray eyes, and she grabbed for the sheet that no longer covered her.

"No, Chase. I'll be fine. You have no need to check me."

The old, familiar irritation boiled up in him, a far more comfortable feeling than the moments of tenderness he'd allowed himself to feel.

"Don't be ridiculous. Someone has to deliver this baby. I am the only option. Unless you think I can do this with a blindfold over my eyes, I suggest you get over your belated prudishness and let me see where the baby is."

"No!" She shook her head back and forth and held her gown tight against her body. She continued to deny him until another pain overtook her. He watched every muscle in her body tense against the contraction, fighting it instead of allowing it to happen. A startled, pain-filled gasp coincided with a gush of clear fluid that spread across her gown and soaked both her and the bed linens. She fainted again.

Chase wasted no time. He struggled to remove the heavy, clinging flannel, but after just a few seconds impatience got the best of him. He grabbed the neck of the gown and ripped it down the middle. As the fabric separated, deep in his mind a resentful thought occurred to him: This was only the second time he'd ever seen his wife naked.

Another contraction hardened her stomach, but this time Elizabeth failed to come out of her swoon. Alarmed, Chase waited a full minute, until her stomach rounded, a sign he'd already come to learn meant the pain had subsided. Without wasting a second, he slid his hand into the birth canal, hoping to feel the baby's head.

Nausea turned his stomach and sweat ran in rivulets from his temples when he reached into the birth canal, searching for signs of a head, and came in contact with a tiny, perfectly formed foot.

"Dear God! Help me!" he prayed heavenward. "Send someone to help me!"

Chapter 1

JANUARY
1997

Barrett Overbrook stood across the
street from the church, the icy, driving rain already soaking through her red cashmere sweater and short black
skirt, stinging her face like hundreds of tiny needles,
carving frigid trails down her back. She'd left her coat in
the rental car, as well as her umbrella. She didn't really
feel the rain anyway. She didn't feel anything at all.

Through the cold downpour, in the early-evening
gloom, the warm yellow light glowing from the church
windows looked like incandescent bars of gold. Barrett
walked a few feet farther, unconcerned about the puddles she trudged through or the effect on her favorite
pair of suede heels.

The huge glass front of the church revealed six elabo-
rate floral arrangements, two of which flanked the center
aisle. She positioned herself on the sidewalk until she

had a clear view down the aisle, all the way to the front of the sanctuary.

Even with his back to her, Barrett recognized the tall, well-built figure of her ex-boyfriend standing beneath the floral arch. Andrew, handsome as always in his black tux, stood beside the chic, perfectly dressed bride in her designer ivory satin. The name of the designer escaped Barrett. She wasn't into snob appeal. But she knew exactly what the gown looked like, even through the blur of the downpour.

She should. She'd helped her twin sister pick it out.

Elizabeth, of course, had gained permission from Barrett to date Andrew after she'd broken off with him. Within just a few months there'd been an engagement announcement, and Elizabeth had properly requested that her identical twin be maid of honor at the wedding. When Barrett told her she would be in Europe with her job from October through December and would be unable to make the wedding, Elizabeth had managed to appear convincingly disappointed.

But here Barrett was, back a month early because she'd finished the overseas project in record time. She'd flown into Chicago, stopped at her apartment long enough to repack, book another flight out, then catch a cab back to the airport. She'd arrived at Cincinnati's airport in plenty of time to go to the wedding. But instead of going to her parents' home to get dressed, she'd driven around for hours, trying to collect her thoughts and make sense of all the emotions bombarding her.

And now here she stood, in a freezing torrential downpour, watching her sister marry her old boyfriend.

As she watched, her sister turned, then Andrew lifted

the wispy veil. Barrett's stomach muscles tightened. Their first kiss as man and wife.

Her reaction surprised her. Her brain said she couldn't care less, while her stomach wanted to go somewhere and throw up.

Icy streams of water ran down her face and neck, sculpting her hair into inky spikes over her eyes and against her cheeks. An unfamiliar, unexpected burning behind her eyelids jolted her into action before hot, salty streaks of tears could mingle with the rain. While the downpour continued, while the rain sucked every ounce of warmth from her skin, setting chill bumps to dancing and teeth to chattering, she shoved a handful of clinging black chin-length hair out of her eyes and spun around to leave.

"Whoa, there!"

A little old man in a blue-and-green plaid felt hat and a navy overcoat, carrying a huge golf umbrella, did a quick sidestep to avoid being bowled over by Barrett's escape.

"Oh! I'm so sorry!" Barrett grabbed both of his arms to keep him from toppling. She hadn't even heard him approach.

"My fault entirely, little lady. I can never resist stopping and peeping in at a wedding. Warms my heart to see new couples in love starting out in life." He offered a fragile hand to Barrett. "The name's Gideon."

"Barrett Overbrook," Barrett said as she took his hand, surprised at the strength squeezing her fingers.

"You married?" he queried in a conversational tone.

Barrett snorted. "Not hardly." She grimaced at her rudeness and shot the old guy an apologetic look.

"Here, now" —he held the umbrella over her head— "you're soaked to the skin. Why, you'll catch your death. Where's your umbrella, child?"

Barrett waved vaguely down the street. "In the car. I was just going."

"Well, let me walk you. Not that you could get much wetter."

"This is so nice of you," Barrett told him as they headed back down the street. "Do you have far to go?"

The old gentleman placed his hand on her forearm and patted it. She suddenly felt all warm and cozy, like she used to when Nana was alive.

"No. I came into town to meet someone. And I walk every day. Rain or shine, through snow or sleet. Sort of like the postal service." He laughed at his predictable joke. Barrett smiled while she dug through her purse for the car keys.

"Well," she said when they arrived at the car, "I'm sorry I tried to mow you down." She opened the door, slid into the seat, and fired up the engine. "Thanks for walking me to the car. It's raining awfully . . ." Barrett never finished her sentence. She actually forgot what she was saying when she turned and found that the sweet old man had disappeared without a trace. "Gee," she said as she glanced up and down the street, "wish I was in that good a shape."

She yanked the car into drive and had to turn the wipers on high when she pulled out into the street. Dread kept her from turning the wheel when she should have circled the block and headed toward the family home. She didn't want to explain to her parents why she hadn't gone to the wedding, didn't want to hear it described in minute detail. She didn't want to see the pride the Drs. Overbrook had in their surgeon son and med student daughter. Not only had those children followed in their parents' footsteps, but now they were both respectably married and in a position to start producing tiny little doctors of their own.

Barrett, on the other hand, had finished college in three and a half years, then landed an entry-level job with FutureTech Software. Within two and a half years she'd achieved her master's in computer science. This last trip to Europe had gotten her promoted to Senior Director. None of which the medically minded Overbrooks could bring themselves to identify with. She could still hear her father's comment on her degree: "For God's sake, Barrett. Computers?" Like he'd just said a four-letter word.

On the spur of the moment, Barrett swerved left at the fork in the road and took the on-ramp to Interstate 71.

She had no idea where she was headed; she would drive all night if the mood struck her. All that mattered was how liberating it felt to be so close to her family and yet to be driving away from them. Her censuring parents, condescending older brother, and perfect twin sister would never know she'd been within criticizing distance.

She drove northeast toward Columbus, plowing on through the pouring rain. During a brilliant flash of rare January lightning, she saw a sign that read, SERENITY—A BED-AND-BREAKFAST—2.5 MI.

Suddenly the storm, jet lag, the unexpected emotions stirred by her sister's wedding all converged to drain her of her last bit of energy. She whipped the car onto the exit and followed the signs to the inn with the inviting name. Serenity. Just what her troubled thoughts needed. The place sounded like heaven.

It took her at least ten minutes to squint her way down the narrow, winding road. The windshield wipers hammered at top speed, and still she could barely see the pavement between swipes. Finally the high beam of the headlights swung onto a quaint little sign in the shape of a house with matching turrets at each corner that announced she'd arrived at her destination.

And not a moment too soon. Her eyes burned, her tense shoulders nearly touched her earlobes, and her hands hurt from gripping the wheel. The welcome light in the sconces flanking the front door beckoned her to come in and relax. Barrett turned into the drive, noticing as she pulled around to the front door that the sign had been a replica of the house. She yanked her tote bag out of the backseat. The rest of her bags could wait until the rain let up. Just as she was about to make a dash for the porch, the front door opened. A huge, striped umbrella blossomed to its full size, and a pair of galoshes-covered feet carried it to the car.

"I saw you pull up the drive. Thought you might need some help."

"Thanks." Barrett slammed the car door and ducked her head to keep from hitting it on the umbrella as they hustled to the porch.

"Thanks. I was just starting to dry . . . You!" Barrett's gratitude turned to surprise when the same little old man she'd nearly knocked over in front of the church peered up at her as he shook out the umbrella.

"Well, well. Didn't think we'd meet again so soon,"

he said, pushing open the front door and waving her through. He had a certain tranquility about him that made him seem not at all surprised to see her again, let alone in this out-of-the-way place.

"You must be my guardian angel tonight." She laughed. "Are you staying here?"

A calm little smile tilted his lips.

"Nope. I run the place. Just got back myself."

"Huh." Barrett smiled at the old guy. "Small world."

"Isn't it, though?" He slid the umbrella into a painted milk can. "You're in luck. The best room in the house is vacant. How long'll you be staying?"

Barrett blinked in surprise as she followed him through the parlor and into an office. She hadn't thought that far in advance.

"Why don't we do one night at a time? If that's all right with you."

"That'll be fine. Not a lot of guests this time of year." The sweet old man handed her the guest book turned to a new page and motioned for her to sign it.

"Well, Miss"— he looked at the name she'd signed— "Overbrook, the downstairs bedroom is ready." He lifted her tote bag and headed for the parlor. "I'll show you to your room. Do you need anything else out of your car?"

"No, thanks, Mr. . . . Gideon, wasn't it?"

"Yep."

"Mr. Gideon. I've got everything I need for tonight."

He escorted her across the parlor to a door that opened directly onto the bedroom.

"This is such an unusual house," she said, looking around. "It isn't at all what it seems on the outside."

"That's part of its charm, or so I'm told." Mr. Gideon

set her tote bag on the bed, then shuffled back to the door. He waved an arthritic hand. "The home was built in the late 1800s. A simple farmhouse originally. The only source of heat in the winter was the fireplace there." He cocked his head toward the huge fireplace, so unlike the small, shallow things in new homes. "These rooms—the parlor, this bedroom, and the kitchen back there—were the original house. First family turned the attic into three bedrooms when the babies started coming. Then about fifty years ago some wise guy added the turrets to each side of the front to make four more rooms." He stood and stared toward the turret office, scratching the back of his head, as if deep in thought. His fingers left little tufts of thinning hair standing straight out. "Well, I'll let you get settled in. As a guest you have the run of the house. Feel free to rummage in the kitchen if you get hungry. Breakfast will be at eight on the back porch. Another wise guy glassed it in, put tile on the floor and started calling it a Florida room about twenty years ago. But dress it up any way you want, it's still a back porch." The tone of Mr. Gideon's voice spoke volumes about what he thought of the "improvements" made by those "wise guys."

"Thanks." Barrett tried hard not to smile. "Breakfast at eight."

He waved a hand and shuffled off into the darkness in the direction of the kitchen. Barrett shut the door, put her tote bag on the floor, then fell back onto the bed. She closed her mind and stared at the old-fashioned milk-glass light fixture on the ceiling until her eyes burned. Some moth that had met its fate in the light made a silhouette in the fixture. One lone tear inched its way from the corner of her eye into the hair at her temple before she squeezed her eyes shut and willed away the nameless pain.

Gideon watched her stare at the ceiling, his presence unseen and unfelt. His old man's body had returned to its wondrous, angelic form, though he cared not what form he took.

He looked with love on this poor, confused, misguided child who'd lost her only earthly source of unconditional love so many years ago when her grandmother had died.

He felt her confusion, the unbearable sense of loneliness she constantly refused to acknowledge, her sense of being misplaced in the tapestry of life. And he knew without a doubt that, left to lead the life she presently had, she would live a solitary, empty, and eventually bitter existence.

He looked at the girl, twenty-five now and beautiful, with her warm, tawny skin and her silky black hair cut in a horizontal line from her chin. Her dark brown eyes, inherited along with her other coloring from an Iroquois ancestor, sparkled with life when she allowed herself to be happy, which wasn't often.

This was a woman so driven to prove her worth to her family, yet be her own person, that she worked eighteen-hour days, sometimes seven days a week. She'd received such scant love and attention from her busy parents that she'd vowed never to marry and subject more children to such a life, never realizing that she wouldn't be like the clinical parents her mother and father were. A cynicism about love and family had hardened her heart until she avoided anything resembling domestic life. Indeed, this lonely woman who lived to work and sleep had converted her kitchen into an office, with only a small refrigerator and a microwave oven to heat her meals.

Since Barrett's childhood, Gideon had guided her toward what her soul needed for happiness, but she had fought his will with an amazing strength of her own. She forced herself into fierce independence and became more alone with each passing day. He could see now that drastic measures would have to be taken to save Barrett Overbrook from herself.

He felt her begin to drift into an exhausted slumber. But before she could sleep he caused her thoughts to become more disturbing, more confusing, until she roused from her lethargy and rose, troubled, from the bed. She would not sleep this night until he was ready for her to. In fact, she would not sleep this night at all.

Barrett snatched the handle of her tote and swung the bag onto the antique vanity table. She'd been all but asleep just moments earlier, and now she found herself wide awake. She rummaged through the tote, pulling out a silk nightgown and her cosmetics bag, trying not to let her mind settle too long on any one thought. She'd been using that tactic so long she was an expert at it.

But tonight her thoughts defeated her best efforts. Try as she might, she couldn't ignore them any longer.

Why had she not made a go of it with Andrew? Why did she never feel truly happy? Why did everything she touch turn to crap? Yes, crap! For that was exactly what it was. The questions raced through her mind like one continuous ticker tape.

Why, why, why?

Shaking her head to clear it, Barrett tossed the turquoise nightgown across the bed and headed for the kitchen. Maybe a snack would get her mind off things—Mr. Gideon had told her to feel free to raid the refrigerator.

A low-burning lamp in the parlor lit her way to the kitchen, where a nightlight glowed above the counter. She kicked off her still-damp suede heels so she wouldn't make a racket and padded across the modern linoleum floor.

"There's fresh-baked pound cake in the cupboard. Or would you rather have a sandwich?"

Barrett jumped a foot, stifling a yelp of alarm. Once her heart started beating again she looked around for the source of the disembodied voice.

"And there's soft drinks in the icebox unless you want a cup of coffee. Sorry, I don't keep the hard stuff."

She followed the voice and found Mr. Gideon sitting on a cozy, overstuffed couch in a corner of the "wise guy's" glassed-in porch. He held a big glass of milk, and a half-eaten slice of pound cake littered the plate on the coffee table in front of him. The only light in the room was what spilled over from the meager night-light in the kitchen.

He looked up as she stood in the doorway, her hand still pressing against her thrumming heart.

"Or there's fresh fruit. Apples. Bananas. There might still be some grapes in there."

He started to rise, but Barrett waved him back down.

"Don't get up. I'll . . . I'll have what you're having."

"Pound cake to the right of the stove, glasses to the left of the sink." He leaned back into the cushy sofa and took a big swig of milk.

Barrett gathered up her snack and carried it to the porch.

"Mind if I join you?"

"Be insulted if you didn't." Mr. Gideon waggled a hand toward the matching chair across from him. "Have a seat there. Here now, you've got nothing on your feet! And you're still in those damp clothes. Do you have a death wish, child?" He pulled a folded lap blanket from the arm of the couch and tossed it to her. "Put that around you before you sit down."

Barrett set her snack on the coffee table and wrapped herself in the soft blanket. An immediate, heavenly warmth melted the last of the ice running through her veins and warmed her all the way to her toes.

"Thanks. I didn't realize how much I needed that."

"Yep. That's a problem with people. Not knowing how much they need something. So you say you're not married?"

Barrett looked at the old guy for a second and tried to read him. He was an odd one, but strangely enough she felt completely comfortable with him. More than comfortable. Safe.

"No, I'm not married."

"How about your family? Brothers? Sisters?"

"I have an older brother. Three years older. And a twin sister."

"Identical?"

"Uh-huh," Barrett hummed through a mouthful of pound cake.

"You girls have that bond or psychic thread or whatever I hear tell about twins having?"

Barrett shook her head and laughed. "No. I think

somebody made that up. The only thing psychic about me is knowing when I'm going to sneeze."

"You ever switch roles to fool your friends?"

"No, not really. We tried a couple of times when we were really little, but we could never pull it off."

"How come?"

"Well, we're identical in looks, but we couldn't be more different in personality."

"How so?"

"Well, Elizabeth is perfect, and I'm . . . not."

"Perfect?"

"You know. Everything comes easy to her. She never does anything wrong. She always makes the right decisions. You know. Perfect. Mom and Dad never had to get on her case, and Browning never harassed her."

"Browning?" Gideon gave her a puzzled look.

Barrett felt the blood rise in her face, as it did every time people noticed the names.

"Yes. Our parents had the nerve to name their three kids Elizabeth, Barrett, and Browning. They named my brother after Robert and then thought they were being chic instead of stupid when my sister and I came along."

"Well, just be glad they weren't admirers of Edgar Allan Poe. Or the Three Stooges," he said with a half smile.

Barrett nearly snorted the milk out her nose. She managed to swallow, with no small effort.

"You've got a point. I never thought of it that way."

A companionable silence fell between them while Barrett finished her cake. She scrunched back into the softness of the chair, tucked her legs into the seat, and watched the rain run in uneven sheets down the glass walls of the porch.

"Are you and your brother close?" Mr. Gideon resumed their conversation. Barrett thought his voice had the same inflections as Nana's.

"No. Not at all. I guess we just don't have anything in common. He was a bookworm, I was a jock. He went into medicine, I don't even have a medicine cabinet. Elizabeth followed in his footsteps, and Mom and Dad have never let me forget it." Barrett's mind skimmed over memories of Browning helping Elizabeth study, of the two of them with their heads together, fascinated by some medical oddity. Of feeling like the proverbial fifth wheel when her parents joined in the conversation and the four of them dissected the latest medical journal.

"What about your parents? What do they do for a living?" Mr. Gideon rose stiffly from the couch and collected their plates and glasses. "Go on. I'm just putting these away."

"My parents are both doctors." Barrett raised her voice a tad while he rattled around in the other room. "Dad's a surgeon and Mom's an ob-gyn." She waited until he scuffed back in and eased himself onto the sofa. "They weren't around much. I don't remember the five of us ever sitting down to a meal without at least one of them being called away before it was over. They had their hospital rounds and office hours and it seemed at least one emergency or delivery every day. I've wondered a thousand times how they found time to have us kids, or why they even bothered. When they *were* with us, all they did was talk medicine. My gross-out tolerance is so high I could eat dinner off a gurney in the morgue, and there's no doubt in my mind I could deliver a baby if I had to."

"If they were so busy, who took care of you?"

"My Nana." To her horror, Barrett's voice caught in her throat. Even after all these years, the thought of Nana brought instant tears to her eyes. She steeled herself and went on. "My dad's mom. She lived with us 'til I was ten. When she died, Mom and Dad hired a housekeeper." A picture of that rigid old bat flashed through Barrett's mind. "I didn't think I would ever get over missing Nana." And she hadn't. She still missed her grandmother so much she'd get an ache right in the center of her chest if she let herself think about it. She would give anything to be able to lay her head on Nana's lap one more time, to talk to her while those sweet old fingers smoothed her hair away from her forehead.

Barrett scrunched deeper into the seat and pulled the blanket higher, blinking her burning eyes. Thankfully, Mr. Gideon changed the subject.

"So, you're not married. Got a fiancé? Boyfriend?"

Barrett snorted again. She noticed a rude pattern developing here.

"No. No boyfriend. I was too busy studying and working, trying to be more like Elizabeth and Browning, to date much. There's only been one guy I dated more than a few times, but even then we never did . . . get very serious." Barrett's face burned to the roots of her hair at almost confessing her "lack of experience" to this stranger. Why was it so easy to forget who she was talking to? "Anyway, I broke it off. In fact, the couple you saw getting married tonight was my old boyfriend and my sister."

She waited for the inevitable question about why she was out in the rain instead of at her twin's wedding, but the question never came.

Instead he asked, "Don't you want to get married? Have a family?"

Those damn tears were back, along with the urge to snort again. She stifled both. She couldn't believe she was having this conversation with a virtual stranger. But it felt good to talk, almost like talking to her grandmother. If she tried real hard, she could almost feel her grandmother's presence.

"No. I don't ever plan to get married. I'm not into tag team matrimony with separate careers or living my life around someone else's schedule. And the thought of having babies throw up on my shoulder and changing smelly diapers isn't my idea of heaven." The problem was, she couldn't say what her idea of heaven was.

Mr. Gideon nodded sagely while he pulled an ornately carved pipe from his jacket pocket. He patted his chest, dipped a hand inside his pockets, then patted his sides. When he came up empty, he put the pipe between his teeth anyway.

He just sat there and nodded on occasion, as if he understood her completely. He didn't try to point out all the wonderful advantages of having a big, strong man to look after her, and he didn't go off on a tangent about the rewards of parenthood and having children in her old age.

"Well, it's a wise woman who knows what she wants," he said eventually. Barrett had a feeling he spoke volumes by what he didn't say, but she suddenly felt too tired to give it much thought.

"I'm not sure I know what I want, but I definitely know what I *don't* want, and that's a husband and kids. I wouldn't be caught dead married." She stretched, then pulled the lap robe from around her. "Thanks for the snack, Mr. Gideon. I enjoyed the chat."

"You look tired, child. Get out of those damp clothes and get some sleep."

Her elderly host took the lap robe from her and folded it with care. She followed him through the kitchen, gathering up her shoes at the parlor door. Funny, she hadn't noticed the fire burning in the fireplace earlier. And she could have sworn there'd been carpet where her toes now curled under on the cold wooden floor.

I'm so tired I'm not firing on all cylinders, she thought fuzzily.

"Good night, Mr. Gideon," she called as he headed toward the office. He turned, his fist cradling the bowl of his pipe. He smiled at her, a smile so warm and loving, so gentle, that she had to swallow past a sudden lump in her throat.

"Good night, child," he said with a benevolent look. "God bless."

Chapter 2

CHASE FELT BLINDLY, trying to determine if the baby could be delivered. Sweat ran from his temples to drip off his chin or trickle down into his collar. The baby seemed to be firmly lodged, one leg in the birth canal, the other folded in the womb, making it impossible to deliver.

"Oh, God! Help me!" he prayed again, as a new contraction clamped on his hand.

The door flew open with a blast of frigid air and Wes stomped into the room. He blew on his hands and kicked the door shut, then froze at the scene before him.

"Wes!" Chase flicked a blanket over his wife's naked body, then dragged his shirtsleeve across his face to wipe off the sweat, one hand still inside Elizabeth. "Where's Doc Logan?"

"He's at the Smithers place. Their oldest has pneumonia and they think another one's coming down with it."

"What about Alice? Did you stop by the Parkers' farm?"

"She's laid up, sick as a dog. They're waiting for the doc, too. It's snowing, though, and that's bound to slow him down if we get much at all. But Doc says there ain't nothing to delivering a baby. Just tell her to relax and catch it when it pops out."

Chase wanted to scream.

"Look, Wes. I need help here. Elizabeth has passed out and she's not coming to. The baby's coming feet first, but I think it's stuck. I can only feel one leg. You've got to help me. I need to move the baby. Either turn it or get the other leg pulled down."

"What do you need me to do?"

"Hold her down while I push the foot back up."

Wes slid his gaze to Elizabeth's unconscious face.

"She'll kill you if she wakes up and finds me touching her. She'd kill you if she knew I was even in the room right now."

"And she's going to die, along with the baby, if I don't do something. Damn her prejudice! Help me here!"

Wes yanked off his heavy coat and moved to the head of the bed. He placed his big, dark hands on Elizabeth's shoulders, ready to hold her down.

"Now when this contraction stops, I'm going to push up on the outside as well as pushing the foot to the inside. If I can get the foot back in there the baby's position may correct itself."

He felt the grip of the birth canal on his hand loosen, and Elizabeth's distended stomach rounded.

"Now!" He pushed, gently at first, his left hand on her stomach, his right hand trying to feed the leg back into the womb. Nothing moved. He pushed again, harder. Nothing.

"Any signs of her coming to?"

Wes studied her face and shook his head. "Not even a flicker of an eyelash. This ain't good, Chaser."

Another contraction began and Chase stopped pushing. He dragged his sleeve across his eyes and looked at his wife.

Her face looked worse than before. The pale skin now was tinged with gray. He jumped up from his position at the foot of the bed and laid his ear to her chest. He could barely hear a faint, thready heartbeat.

The pain stopped. He went back to pushing, this time with a vengeance. He wasn't sure, but he thought he'd managed to move the leg a bit.

Another contraction hit, closer even than the last. He listened again for her heartbeat, hearing only a ghost of a thud in her chest. Chase looked up into the worried blue eyes of his half brother.

"We're losing her, Wes. We're losing her."

Barrett moaned and tried to remember if she had any aspirin in her tote bag. The cramps had started just as she drifted into that fuzzy netherworld between slumber and wakefulness, and she still wasn't fully awake. When the cramp subsided she reached for the welcome darkness of sleep.

The pain returned, and in that irrational state of half-consciousness she curled into a ball and tried to ignore it. These were the worst cramps she'd ever experienced. After a foggy mental calculation she determined that her period wasn't due. Could she have eaten something bad?

All she'd eaten that day was that slice of pound cake and the glass of milk. Surely the cake hadn't made her sick. Could her lactose intolerance have flared up with just that small amount of milk?

"Ohhhhh," she moaned out loud. Curling into a tighter ball, she peered into the darkness for her tote. It sat across the room on the vanity, a football field away. With every passing moment the pain increased.

She tried to sit up, to make it across the room to the vanity, but the cramp encircled her abdomen like a vise. Should she call for Mr. Gideon? Was anyone else even sleeping downstairs?

She fell back onto the bed when a wave of dizziness crashed over her. The room spun about in a distorted, misshapen blur as she felt herself losing consciousness.

"Oh, God! Somebody help me! Please send someone to help me!"

Barrett heard voices just seconds before another pain ripped through her.

"Help me!" she screamed, then screamed again from the pain.

"Hold her down, Wes! I've just about got it!"

She felt the pressure of hands increase on her shoulders. She opened her eyes, panting in agony, and looked straight into the face of a blue-eyed black man.

"She's awake, Chaser."

Terror momentarily froze her. When she could move she jerked her gaze downward and had to fight not to pass out.

Dear God, what's wrong with me? Her stomach rose before her, enormously swollen. Pain wrapped around her like a straitjacket. A man sat at her updrawn knees, one hand on her exposed stomach and the other . . .

This has to be a dream! A nightmare. It's not really happening!

"One more time, Elizabeth, and I should have it. Has the pain stopped?"

She stared, wild-eyed, at this man. He thought she was Elizabeth?

White-hot agony blinded her again, even worse than before, as he shoved with both his hands. She felt as if she were being ripped in two. She screamed. She cursed with every foul word she'd ever heard. She panted and cried until he finally stopped shoving. He pulled his hand from inside her and she nearly fainted at the dark-red blood smeared nearly to his elbow.

"All right, Elizabeth. The baby's turned. With your next contraction I want you to push as hard as you can."

As he spoke, her stomach tightened. The pain seized her. An overwhelming urge to bear down gripped her. While she screamed, while she pushed to rid her body of whatever was causing this agony, she kept telling herself to wake up.

"Push harder!"

The black man shoved her into a sitting position. She redoubled her efforts. She closed her eyes and pushed so hard that a hissing moan rose from the depths of her lungs.

Something shot out of her, and the agonizing pain subsided in sudden relief. She opened her eyes, wheezing for breath.

A nightmare! This is a hellish nightmare!

A baby's head protruded from between her legs! The

man at her feet wiped blood from its waxy face, then looked up at her.

"One more push. Can you do one more?"

The pain came back then. Without being told a second time she closed her eyes, bearing down with all her might.

The baby slipped from her in blessed, glorious release. Barrett fell back onto the sweat-dampened sheets and waited to wake up. Surely the dream would stop now.

She felt something else slide from her body, but that was nothing compared to what she'd already endured.

"He's not breathing, Wes. He's getting bluer by the minute."

Barrett lay there, willing herself back to consciousness, ignoring these figments of her imagination.

When she heard a smack, her eyes flew open. The man at her feet held a slippery, blue-tinged baby by its scrawny rib cage. Would this nightmare never end?

The black man stood rooted at her shoulders, his strange eyes wide with a helpless look.

Barrett struggled upright when the man jostled the limp body. Her muscles ached, her abdomen felt as if a prizefighter had used it for a punching bag. Her raw throat rasped when she spoke.

"Give it to me. Lay it here on the bed." When the man hesitated she yelled, *"Now!"*

He quickly placed the baby beside Barrett, and all that CPR training her parents had insisted on kicked in. Not wasting a second, she tilted the tiny head back and dipped her finger into its mouth to clear the mucus. She placed her mouth over the baby's mouth and nose, then blew little puffs of air into its lungs. She stopped, found a faint, sporadic heartbeat, then breathed for it again. Not much more than half a minute passed before a weak whimper rose from the little body. The whimper grew stronger, and stronger still, until an angry wail reverberated through the room.

Barrett fell back against the sheets, exhausted from that minor exertion.

"Wrap a blanket around it. It's cold in here." Her mind shut down, numb from her ordeal. She didn't understand why she couldn't control this dream. It all felt so real— the pains, the baby's soft skin still wet from its birth, the chill in the room. She could even smell wood smoke and hear the pop of pine burning in the fireplace.

She just wanted the oblivion of a dreamless sleep. She felt warm, cozy covers being pulled up to her chin. Her body relaxed, the aches lessened, and a welcome black fog enveloped her in sleep.

While Wes tucked the covers around Elizabeth's abused body, Chase snatched a tiny, soft blanket and fumbled with swaddling the baby. After several seconds of wrapping and unwrapping, the result of his efforts looked more like a wad of dirty laundry than a baby in a blanket. The newborn's stiff-legged wailing quieted to the sound of a whining puppy for a moment, then started back up stronger than ever.

"I think you ought to pick it up, Chaser." Wes still stood guard at Elizabeth's head, his wide blue eyes fastened on the baby as if it were a coiled rattler.

Chase paced for a few seconds, dragging his fingers through his hair, then stopped.

"Yeah. I guess I should pick it up." He eyed the squirming blanket, then looked back at his half brother. "Then what?"

Wes shrugged. "He probably wants to eat." He turned and glanced at Elizabeth. "But I don't think she's in any shape to nurse him now. Let her rest a while. What's that pile of stuff over there? Should we put some clothes on it?"

The cries coming from within the sloppy folds escalated again to an alarming scream.

If the baby didn't stop crying it would wake Elizabeth, and Chase knew she needed rest more than anything else right now. Gingerly, he worked his fingers under the wad of fabric and lifted the nearly weightless mass off the bed. The crying subsided to a whimper as he held the baby at arm's length only inches from the mattress. He looked around with uncertainty, then pointed with his chin toward the sofa.

"Put a pillow over there. We'll lay it down to put some clothes on it."

Finally leaving his post, Wes snatched a big feather pillow from the bedroom, then patted it down on the sofa. Chase moved the baby, still holding it at arm's length, and placed it in the fluffy white nest.

"Let's see what we've got here." He rifled through the pile of baby things. At the bottom lay a neatly folded stack of white cotton squares with several safety pins fastened to the top.

There could be no doubt as to the purpose of these things. How quickly did one need to put a diaper on a newborn? Immediately after birth? After it ate? To be on the safe side he reluctantly decided the diapering should be done as soon as possible.

When unfolded, the diaper looked nearly as large as the baby blanket. He held it up and shot Wes a questioning glance.

His half brother eyed the dangling white flag for a second, then his pale eyes lit with inspiration and he snapped his fingers.

"I know this one! My sister folded those things up into triangles. You just keep folding 'til you get the right size."

Chase had a little inspiration of his own.

"Show me."

Unfortunately, Wes was one step ahead of him. He patted the air with the palms of his hands and backed away. "Oooooh, no. You get to do the honors. That's *your* youngun."

Bitterness spiked through Chase at Wes's words. His hackles rose for a moment, but he fought to calm himself. Wes didn't know the story. No one did.

The whimpers became more insistent. Chase shoved all his thoughts to the back of his mind, folded the square to opposite corners, then folded it again. The triangle still looked huge for such a puny, squirming scrap of humanity, but he slipped it under the tiny bottom anyway. Wes, who had unfastened a pin and now hovered at Chase's shoulder, handed the pin over and supervised with enthusiasm.

Once the diaper's corners were all safely secured into a somewhat haphazard lump, Chase surveyed his efforts. It would do until Elizabeth could fix it. Of course, she would know the perfect way to pin a diaper. Hell, even after nearly dying, she had managed to save the baby's life where he would have failed. Where in the name of God had she learned that maneuver?

"Here, put this thing on it." Wes held up a little cotton shirt, which looked even smaller dangling from his massive hands. Chase took one of the clean diapers and gently wiped as much of the waxy, white film from the baby's body as he could before putting the shirt on him. Next came a delicately embroidered nightgown, each and every stitch placed lovingly by his perfect wife. A pair of booties, of course crocheted by Elizabeth, were the last things Chase bothered with before wrapping the baby back in the blanket.

He sat back, satisfied that the child was adequately dressed. Wes busied himself with stirring the fire and laying on a few more logs, then disappeared into the kitchen. It was only then, when Wes was gone and Elizabeth lay asleep, that Chase allowed himself to *really* look at the child he'd just helped into the world.

The baby's tiny hands and feet made jerky little bumps beneath the blanket. Strange smacking noises replaced the whimpers for the time being.

He definitely has the Alston coloring. Chase studied the baby's mop of thick black hair. Only time would tell if he would have the Alston eyes, a pale golden brown so light they were more the color of amber. Chase searched the miniature face for other family traits.

A sick knot tightened in the pit of his stomach. What would it matter if the baby had the black hair and amber eyes of the Alstons? He could inherit every form of family resemblance, and Chase would still never know if the child was his son—or his nephew.

"Elizabeth."

Barrett stirred, moaned, then pulled the covers higher and ignored the voice talking to her sister.

"Elizabeth."

A hand gently shook her shoulder.

"I'm Barrett. Go 'way," she mumbled. It'd been ages since anyone had confused her with her sister, but Barrett's exhausted state allowed the thought little more than passing notice.

"The baby needs to eat, Elizabeth."

Irritation at being mistaken for her twin dragged Barrett into semi-wakefulness. Then the mention of a baby brought back the horrible nightmare she'd had during the night.

"Elizabeth." The quiet voice held a trace of impatience. It sounded like the voice in her nightmare. Surely she couldn't still be dreaming. Surely . . . The sound of footsteps faded as he walked away.

She opened her eyes and peered through the gloom of the dimly lit room. *This is definitely a dream.* She lay in an old rope bed that had been set up in front of a fireplace—the fireplace in the parlor of the bed-and-breakfast! As her eyes adjusted to the weak glow of a kerosene lamp, she could make out the dark rectangle of the doorway to her bedroom. To her left lay the kitchen. She could even smell food cooking. But a creepy feeling made the fine little hairs on the back of her neck stand on end when she looked for the office off the parlor and found a wall instead of a doorway.

She studied the room more closely. Oil lamps and candles. No sign of electric lights. Not even switches on the wall. No telephone. Instead of the plush mauve carpet, a large oval rag rug covered the floor. The furniture had changed. A rifle leaned against the wall next to the front door. The room looked like it might have looked a century earlier.

This is a dream! Change it! Just wake up!

"So, you're awake. How are you feeling?"

Barrett jumped at the sound of the voice. The sudden movement sent dull pains shooting through her bruised abdomen. The man in her nightmare walked to the side of the bed, a quilted bundle in his arms.

He would have been heart-stopping handsome with all that thick black hair and a face that could advertise men's cologne, if only a smile had dared to curve his lips. But he just looked at her with eyes the color of scorched butter.

"I thought you might like to see your son. You'll need to feed him as soon as we get some food in you."

She could only stare at this man, this figment of her imagination.

"Wes," the man called toward the kitchen, "is Elizabeth's supper ready yet?"

That did it! Fear, fatigue, and anger got the best of her. It was time to take control of this dream. She elbowed herself into a sitting position, hauling the covers up with her, ignoring her nakedness and the soreness in her stomach.

When she spoke, she fought to sound as brave as her words. "Look! I don't know why you're calling me Elizabeth. I'm sure there's some Freudian reason for that.

But if you don't mind, the least you can do is call me Barrett. Okay?" When the man simply stared at her she repeated it louder: "Okay?"

He shot a glance toward the kitchen, then returned his gaze to hers. The regulator clock on the wall ticked. A log in the fireplace fell with a burst of orange sparks. Cooking utensils clinked against each other in the next room.

"You want me to call you Barrett," he finally stated, his black brows so close they looked like raven's wings.

"I don't think that's asking too much."

"Why do you want to be called Barrett?"

She took a deep breath and fought to steady her voice. "Because that's my name. So humor me, why don't you, and call me by my name!" Falling back against the pillows, she belatedly yanked the covers to her chin and stared at the man, too frightened and angry to be embarrassed. "And where are my clothes?"

The man's raven-winged brows did come together then. He narrowed his eyes and stared at her with a questioning look, as if she'd just grown a second head and he couldn't figure out what to do about it. Without saying a word he turned on his heel, disappeared into the bedroom, then reappeared seconds later carrying a long-sleeved flannel nightgown with pink flowers along the yoke and a ruffled hem. He tossed the homely thing onto the bed.

"If you need help putting it on, call me. Then you need to eat so you can feed the baby before he starves to death." He disappeared into the brighter recesses of the kitchen, still carrying the bundle that Barrett assumed was the baby. She wanted to yell at him that the gown wasn't hers, but modesty won out. She pulled the heavy thing over her head, shoved her arms through the sleeves, then dragged the scratchy flannel down under the covers.

Her fingers brushed against her tender stomach, a stomach that should have been rock-hard from daily sit-ups but instead felt as mushy as a marshmallow. She lifted the layers of covers and stared, aghast, at the expanse of stretched, loose skin that rippled across her stomach with every hesitant touch of her finger. She gingerly poked her lower abdomen, horrified when her finger sank into the skin as if into a mound of pasty-white bread dough. This couldn't be her body.

The rattle of dishes momentarily drew her attention.

The man with the golden eyes stood just inside the parlor, the wooden tray in his hands bearing a glass of milk and a bowl of something steaming and fragrant.

He stared at her intently, his brow lowered yet again. Barrett fought down the embarrassment at being caught poking at her stomach. She returned his look with what she hoped was a defiant glare.

"What?" she said.

He simply schooled his features into indifference and continued into the room.

She couldn't figure this dream out. Her first thought upon waking and finding the two men there had been that she was about to be raped. But no sooner had she formed that thought than she'd seen the huge, swollen belly where her hundred-crunch-a-day stomach should have been, and she realized she had to be dreaming. Why or how she'd dreamed such a painfully believable labor and delivery she had no idea. No doubt this whole nightmare, including the baby, stemmed from watching her sister marry her ex-boyfriend and the turmoil of emotions that event had stirred up over the past weeks.

The man placed the tray on a high table next to the bed.

"Do you need help or can you feed yourself?" he asked in a voice that conveyed how little he cared.

"I think I can handle feeding myself," she said, exactly mirroring his lack of emotion.

Not a flicker changed in his features as he handed her the bowl of beef stew. She studied him while he placed the milk within reach before bending at the hearth to stir the fire. Since she couldn't seem to wake herself up, she decided to try and make sense out of all of this.

"So. Who are you supposed to be?" she asked, a chunk of meat on the spoon hovering at her lips.

His body went completely still, the poker frozen in mid-jab. She couldn't see his face, but the muscles across the expanse of his shoulders seemed to bunch into tight knots. He slowly pivoted his head so that his pale eyes pierced her with a suspicious gaze.

"I beg your pardon?"

"Who are you? I know this is *my* nightmare, but I can't figure out who *you're* supposed to be. And the black guy. . . I'm not even going to try to figure *him* out." She kept her tone light, but this whole sense of reality sparked a flicker of doubt about whether or not this was a dream.

The man speared the glowing log with a final, vicious jab, then rose to his full height and faced her.

"I don't have time for your games, Elizabeth—"

"Barrett," she reminded him.

He glared at her. "If you are attempting to make our marriage more of a farce than it already—"

"Marriage! You're my *husband*?" Her stomach tightened under all that loose skin. What could *that* mean?

He continued to glare at her in absolute silence.

"I know! It must mean that I really *don't* want to be saddled with some demanding husband and baby. I was right when I told Mr. Gideon I didn't—"

The man snatched a heavy winter coat off a peg and stalked to the door. With his hand on the knob he turned and looked at her with loathing in his eyes.

"Marry in haste, repent in leisure. That has been a litany in my mind since our wedding night. Now it looks as if you've taken up the same chant, Elizabeth, but I'll ask you to repent in silence!"

"Barrett!" she corrected.

He turned and yanked open the door, then rattled the windows when he slammed it on his way out.

"Temper, temper," Barrett mumbled to herself. She turned her attention back to the delicious imaginary food, which, amazingly enough, seemed to satisfy the very real, gnawing hunger that had overtaken her while she slept . . . or dreamed she was sleeping. She shook her head to clear it. This was getting *way* too confusing. And much too real.

"S'cuse me, Miss Elizabeth."

Barrett looked up to see the blue-eyed black man's head poking out of the kitchen.

"You done?"

She scraped the last bit of stew from the bottom of the bowl.

"Actually, this is so good I wondered if I could have some more."

His surprised look raised his dark eyebrows clear to his hairline.

"Why . . . sure," he said, as if he had never before heard such a request. He disappeared with her empty bowl and returned seconds later with a refill, along with a thick slice of bread balanced on top.

"Thanks." She took the stoneware bowl, then bit off a corner of the bread. "Ummm. This is good."

"Chaser forgot the bread last time." He handed her a cloth napkin, then turned to leave.

"Chaser? His name's Chaser?"

The man stopped in midstride. Eyes the color of a robin's egg slid to her face. He studied her, as if trying to take her measure.

"So I'm married to a man named Chaser," she said to no one in particular. "Probably comes by the name naturally. And who might you be?" She waited for an answer, but he just continued to stare at her. "I mean, if Chaser is the husband I don't want, and that baby, wherever it is, is the child I never want to have, then that would make you . . ." She waited for him to complete her sentence.

"Wes."

"Wes?"

"Wes."

"Hmmm. And what part do you play in this nightmare, Wes? And why in the world would you have blue eyes?"

Wes's flawless, caramel skin developed mottled

patches of red. For some reason, he appeared to be angry with her.

"Miss Elizabeth, you've never liked me, but—"

"Barrett."

"What?"

"I want to be called Barrett. Not *Miss* Barrett, either. Just Barrett. And I have no reason not to like you. I don't even know you. Do you work for Chaser?"

He looked at her as if she'd lost her mind. "You know we're half brothers."

"Half brothers?" How weird, she thought. What could *that* mean—dreaming of an ill-tempered husband with a blue-eyed black brother. "And why do you have blue eyes?"

He pinched the bridge of his nose and shook his head.

"Because my mama had blue eyes. And she had blue eyes because my granddaddy, her white master, had blue eyes. Chaser got hazel eyes, like our father's."

Well, apparently she'd dreamed up a couple of figments with complete histories of their own. How odd.

Before she could ask Wes any more questions, the front door flew open and slammed against the wall. Chaser barged in with a snowy armload of firewood, kicked the door shut, stalked to the hearth, and dumped the load into the wood box. At that moment a high-pitched, angry cry rose from the depths of the kitchen.

"I put him in a basket next to the stove, Chaser. I'll get him." Wes ducked into the kitchen, obviously glad to end the interview.

"You'll have to feed him, Elizabeth, whether—"

"Barrett."

Her so-called husband closed his eyes and pinched the bridge of his nose, much like his half brother had done moments earlier.

"I'm trying very hard not to lose my patience, since you've just come through a very difficult birth—"

"Then just humor me, Chaser. Call me Barrett, and I won't be endlessly correcting you." She tried to give him a smile that conveyed how completely logical she thought her request to be, but he just stared at her with narrowed eyes.

Wes walked into the parlor, jostling the blanket, from which indignant screams emanated.

"He was born two hours ago, Eliz . . . *Barrett*. He needs to nurse."

"Nurse!"

Chaser looked toward the heavens as if sending up a silent prayer.

"How did you plan to feed him? Give him a knife and fork and sit him down at the table?"

"But I don't know anything about nursing! Why on earth would I have a nightmare about nursing a baby?"

"That's enough!" Chaser shouted. He took a deep breath, apparently to calm himself, which didn't seem to be working, then blew the breath out slowly as he took the livid baby from Wes. "Though I will not argue that we are certainly living a nightmare, you are *not* dreaming anything. You are wide awake, with a hungry new son who needs to be nursed. How hard can it be? Put the child to your breast and let him nurse!" He handed her the screaming bundle so quickly that she took it without thinking. "We will give you all the privacy you need. Call when you've finished."

Barrett sat there for several seconds, holding the loud, squirming bundle as if it were a handful of nitroglycerin. The longer she held it the harder it cried. The tiny face visible among the many folds of the wadded quilt turned beet red as it stiffened its scrawny body and screamed until its voice quivered.

"Okay, okay, okay," Barrett conceded. If she didn't try to nurse this "baby" Chaser would be back in here, and then she'd have two males screaming at her. Besides, all she wanted to do was shut it up so she could go to sleep and get out of this dream.

She propped the fidgeting, screaming newborn in the crook of her arm while she fumbled at the buttons on the front of her gown. Pulling the heavy flannel aside, she ineptly moved the baby until her bare breast accidentally brushed his cheek. Immediately, the tiny mouth zeroed in on its target, latching on with a vengeance, tugging greedily and noisily as if it had known exactly what to do all along.

Barrett jerked her head back in wonder. What an absolutely realistic sensation! She actually felt as if a baby were nursing at her breast—or at least what she imagined that would feel like. There was nothing sensual about the sensation. Of course, she experienced no sense of maternal instinct either. Scrunching down into the mound of covers, she watched the tiny lips encircle her distended nipple, the little pink tongue visible in the corner of its mouth working to draw sustenance. Barrett watched, fascinated at the natural instincts of this newborn.

"You know," she said as she tilted her head back and gave the baby a serious look, "this isn't good for my reputation. You're the first guy I ever let get this far, and I don't even know your name."

Totally unimpressed, the baby continued smacking away at her breast until he deemed it no longer of interest. As quickly as he'd found the nipple, he released it and began whining like a lost puppy.

Now what? In the recesses of her mind Barrett remembered playing with a baby doll and being told it must be "burped." Well, it wouldn't hurt to try. She inexpertly joggled the baby around in an effort to get him to her shoulder, when a belch that would have done a dockworker proud blew from between his pink Cupid's-bow lips.

She giggled at such an incongruous noise coming from such a minuscule creature, and her spirits brightened for the first time in weeks.

"Okay, big guy, do you want dessert? Better get it while you can 'cause I don't plan on being here when I wake up."

She transferred the baby to her right arm and guided him to the rest of his meal. He took to that breast with the same noisy enthusiasm he'd had for the other. Barrett turned on her side, the baby cradled in her arm. The vigorous tugging at her breast caused mini-contractions in her uterus. She relaxed her body, the warmth of the covers seeping into her muscles and soothing the aches in her abdomen. The tugging seemed to slow somewhat. Her body cried out for sleep as exhaustion overtook her. She allowed herself to be swept into the black oblivion, her last thought being that this would be one dream she wouldn't have trouble remembering when she woke.

*   *   *

Ah, Barrett, my child, I fear you are in for a rude awakening.

Gideon stood with his magnificent presence glowing around Barrett's bed as she fell into an exhausted sleep. The baby continued to nurse, though not with the fervor Barrett's inexperience led her to believe. No, the ordeal of his birth had left the tiny new soul weaker than Gideon liked. With his aura—his celestial halo—emanating from his being, Gideon gently touched his hand to the baby's heart, lending a strength to the newborn that would ensure his survival. Barrett he left to heal on her own. He wanted this determined, independent soul to be forced to rely on someone else, if only for a while.

My iron-willed child, if you had not been so fiercely determined to stand alone, I would not have been forced to remove you from a world in which you could do just that. Learn well.

Chapter 3

CHASE STOOD IN the doorway between the kitchen and the parlor, spellbound, disconcerted, and confused. He'd come to see if his wife needed him to take the baby, but the scene he encountered made him hesitate.

Firelight cast a dancing, rosy glow upon the two occupants of the bed. His wife held the child to her breast, watching it nurse with a look of wonder. Her face had never looked so soft, so vulnerable in the eight and a half months they'd been married. The usually tight knot of hair atop her head had loosened to a curly mass during childbirth, and large, spiraling wisps fell in beguiling disarray around her face.

"You know, this isn't good for my reputation. You're the first guy I ever let get this far, and I don't even know your name."

She spoke to the baby in a lighthearted, teasing manner in which he'd never heard his wife speak. And what did she mean about letting a man get that far? Chase knew that at least two men had gotten that far, and farther. His brother and himself.

He watched her giggle when the baby erupted with an enormous burp. He found his feet rooted to the floor when she offered her other breast for the baby to nurse. Who was this smiling, laughing, teasing woman? He hadn't known this side of his wife existed, and it irritated him to feel a twinge of jealousy rise up. Perhaps she was delirious from the ordeal of the difficult birth.

The fact that she had survived the birth at all still surprised him. One moment her unconscious face had turned deathly white, her heartbeat all but nonexistent. In fact, Chase had believed she'd breathed her last breath. Then the next moment she'd screamed with an energy even *he* would have been hard-pressed to rival. And those curses! She'd turned the air blue with the curses spewing from her righteous lips. Up until that moment the strongest word he'd ever heard her use had been "fiddlesticks."

And now she wanted to be called Barrett. What possible explanation could there be for such an odd request? Perhaps she was suffering from a fever. Childbed fever had claimed its share of women, he knew.

Even as the thought occurred to him, he realized that this woman who never had a hair out of place, never allowed a speck of dust to settle on the furniture, never let a dirty dish sit or a spot linger on clothing, now lay on sheets still damp from birthing waters and blood.

Without a second thought Chase crossed to the bed in front of the fire. The baby and his wife had both fallen into the sound sleep of the exhausted. He gently felt her forehead for signs of fever. He had to smooth several dark, curly tendrils back from her brow, but her skin felt cool, healthy . . . soft. She turned her head in her sleep and nuzzled his palm with her cheek. He jerked his hand away as if the touch of her burned him.

Elizabeth sighed and shifted slightly. The movement took her breast out of the baby's now-slack mouth. Chase averted his gaze when a frisson of heat shot through his body, irritating him as much as arousing him. With an impatient jerk, he pulled the edges of her gown together.

For God's sake, after eight and a half months, the sight of a cow's udder would excite me.

"Chaser." Chase jumped and turned around, feeling like a little boy caught peeping through keyholes. Wes stood in the doorway of the kitchen, his arms reaching heavenward in a mighty stretch, his tonsils nearly visible from his enormous yawn. After giving his eyes a thorough massage with the heels of his hands, he blinked through half-closed lids. "You need me for anything here before I turn in? S'been a long day."

"No. Go on home. After I pull these sheets out from under Elizabeth, I'm going to try and get some sleep, too." Then, as an afterthought, "If the cottage is too cold you're welcome to sleep here."

Wes flicked a glance at Elizabeth. "Nah. I'm tougher than you, little brother. I'll be fine. You need any help doing that?"

"No." Chase shot a glance at the bed. "My perfect little wife made a birthing bed. There's a canvas under the damp sheets and clean bedding under the canvas. All I have to do is peel the soiled ones off. But you can put the baby back in his basket on your way out."

"I still don't understand why you didn't build him a cradle. A baby ought to have a cradle," Wes grumbled.

Chase fought the familiar irritation that had come to be his constant companion. He scooped the sleeping infant up into his arms and handed him to his cantankerous uncle.

"You build him one," he said with total lack of emotion before turning back to his task. "Wes?"

Wes stopped his grumbling journey to the kitchen.

"Yeah?"

"Does she seem different to you? I mean, besides her cursing and screaming and wanting to be called Barrett? She called me Chaser tonight. Not Chase." He eyed the subject of their conversation. "What do you suppose that means?"

Wes peered at Elizabeth's sleeping form, then shrugged.

"Why should it mean anything? Maybe it's just that motherhood agrees with her. Hasn't she always been a good wife?"

"Yeah." Chase turned back to the task of caring for that wife and sighed. "Just perfect."

An ear-piercing wail jolted Barrett out of a luscious, sound sleep.

"Dear Lord, will this nightmare never end?" she asked aloud as she attempted to elbow her way to a sitting position, glancing around the now-familiar parlor. Dull pain shot through the weak muscles of her abdomen. She fell back against the pillows, giving up any attempt to rise. Only then did she realize she was not alone in the bed.

Chaser slept next to her, one arm flung above his head to rest on the pillow, the black shadow of whiskers on his jaw matching his tousled black hair. Not for the first time, it occurred to Barrett how handsome she'd dreamed this man. The sight of those black lashes fanned in sleep across tanned, masculine cheekbones, the manly dark stubble—everything about him added up to a guy so good-looking he could hurt a girl's eyes. The kind of man women did double takes over.

As she watched, the screams from the baby intensified. Chaser jerked awake, and without so much as looking in her direction—in fact, pointedly *not* looking at her—he rolled out of bed, staggered to the basket, and picked the baby up.

"Maybe he's not as handsome as I thought," she mumbled to herself when his face, absolutely devoid of emotion, appeared on her side of the bed. Tiny hands and feet flailed within the blanket he carried against his bare chest. She let her gaze drop to take in the rusty, faded long underwear hugging Chaser's waist with little more than faith keeping them up.

At least she could dream *some* things right.

"Do you feel up to changing his diaper?"

Barrett cocked one eyebrow at such a ridiculous question.

"I think not," she answered in a tone that told him what she thought of the suggestion. "But I do have to go to the bathroom. And please don't tell me I've dreamed up a place with an outhouse."

Chaser just stared at her for a moment and shook his head. He walked into the bedroom, still jostling the baby, and returned several minutes later, fully dressed, with the baby in one arm and what Barrett knew could only be a chamber pot in his hand. Her face burned clear to the roots of her hair.

"You can't be serious."

Chaser fidgeted with irritation.

"Look, Elizabeth—"

"Barrett!"

"Damn it! There's a foot of snow on the ground, and since I doubt you can walk across the room, there's little chance you'll make it across twenty yards of snow to the privy. I'll change his diaper while you avail yourself."

Barrett eyed the porcelain convenience while Chaser snatched a diaper from the stack. She glared up at him through narrowed, warning eyes. It was this or nothing.

"Then go into the kitchen to change him."

"With pleasure."

"And don't come out until I call you!"

"You flatter yourself, madam!"

Pig!

After what seemed like hours to Barrett's burning face, tender stomach, and weak limbs, she finally replaced the painted porcelain lid and slid the ungainly thing out of sight. Since she'd now found another area on her body even more tender than her stomach, she perched very gingerly on the edge of the bed, worrying about the latest problem she'd discovered.

"Is it safe to come in now, or do I risk having the contents hurled at me?"

Barrett jerked her gaze to the doorway, but true to his word, he remained out of sight.

"It's safe," she mumbled. When he entered with the baby in his arms, she kept her seat on the edge of the bed, trying not to cast nervous glances at Chaser. Why was she so nervous? Why was she embarrassed? For Pete's sake, it was only a dream. Just come out with it!

"Chaser, I need . . . uh . . . I need some . . ."

"Some what?"

She chanced a quick glance at him. He seemed only mildly irritated.

"Well, I don't know. I'm not sure what women used in the old days."

"Used?"

His brows drew closer together in a scowl. She suddenly found the task of fitting her thumbnails together to be intensely interesting.

"You know. I need . . ." She drew in a deep breath, let it out, then spoke to a shadow on the ceiling, "I'm bleeding. I need something for the blood. What do women here use when they have their periods?"

"Periods?"

Lord, was he dense! "Monthly courses. The curse. On the ra . . . well, you get the picture."

Chaser made no sound at all. When she looked at him, his face was the shade of a Caribbean sunburn. He turned his back to her.

"I have no idea what women use here, or anywhere else for that matter, Elizabeth. I haven't made it a habit—"

"The name is *Barrett*!"

He spun around and glared at her. The sudden movement startled the baby, and an angry whine escalated the tension. Chaser jiggled the infant and continued to glare.

"I have no idea what women use, *Barrett*!"

"Well, what did I use before I got pregnant?"

"I wouldn't know, *Barrett*. You've not had a monthly cycle since we've been married. Remember, *Barrett*?"

"No, *Chaser*, I don't remember! All I remember is waking up in the middle of this nightmare with your hand rammed in me clear to my teeth and Wes shoving my shoulders through the mattress! *I'm* the one whose vital organs you tried to rearrange, not the other way around, so why don't you cut the attitude and pretend for a minute you're human? I just asked a simple question!"

He studied her, more questioning now than angry. Uncomfortable under his scrutiny, she glanced about the room for a solution to her problem without his help. At last her gaze fell upon the stack of cotton diapers, and she wanted to bang her head for not thinking of it before. She managed to stretch her reach and pluck one from the top. Setting her chin and skewering him with a defiant look, she folded the cloth lengthwise several times before saying, "Do you mind? A moment of privacy and then I'll feed your precious son."

If she had kicked him where it hurts, she didn't think he could have looked more enraged. He laid the baby on the bed beside her, stomped to the door, and yanked it open as he snatched his coat from its peg. A chill wind rushed through the open portal, causing goose bumps to dance on her arms.

"I'll give you all the privacy you need, and more, *Barrett*. See to . . . my precious son." With that last word—spoken like a curse—still hanging in the air, he slammed the door behind his retreating back.

The sharp sound jerked the baby into a livid, stiff-legged wail. Barrett had no time to fling a few curses of her own. She hurried to get the cloth into place, making a mental note to figure out how to keep it there later. Scooping the squalling infant up in her arms, she freed one breast and brought him to it. As before, he zeroed in like a heat-seeking missile, and in moments his cries turned into the gentle smacking noises she'd already come to recognize and enjoy in an oddly detached way.

She watched him nurse with a sense of awe. How could she dream so vividly of something she knew nothing about? Childbirth, nursing, even the feel and smell of this baby all seemed so real.

"You don't even have a name, little baby," she whispered to the contented infant. "Or if you do, your daddy hasn't bothered to tell me."

Her tiny audience ignored her, his minuscule fist kneading her breast while he nursed.

Barrett sank back into the pillows and forced her body to relax. She stared at the fire still burning low in the grate and tried to empty her mind. She refused to allow the insidious thought to take root that this wasn't a dream at all.

For two days Chaser was only a shadow on the wall and a low voice in the kitchen. Wes came over from his cottage every morning and brought Barrett her meals. He moved the baby's basket next to her side of the bed. He brought her clean gowns and basins of hot water in which to bathe. He changed the baby's diapers and, much to her embarrassment, emptied the porcelain container hidden under the bed. Barrett had no idea where Chaser spent most of his time, or where he slept. And she didn't care. She just knew it wasn't with her, thank God.

Though she didn't see him, she heard him. The incessant sound of wood being chopped rang in her ears for hours, then the thud of it being stacked set her nerves on edge.

She could hear his low murmurs while he and Wes talked during their meals. She heard the sound of water being poured, over and over again, then the unmistakable sigh of contentment as Chaser slid into a hot bath.

She tried not to let that picture grow in her mind. Tried to ignore it and think about something else—anything else. But the gentle splashing, the humid smell of bathwater and clean skin, the occasional deep sigh, all sabotaged her best efforts to banish him from her thoughts. Two nights in a row she listened to him bathe, and two nights in a row she vacillated between fear, anger, and . . . something she refused to name.

These were her thoughts as she woke on the third morning to the sounds of the fire being stoked and the baby stirring in his basket.

"Mmmmm. Thank you, Wes," Barrett said as she snuggled deeper into the covers.

"The name is Chase," the deep voice returned in exact imitation of Barrett.

Her eyes flew open to the sight of Chaser's broad shoulders and back muscles flexing as he laid several logs on the glowing coals in the grate. Balanced on the balls of his feet, his wrist resting on a knee, a wedge of wood dangling from his fingertips, he turned far enough to look at her over his shoulder. Eyes the color of dark-gold glass sparkled at her for the first time with a trace of humor, as if he were calling a truce.

That single look set a whole swarm of butterflies free in her stomach. Suddenly she found herself wishing she had a big tube of Colgate and worrying about whether or not she had a bad case of pillow head. She gave him a weak, insecure smile.

What a surprising reaction! Normally she adopted a "take me or leave me" attitude with men. Not that she wasn't conscious of her appearance, but she never worried about what men might think except on a professional level.

The baby squirmed in his basket, emitting little fussing noises that Barrett had already classified as his "early warning system." Relieved to have something to focus her attention on besides that golden gaze, she rolled to the edge of the bed and sat up.

And immediately panicked. Something was wrong!

As she came to a sitting position and the baby increased his fussing, her breasts began to tingle, then to ache with all the pain of an abscessed tooth. She shifted her gaze to Chaser, and the trace of humor in his eyes changed to concern.

"Eliz . . . Barrett, what's wrong?" He moved to her side in an instant.

Dear heaven, it even hurt to put her arms to her sides! Her breasts, harder than those on a marble statue, ached enough to bring tears to her eyes.

"Chaser! What's wrong with me?" Without thinking she grabbed his hand and placed it on her swollen breast. The heat of his palm felt good against the aching throb. She searched his face for signs of alarm, but instead she felt him shudder, saw his lids drop closed for a moment before he swallowed hard and removed his hand.

"Your milk has come in, Eliz . . . Barrett. Nothing more. This is normal."

"My milk? My milk?" she squeaked, certain he must be mistaken. "I've been nursing the baby for two days!"

"I know. That was something else. Something richer. Believe me when I tell you this is normal." He stood, stiff-backed, his eyes shuttered now with his usual emotionless gaze. "All nursing creatures experience it. It's hard to raise farm animals and not know this. To tell you the truth, I'm rather surprised you didn't already know."

"Excuse me?" Barrett couldn't believe the change in him. She felt as if the temperature of the room dropped twenty degrees when he looked down at her. "I'm sorry, but could the guy who was here just a second ago please come back? I liked him better."

Chaser studied her for a moment, then went back to building up the fire.

"If you don't feed him soon, he's going to start screaming," he said with his back to her.

Fighting an uncharacteristic burning behind her eyelids, she lifted the baby to her swollen breast. Just the brush of his tiny lips increased the throbbing. She thought she would scream as he struggled to get the hard, unyielding nipple into his mouth. Finally he settled down to nurse. She watched, flinching each time his little fist touched her. Within a few seconds, white, watery milk dribbled from the corner of his mouth to run down her breast and onto her doughy stomach.

She closed her eyes, squeezing back the threatening tears. Good Lord, she wanted to go home!

A huge fire now roared in the fireplace. Chaser rose, dusted his hands on the seat of his buckskins, then turned back to Barrett. He stepped away from the fireplace, as if ready to leave the room, but his gaze caught and locked on the baby nursing at Barrett's breast.

The pain was so intense, she swallowed her pride and looked up into his face. He'd been right about the milk.

"Will it always hurt like this?" She mentally kicked herself for the quiver in her voice and the hot tears that welled in her eyes.

He looked at the floor and shook his head. At least he didn't seem so rigid.

"I don't think so," he said, looking back at her.

They stared at each other for several seconds. Barrett finally broke the gaze to glance down at the baby.

"What's his name?" she asked in a quiet voice.

The fire popped and cracked. A dog barked somewhere outside. The clock on the mantel ticked, and the baby made little sounds in his throat as he swallowed, but his father never answered. Barrett looked up at Chaser, who hadn't moved except to draw his brows together in a hateful scowl.

She ignored his blistering glare. This man had the mood swings of a manic-depressive.

"Don't tell me you haven't named him," she said. "I thought all fathers were anxious to name their sons. Let me guess. You've named him Chaser, Jr."

He jerked back his head, as if slapped, and sucked his breath between his teeth.

"You know as well as I that my name is Chase, not

Chaser, though I admit I have no idea why you've suddenly taken to calling me that when you've always refused before. Just because Wes calls me Chaser." He leaned down, his gaze glittering with malice. When he spoke, his warm breath ghosted across her face. "Name him for his father?" he asked, his head deceivingly tilted in question. "That would be easier if we knew which one of us had fathered him, wouldn't it? Or maybe you know and have forgotten my brother's name as quickly as you've forgotten your own, *Barrett*. In that case, let me refresh your memory. Name him Aidan."

Chase worked like a man possessed, mucking out the stalls, throwing down fresh straw, feeding the livestock. He'd stripped off his heavy coat and worked in his worn flannel shirt. Clouds of warm, moist air puffed from between his lips with every breath in the frigid barn.

What was she up to? The sweet taste of satisfaction he'd had when he told her to name the baby Aidan turned bitter when she'd looked at him, confusion creasing her brow. The look had been genuine enough. The woman had missed her calling. With such a flair for acting, she could have trodden the boards to fame.

He was tired of the emotional ups and downs he'd suffered the past few days. After his initial rage on their wedding night, and again when she told him she was pregnant, he'd settled into a certain irritated boredom for eight and a half months. Irritation at having been cuckolded by his brother, boredom at the quiet, industrious, dutiful, *perfect* wife she'd become to try and make it up to him.

So bored with her fixed smile, her even, subdued

temper, her nearly sterile housekeeping and ability to do everything well, he'd found himself doing little things just to get her goat. He made sure he never wiped his feet if he could track something in on her pristine floor. He dirtied a clean glass every time he got a drink of water instead of using the dipper. Some days he found he was *very* thirsty. He would leave a trail of dirty clothes on the floor or sit on the bed just to wrinkle the counterpane. The list was long indeed. And childish. And all his petty attempts only made him feel small, while his wife continued to be every man's dream.

Yes, he'd married every man's dream. Appealing to look at, at least before she started scraping her hair into that hated lump and wearing dull clothes the color of mud. She kept a spotless house, cooked better than she cleaned, and lived with the frugalness he'd chosen as a lifestyle after leaving his family's South Carolina estate to make his own way, to get far away from his grasping brother.

And he hadn't touched her since their wedding night, when he'd made love to her once as a tender, caring husband, once as an enraged cuckold.

Chase shook off his troubling thoughts. If he allowed himself to think too long it would fuel his anger all the more. And anger was an emotion he couldn't afford to indulge in if he was to live in peace with this woman.

He tossed the pitchfork into the loft and grabbed the ladder to climb up behind it.

"Chaser?" Wes's voice followed the creak of a rusty hinge. Chase stepped back onto the packed-dirt floor.

"Over here."

Wes moved into a dusty bar of light.

"The doc finally made it. You want to come in and talk to him?"

Chase was in no mood to talk to the doctor. A pompous ass if ever there was one, the man flew into rages when any detail about his practice was questioned.

"No. Just have him check her and the baby. If he needs to see me I'll be out here." The thought of having to enter a barn should deter that puffed-up medicine man. He started back up the ladder, then stopped. "Wes?"

"Yeah?"

"She still treating you different? Nice?"

Wes nodded and scratched his head. "Yeah. She even asked me to sit down last night and keep her company for a spell. We had us a nice little visit." He hesitated a moment. "That all you want, little brother?"

Chase just nodded, though what he really wanted was answers to a great many questions.

He spent the next several minutes rearranging the hay in the loft before realizing he hadn't thrown one forkful into the stall below.

Damn!

He heaved a few forks of hay over the side, then swung down the ladder and pulled his coat on before heading to the house. His boots crunched on the firmly packed snow, the sound loud in the muffled silence of the white-blanketed landscape.

The woman had gotten under his skin more in the last three days than she had in all the months of their marriage. What in the world had happened to change her so? It was as if she was a different person. Surely childbirth didn't change women so dramatically. At least he hadn't found that to be the case in other women he had known.

An outraged cry erupted from within the house, followed seconds later by a loud crash.

Chase pounded down the snowy path, tore through the back door, then slid on ice-covered soles across the kitchen floor. He came to a stumbling halt when his boots hit the rag rug in the parlor.

His wife sat on the edge of the bed, glaring daggers at the doctor, the baby wrapped protectively in her arms. Wes looked up at Chase from where he knelt, picking up large chunks of porcelain chamber pot. The tiniest hint of a smile curved his brother's lips. The doctor, his face a mottled red above his scraggly beard, was hurriedly flinging on his greatcoat and muffler.

"Alston, your wife is mad!"

"Mad!" Her shrill voice cut through the tension as she rocked the baby on the edge of the bed. "I'm not the one who said he just came from treating pneumonia cases and wanted to examine a baby without even washing his hands! You're lucky the chamber pot was clean, you quack!"

"She hurled it at my head, Alston! Hurled it right at my head! And nearly hit me. Take your woman in hand, sir! Are you going to allow her to behave in this manner?"

"Allow? Allow?" His wife stood shakily, the baby still clutched against her chest. "He doesn't 'allow' me anything, Dr. Quack! No one dictates my behavior to me. No one takes me 'in hand.' And no one touches me or this baby without washing his hands. Are you so ill-prepared as a doctor that you've never heard of—" She stopped in midsentence and turned to Chase. "What year is this supposed to be?"

"Supposed to be?" he asked, confused by this non sequitur, and by the fact that she had to ask.

"See what I mean, Alston? She's mad!" The doctor pointed at her with his medical bag.

"Damn it! What year is it?" she insisted.

"1887," Wes's calm voice offered.

"Thank you, Wes. Have you not heard, Dr. Quack, of Florence Nightingale? Sanitary conditions? The Crimean War? I *know* you people learned something about sanitation during the Civil War."

"You dare to tutor me in medicine, Elizabeth Alston?"

"I have more knowledge about medicine in my little finger than you could scrounge up in your entire ample body! And the name is *Barrett*!"

"Dr. Logan, please!" Chase finally found his voice, after having been left speechless by this fiery side of his wife. "Could you be more professional and refrain from arguing with your patient? And Barrett, sit down before you fall down. You're weaving like a drunkard."

Barrett continued to stand, no doubt because he'd told her to sit. She did, however, lay the baby in his basket and cover him with a blanket. Then she straightened to glare again at the doctor.

How odd. He actually called his wife Barrett without even thinking. Even thought of her as Barrett. Perhaps because she didn't even slightly resemble the Elizabeth of just a few days ago. He shook off his ill-timed musings when the doctor flung the door open with a dramatic flourish.

"Alston, I'll be back only when you have taken control of your wife." Without waiting for a response, and leaving several pieces of his medical paraphernalia behind him, the doctor went out, the door slamming behind him.

The blown-glass chimney of a hurricane lamp exploded against the door almost before it closed. Chase rushed to grab the rest of the lamp from Barrett's hand before it met a similar fate.

She relinquished the lamp but staggered weakly, yet determinedly, toward the door.

"Barrett!" Chase grabbed a handful of his wife's flannel gown and yanked her back against his chest. His arms wrapped around her as she struggled to free herself. "Your feet are bare! You'll cut them to ribbons before you ever get to the snow outside! What is wrong with you?"

"That male chauvinist pig! Running out of here like a weasel! I'll tell him what I think of him and his quack medicine! And his chauvinistic attitude! Let me go!"

Barrett squirmed in his grip and he turned her to face him. He had no idea what she was talking about. All he knew was he had to keep her from the thousands of splinters of glass that winked up from the floor in front of the door.

"Barrett, stop it!"

She shoved against his chest, trying to break his hold. Her hair fell in dark, springy ringlets over her shoulders, her face flushed a rosy hue. Whatever he might have been about to say flew from his mind at the sight of this woman, who didn't look at all like his wife. The tight knot atop her head hadn't been in evidence since the day of her lying-in, but he hadn't stopped to look at her long enough to realize what a miraculous change the absence of it wrought. She glared up at him as she struggled, her gray eyes lit with more life than he'd ever seen in them. Her flawless skin rivaled the dew-kissed petals of a pale pink rose. Her lips looked soft and warm and inviting. Her struggles eased and he found himself gazing into his wife's eyes.

An ache started deep down inside him and slowly crept into every part of his body. The ache intensified and centered low, where her belly pressed against him. She continued to look up at him, her eyes growing soft and heavy-lidded. Her most minuscule movement sent a charge rippling through his limbs, and he felt as if it would shoot right through his fingertips. Did she feel it too? Did she ache for his lips to touch hers, for his tongue to seek hers out, for the heat of his hands to burn trails along her skin?

She did. He was sure of it.

He could feel her want, almost as tangibly as his own. He lowered his head, never taking his gaze from hers, waiting for a sign of prudish embarrassment that never came. Her eyes fluttered closed as she tilted her head up, her lips parted in welcome. That small gesture caused an explosion of sweet agony and he fought to remain gentle, tender. He could feel her warm breath, shallow and rapid, as it caressed his face. When his lips settled lightly against hers, a searing flame rose from within him, threatening to engulf him in a blind frenzy.

"Ow! Damn!" came a voice from the fireplace.

Barrett self-consciously jerked away from Chase,

who spun around to drill his brother with a withering look.

"What . . ." Chase had to clear his husky throat. "What is the matter?"

Wes looked up at him from his crouched position, thumb in mouth, with an apologetic, then devilish grin.

"Cut my thumb on a piece of chimney," he said and produced a bleeding thumb to prove it.

"Oh, Wes!" Barrett exclaimed. "That looks bad! Come in the kitchen and let me clean it."

Barrett headed for the kitchen without a backward glance while Wes stood and shrugged apologetically. "Sorry, little brother. I wasn't paying attention."

"Oh. Dare I ask what you *were* paying attention to?"

"Well, I think you and I both know the answer to that," his blasted brother had the gall to answer with a broad smile. "Sure didn't mean to interrupt, though."

Chase could not find the same humor in the situation that his half brother so obviously did. Maybe a dunk in the nearest snowbank would cure Wes of his good humor. Or maybe Chase would just dunk himself in it. The heat of his body right now would melt the snow quicker than a spring thaw.

"Excuse me," Barrett called from the doorway of the kitchen, holding another lamp, "could somebody show me how to light one of these things?"

After letting out a frustrated, unintelligible noise, Chase had crunched through the broken glass and slammed, coatless, out into the winter morning. It occurred to Barrett that the front door had yet to be closed quietly since she'd appeared in this place.

"What's his problem?" she asked toward the door, more to herself than to Wes. When she looked back, Wes shot a smiling blue-eyed look over his shoulder at her. Those incongruous eyes of his seemed to have the wisdom of the ages in their depths. They made Barrett shiver.

At least now she *could* shiver. A few minutes ago she had thought she would spontaneously combust. She could see the tabloid headlines: WOMAN BURSTS INTO FLAMES IN ARMS OF NIGHTMARE LOVER.

Or maybe "dream lover" was more like it. He'd certainly felt like a dream, holding her against his solid chest with those warm, strong arms, looking at her with his strange golden eyes as if he wanted to reach right into her soul and pull out her innermost feelings, then wrap them both in those feelings like a soft, warm blanket.

She followed Wes and the now-glowing lamp into the dimly lit room. Her fuzzy, cozy thoughts stopped when Wes turned up the lamp wick and the cheery yellow glow joined with the thin winter-morning light to illuminate the kitchen.

All those hours she'd lain in the parlor, listening to Chaser and Wes murmur in low tones, she'd imagined the kitchen as she'd left it with Mr. Gideon . . . a sink, a stove, electric lights, a microwave and refrigerator, all completely modern. Even though the dream parlor only vaguely resembled the real one, it had never occurred to her to visualize the other rooms equally changed.

How odd that she would dream a kitchen with so much historical detail when she'd gutted her own kitchen and turned it into an office. A microwave and mini-refrigerator were a far cry from the work this room would involve.

As Wes walked over and yanked the handle of an old-time pump, Barrett scanned the room, mentally cataloging all the differences and realizing that this, the dream room, had very few similarities to the real room. The stove here was a black monster of a thing, with doors all over it and occasional orange flames shooting out of round holes on top. A box of firewood sat close by. The sink, nothing more than a big galvanized tub with a drain, got its running water from the pump beside it. A big, round, serviceable pedestal table sat in the middle of the room, with four ladder-back chairs slid neatly around its edge. Dried fruit hung on strings from the ceiling. Dozens and dozens of jars with canned food in them lined the shelves against one wall. Crocks of every shape and size neatly flanked the canned goods. Barrett walked across the icy floor, her bare feet encountering little puddles of melted ice here and there from Chaser's skating entrance into the parlor. She curled her toes under and tried to walk on her heels.

"This floor's colder than Mother's subzero refrigerator," she muttered. Immediately Wes left the job of rinsing his thumb and guided Barrett to a rag rug in front of the stove.

"Here now, Miss Eliz . . . Barrett. You stand on this rug and I'll bring you a chair to sit by the stove."

"No, Wes. I came in here to dress your cut, not to be babied. Now here, let me see your thumb."

Wes looked at his thumb from several angles, then dropped his hand back to his side.

"It's just a scratch. It don't need no attention."

"Hey, I'm the one with the medical background, even if I did get it all across the dinner table. Now let me see that cut. Do you have any Band-Aids? Peroxide?"

Wes stared at her, squinty-eyed, for several seconds.

"You want a bandage?"

"Yeah."

He shrugged, squinted at her one more time, then disappeared into a pantry off the kitchen.

Barrett looked around at the room again, noting the bathing tub in the corner next to the stove, the shaving necessities, a shaving mirror on the wall. A glimpse of herself in the shiny silver caught her attention and she walked over, toes curled, to look closer. She stared in awe at her reflection.

And froze. Why would she be dreaming that she looked like someone else?

The woman staring back at Barrett had dark-chestnut corkscrew curls, totally unlike Barrett's silky straight black chin-length hair. She'd realized yesterday that her hair was long and curly in this dream, but she'd never imagined she looked completely different. The skin of the woman in the mirror looked as if it had never seen the kiss of the sun, but Barrett had a naturally dark complexion. Eyes that should have been the dark brown of her Iroquois ancestor were instead a soft, deep gray, the color of rain clouds in a summer sky.

Her dreams had always been weird, but this one bordered on ridiculous. The baby. The husband. A black brother-in-law. She was dreaming details she shouldn't have any knowledge of. The whole experience felt much too real. Why couldn't she wake up?

"Could you answer me a question?" Wes's voice came from within the pantry.

"What is it?" she asked, distracted as she looked at the mirror.

"What's that thing the floor's colder than? That zero fridgadoor?"

Barrett stared into the soft eyes of the reflection. An icy, ominous tendril of dread trickled down her spine. Why 1887? Why a baby? Why the past?

Why couldn't she wake up?

Chapter 4

"IT'S TIME TO get up."

Barrett jerked completely awake when the sound of logs being tossed—or rather slammed—on the fire accented the statement.

"What?" she groaned. "I didn't ask for an oh-dark-thirty wake-up call." She rolled over, pulled the quilt over her head, and scrunched deeper under the covers. For two seconds. Then the quilt flew to the foot of the bed. The frigid air caused instant chill bumps. "Hey!" She scrambled to drag the quilt back over her. "Why are you waking me up? Isn't that the baby's job?"

"Since you insisted you would not lie in any longer, I assumed you would want to go to church. You'll need the extra time now."

"Church?" Barrett fought to clear the cobwebs from her sleepy mind. She hadn't been to church since Nana died. "You go without me. I'm sleeping in." She covered herself again and curled into a warm little ball. This time the quilt came completely off the bed. "Hey!"

"We're *all* going to church. The community thinks

we're a happy little family, and they're going to keep thinking that. You were up and around yesterday. You even got dressed. You seem to be recovering well. If you insist you don't need to stay abed, we're going to church, so get up and get ready."

By the time Chase finished yapping, Barrett was sitting gingerly on the edge of the bed, the handmade quilt wrapped around her, as she glared up at the demon, manic-depressive, dual personality . . . The man whose kiss she had ached for just yesterday.

She glared again at Chase's retreating back. She'd been about to dig in her heels and tell Mr. High-and-Mighty where he could go besides church, but this morning she just didn't have it in her to do battle with his will. Life would be easier if she just got up and went with them.

"You ready for your breakfast, Miss El . . . Barrett?"

Barrett gave Wes a weak smile and nodded before his head disappeared back into the kitchen.

She peered over the edge of the baby's basket and watched the little guy start to squirm. She snatched a diaper off the stack, for her own purposes, and two safety pins to anchor the folded fabric to the ridiculous, voluminous drawers.

If I can dream up a surly husband, a newborn baby, and a sweet black brother-in-law, why can't I dream up a pair of nice snug French-cut panties and a box of Kotex?

Ignoring the nasty little voice in the back of her mind that said, "Are you still so sure you're dreaming?" Barrett turned her attention to the armoire.

The dull gray dress she'd worn the day before was out of the question for church. Most of the clothing in the armoire, however, was equally dull, if not in color then in style. She finally found a passable forest-green gown and also a beautiful sky-blue one way in the back. She pulled out the blue frock and held it up against her in front of the long cheval glass.

The shade of blue was perfect for the coloring of the woman in the reflection. Barrett had studied herself in private yesterday after making her discovery in the shaving mirror. The face didn't look familiar, so she wasn't dreaming she was someone she knew. She had inventoried her entire body, from her legs, feet, and hands, to the dishearteningly flaccid muscles and skin of her stomach. No part of her body looked like the one she'd lived with for twenty-five years, and the more she stared into the face of her reflection, the more cracks developed in her dreaming theory.

"Are you planning to wear *that*?" Chase opened the door and strolled in as Barrett gave a violent start and spun around.

"Did you ever hear of knocking?" She didn't try to keep the acid out of her voice. He went on as if she hadn't spoken.

"Because wearing the gown you were wed in might give me the wrong impression. I might start getting husbandly ideas."

Barrett cocked an eyebrow at his sarcastic tone and surly stance. She swept a long, cool gaze over his tall, achingly handsome body. He had treated her with nothing but disdain from the very first moment, as if she were beneath contempt. She didn't even try to soften her words.

"Oh, yeah, right." She molded the gown tighter

against her waist and went back to looking in the mirror. "Like you've done so many 'husbandly' things from day one. Excuse me if I don't break out in a virginal cold sweat."

She tried to show absolute outward calm, fighting down the ricocheting laser beams of heat caused by the images of his words.

"Virginal? What an unfortunately inaccurate description. Would you care to break out in another type of sweat?"

She whirled back around to face him.

"Why would I? It's the only kind I know."

A high-pitched, angry whine pierced the tension-filled air between them. Chase cocked a brow at her and smirked.

"Tell that to Aidan."

"Elizabeth! Chase! My soul, Elizabeth, you should still be abed. But my, don't you look fetching! That shade of green becomes you. And your hair! I never knew it was so long and curly. Were you too tired to put it up, dear? Little ones can be so exhausting. Let me see the little fellow. My soul, isn't he handsome! Just like his father. I would have brought food and come to help out, but we were only able to get out today. Don't you hate snow?"

A tiny bird of a woman, dressed as brown as the wren she resembled, flitted around Barrett and Chase outside the church, peeling back a corner of the blanket and cooing at the baby.

"What name did you decide on?"

"Name?" Barrett shot a sideways glance at Chase, but he simply looked at her with as much interest as the woman did. She had no idea why he'd gotten so hot under the collar when she'd brought up the subject of a name earlier, and she wasn't about to tempt fate by bringing it up again here. And why had he told her to name the baby after his brother? "Well, we haven't decided on a name yet."

"Oh? No name? Well. Of course. My soul, he's not that old. There's plenty of time. A man's name is the most important thing he starts out in life with."

"I couldn't agree more, Carrie," Chase volunteered. "And we want to make sure the little one's name fits him, don't we, darling?"

Barrett looked up at Chase and her stomach did a little flip. His tender smile, she knew, was for the benefit of the onlookers, but, oh, what magic it worked on her senses. His hair, the color and sheen of polished coal, fluttered in the frigid morning breeze. His smiling amber eyes looked even lighter, framed as they were with lashes as black as his hair. She fought an almost overwhelming urge to reach up and trace her fingertips along his jawline, a jaw that would show signs of five o'clock shadow long before that time. Oh, why couldn't he smile more often? And why couldn't he mean it? Why had she dreamed up a husband who didn't even like her?

"Barrett, my child, how good it is to see you again! And how wonderful that you're already up and around," said a voice behind her.

The hair rose on Barrett's neck as she turned and scanned the group of well-wishers who had gathered around them. The crowd parted like the Red Sea, and a small, elderly gentleman dressed in black moved toward her with his arms outstretched.

"You've met my wife, sir?" Chase asked.

"Oh, yes. In another time and place. In my profession it's hard to keep track of all the places I've been."

"Your profession?" Barrett asked, not sure if she really spoke aloud. Her head spun crazily and a hum suddenly roared in her ears. The man standing before her was Mr. Gideon. Why in the world would she be dreaming of Mr. Gideon?

"My soul, Reverend Gideon, you haven't passed through as one of our traveling ministers here for years!" the woman named Carrie piped up. "You must have met Elizabeth in South Carolina, where she's from . . . did you say 'Barrett'?"

"Why, yes, dear, I did. And what's this handsome fellow's name?" he asked, lifting the corner of the quilt that shielded the baby's face from the cold.

"We're thinking of calling him Aidan," Chase volunteered with a suspicious look at his wife.

"Adam? A marvelous name. Good enough for our Lord's first human creation and perfect for such a strapping heir as is your first son. Adam, God will smile on you, my son, as He has smiled on your mother and father. Will we be christening young Adam this fine morning?"

No one corrected the minister after such a fine speech. Chase showed no interest in mentioning the error. Barrett felt as if a heavy fog were smothering her mind. She looked to Chase, who must have agreed to the christening, then she felt herself being guided by him into the tiny church.

Wake up! Wake up now, stupid! Roll over and open

your eyes and be back home, or at the inn, or anywhere
in 1997!

As she tried to wake herself, the congregation took
their seats. She and the baby, Chase, and Wes stood at
the altar with Mr. Gideon. A murmur of voices passed
back and forth in front of her, but she heard nothing but
the hum in her ears, punctuated by her heartbeat, and her
silent chant to wake up. Wes said something to Chase,
who turned to her and squeezed her arm. She tried to
focus on his words.

". . . suggested Robert. It doesn't matter to me."

She looked up at him, not quite comprehending his
words. He narrowed his eyes in disgust, then nodded to
Mr. Gideon.

Barrett had never concentrated so hard in her life.
Everyone around her receded from her vision as she
willed herself to wake up. She felt the baby being taken
from her arms, heard the drone of a voice as if from a
distance. She blocked out the feel of the corset tied
loosely around her middle, blocked out the pain at her
ankles where the button-top boots had already rubbed a
blister. She refused to think of Chase's angry impatience
when she had asked him to show her how to button them
this morning. She blocked out everything except the vision of waking in her bed at the inn.

". . . I christen thee Adam Robert Alston, in the name
of the Father, the Son, and the Holy Ghost."

Suddenly the baby was back in her arms, Chase and
Wes and Mr. Gideon were back, the congregation of
thirty or forty were all smiling at them. Barrett felt tears
suddenly burn to be released, but she stiffened her resolve and swallowed hard.

Chase escorted her down the center aisle to a pew in the middle of the church. She inched her way in far enough to leave room for Chase and Wes, then let herself drop to the wooden seat. Pain immediately shot through her in a sickening swirl. The damage caused by the birth had not yet healed, and the bare wood of the pew was too hard for even a dozen petticoats to soften.

"I'd like to begin this morning by saying how glad I am to be back in this beautiful part of God's world. I'm Reverend Gideon, for those of you who don't know me, and I have heard nothing but wonderful things from fellow ministers fortunate enough to have been sent here. We hope to find a permanent pastor for you soon, since your church has grown so much in the last year."

Barrett barely heard his words. She stood when everyone stood. She moved her lips when everyone sang. She bowed her head when everyone bowed theirs. She felt strangely disconnected, and she didn't know why. Every time she looked up, Mr. Gideon's eyes were on her. Then finally she couldn't look away. She tried to block out his words, but they came in loud and clear.

"You've heard the phrase 'God works in mysterious ways.' What seems to be a nightmare to some, a tragedy, is actually the passing of a soul into a better life, be it here on earth or to our heavenly reward. A tapestry, if viewed from the wrong side, is a jumble of loose ends, knots, and threads that cross in what appear to be random directions. Some of these jumbled areas are the nightmares of our lives. But turn the tapestry over, and view it from the right side. The jumbles turn into a beautiful picture, with every stitch well thought out by the person who created the masterpiece. In our case, life is the great tapestry, and each one of our lives is a thread. Look closely. You'll also find the threads to be of varying lengths. Some short, some long, some extremely long. No matter the length, each and every thread serves a purpose by contributing to the tapestry in one way or another. Some threads cross, some never meet, and some intertwine to make the final result even more beautiful. There are times, though very rare, when the Master Weaver removes a thread in order to use it somewhere else, to complete the picture and to keep the thread strong."

Mr. Gideon's eyes remained on her, only her, as he spoke. Barrett wanted so badly to look away, but he held her gaze with an irresistible force. Her stomach churned as his words sank in and their meaning became clear. Suddenly she felt as if the tangled, loose threads of her life had just snarled into a tight knot. But she must be wrong! He couldn't mean . . .

Mr. Gideon left the pulpit and walked down the aisle, continuing to speak. He stopped in front of her, and finally she was able to look away.

Chase and Wes, everyone in the congregation continued to look toward the pulpit as if he'd never left.

"Don't fight it anymore, Barrett. You've known for a couple of days now. You just won't accept it. You're not dreaming. You're really here, in 1887, with a baby and a husband."

"No . . . I'm . . . I can't . . ."

"You are."

"This is insane! I'm dreaming you!"

"No, Barrett. I'm an angel. A guardian angel. Yours."

"Mine?"

Mr. Gideon smiled at her, a smile full of peacefulness and serenity. As he smiled his body began to transform, to slowly become larger than life. Her mind swam at the sight of his old man's body strengthening and growing into celestial perfection. His face, more perfect than Michelangelo's greatest masterpiece, seemed to glow with a light from within. And no sooner did the sight of him register in her mind than the form of Mr. Gideon returned, innkeeper and traveling minister.

She tried to convince herself this was just part of her dream, but something told her, deep in her soul, that it was all too real.

She truly was in 1887, with a husband and child.

"I . . . I don't understand. Why me? How did this happen?" Barrett looked first at Chase, then Wes, then turned in her seat to view the rest of the churchgoers. Every one of them continued to watch the pulpit. Children squirmed in their seats, parents quickly quieted them, but no one looked at her and Mr. Gideon.

"You've been a challenge to me, Barrett, almost from the day you were born, but especially since your grandmother died."

Barrett drew in her breath, blinking back the scalding tears that memories of Nana always brought.

"What does Nana have to do with it?"

"You closed yourself off. You had no one to turn to for love when she died, so you learned to turn to no one. Ever. That's a dangerous thing for a human to do. And you fought me with every person I put in your path. I thought for a while that Andrew might draw you out, but you were too independent to open yourself up to anyone. I had to bring you to a time and place where you'd be helpless. Where you'd be forced to lean on someone who could help you become the person you were born to be."

Barrett began to shake. She trembled more violently with every new disclosure.

"*You* brought me here? So I could lean on someone? Is this 'someone' supposed to be him?" She flicked a disdainful glance toward Chase. "Because I gotta tell you, you picked one warm, caring, tender individual for me to warm up to."

"Learn while you're here, my child. Become the person you've kept locked away in your heart, starving for love. Open yourself to the family—"

"When can I go back? What do I have to do to get back to my time?"

"You're here to learn, Barrett. Everything that happens in life is a learning experience. Learn to trust these people. Allow yourself to love—"

Anger such as she had never experienced exploded deep inside her, growing like a balloon until she was sure her head would burst from her rage.

"Did I ask for your help? Did I ever once pray for help for my pitiful, sterile life?"

"No. And that's not natural. You've turned to no one when you've needed help, no matter what the circumstances." His tone remained calm, serene.

"How dare you!" She stood, knees trembling. Her fists clutched the blanket wrapped around the baby, her knuckles ached with the force of her grip. She wanted to go for the throat of this . . . this life-wrecker! "Who do you think you are, to come barging into my life, screwing around with it? I didn't ask to be sent back to a time

I know nothing about to live with a man who can barely tolerate me. Damn it, I never asked for anything!"

"No. Someone else asked on your behalf."

Barrett snorted in disbelief. "Who?" Her family wasn't the praying kind. And she couldn't think of any friends close enough to care.

"Your grandmother." Barrett fought back an immediate stab of grief. "I was there, in the hospital room, the day she came home to us. I allowed her to see me. She asked me then to watch over you. But I've always been with you. Remember the time when you were eight and you got separated from your brother and sister and grandmother at the zoo? You didn't know there was a man following you. Your grandmother was frantic. I led her to you before the man could take you. And the time you drove all night to get back to college after that argument with your sister, did you know you fell asleep at the wheel? Did you know I had to make you hit two bumps in the road to wake you? I was there, Barrett, when you stood outside your sister's wedding—"

"I don't want to hear this!" Barrett would have covered her ears if she hadn't been holding the baby. A desperate, numbing panic seized her. Her heart drummed an erratic beat in her ear. "Look, Clarence, if this is some bungled attempt to earn your wings or something, I'll go ring a bell for you until you get them. Just send me home first!"

In a flash, Mr. Gideon changed again into the celestial creature she'd glimpsed moments before. His beauty was so awesome it hurt her eyes to look upon him. He stood so tall that he loomed over her, and with a benevolent smile and tilt of his head, he seemed now to grow even larger. She watched, transfixed and incredulous, as a magnificent pair of cloud-white, incandescent wings rose behind him, then spread to a span of more than twice the height of a man.

"I'm a celestial being, Barrett, created by God to live forever and guard His creatures, *not* a human who has lived and died. There is no bumbling around by a confused mortal soul trying to earn his 'angel's wings' by doing good deeds after death. That's just a Hollywood myth. Guardians have no mortal tendencies such as pride or jealousy or indecisiveness. Our only two emotions are unconditional love for those we look after and unconditional hate for the evil in the world.

"You're here to learn to love, Barrett, and to allow yourself to be loved."

He turned, his wings now folded, and suddenly became Mr. Gideon again.

Never in her life had Barrett been at such a loss for words. She watched the old man start back up the aisle and knew she had to do something.

"Wait!"

He turned back to her.

"You can't drop a bomb like this on me and then turn around and walk away!"

"The deed is done, child. It is for the best."

Barrett couldn't believe her ears.

"Excuse me if I don't agree. I think *I* know what's best for me, and being zapped more than a hundred years into the past isn't on my top ten list of things best for Barrett. You've got to send me back! I don't belong here!"

Mr. Gideon remained silent, simply looking at her. That serene, benevolent smile made her crazy.

"You had no right to do this to me!" she screamed. She didn't care if the others could hear her or not. "I didn't ask for help! I didn't ask to come back here! I demand that you send me back!" She stomped her foot for emphasis. "Immediately!"

After her tirade, the silence of the room nearly thundered. But no one seemed to notice her standing there, screaming at the minister. Skirts rustled, someone in the back sneezed, then blew his nose. Chase hid a yawn behind his fist. The whole scene was so surreal that she had to fight back a growing sense of hysteria.

Finally Mr. Gideon held out his hand to her and uncurled his fingers. In his palm lay a glittering, heart-shaped locket on a chain so fine and fragile it looked to be spun from golden spiders' webs. She frowned at the thing and waited for him to explain.

"This is your heart, Barrett." The locket slowly opened. "It's empty, begging to be filled with love." The locket closed again, and he took the chain in his fingers and fastened it around her neck. "When the heart is full, when you've learned to love, you can go back. All you have to do is open your locket, and your heart." With those words, he started back up the aisle to the pulpit. Barrett quickly sank to her seat, laid the baby on her lap, and popped the locket open with her fingernail.

Nothing happened.

"Only when your heart is full, Barrett. Not until then," he said with his back still to her. When he reached the pulpit, he turned, raised one arm, and said, "Let us pray."

Barrett released a loud, irritated sigh. Chase speared

her with a sideways look from beneath his bowed head.
Two old ladies in the pew in front of them turned and
glared at her.

She wanted to scream. Wanted to cry. Wanted to put
her fist through a wall. Never had she felt so helpless
and frustrated. Never had she felt such lack of control.

She glared at the man leading the prayer. If he thought
he had her beat, he had another think coming.

Chase watched his wife from the corner of his eye as he
drove the wagon home and chatted with Wes. Reverend
Gideon's sermon had teased his imagination. His life
could certainly be described as a tangle of loose ends
and knots. Could he ever hope to turn it around to the
beautiful side of the picture?

Amazingly enough, in the last few days he'd felt
more attracted to his wife than he had since he'd met
her. She almost seemed to be a different person. Gone
was the meek, quiet, perfect woman she'd become after
their wedding night. Not that Elizabeth had ever been a
searing temptress, but her feeble attempts to make up
for her infidelity had succeeded only in making her
mind-numbingly boring. But almost since the moment
the baby had been born she'd become fiery, outspoken,
and entirely too attractive for Chase's own good. He almost wished she would put her hair back into that se-
vere, hated knot atop her head. At least then he wouldn't
want to tangle his fingers in it to see if it felt as soft and
springy as it looked.

He glanced up at her now. She'd refused to wear a
bonnet this morning, saying something about having
"hat hair"—whatever that was—when she took it off.

The sun glinted off the cloud of chestnut ringlets, bringing out little sparkles of red and gold. A wisp here and there lifted in the breeze or swirled to caress her cheek. The day had turned unseasonably mild, melting the last of the snow, and she had unclasped her cape and let it fall behind her. At first glance she seemed relaxed, but he knew her well enough now to know that something was disturbing her. Their relationship was such that normally he wouldn't bother to probe. But for some reason this time he did.

"What did you think of Reverend Gideon's sermon?"

Her face tightened before she looked at him. "It was all right, I guess." She turned away from him.

So much for probing. He'd opened the door and she'd closed it in his face.

The baby had slept peacefully throughout the morning in his mother's arms, but now he began to make little fussing noises. Barrett jiggled him—strange, how he thought of her as Barrett now—but the little one refused to be soothed. Before long his fussing turned into a full-fledged hungry wail.

"What in the world?" A note of panic invaded Barrett's voice. She shoved the crying baby into Wes's arms and looked down at her bodice. She looked up at Chase with a bewildered expression, then back at her bodice.

"Whoa—whoa!" Chase pulled the horse to a stop. "What's wrong?"

"I don't know! There's this kind of hot tingling, and my breasts are aching! Throbbing! This has never happened before! Oh, no!" Chase followed her gaze to her bodice. Two dark circles appeared at the tip of each breast and grew rapidly into huge damp spots. The smell of milk drifted on the air. She pressed her palms tightly against herself and looked at Chase. Before the birth she would have choked before uttering the word "breast."

He glanced up at Wes, who discreetly occupied himself with quieting the baby.

"We're almost home. You can feed him then." He clucked the horse into a trot.

He'd never seen anyone look so dejected. Her shoulders slumped forward, and she looked ready to cry.

Chase was utterly baffled by his wife. It wasn't like her to be so ill-prepared. She'd been the epitome of knowledgeable efficiency before the baby was born, right down to making the childbirth bed and canning strained vegetables for him to eat when he got older. He couldn't believe she prepared with such thoroughness up to the birth, then didn't bother to find out what to expect afterward.

"Perhaps you should visit Alice Parker. She helped you prepare for the baby. She can help with unexpected things like this. With eight children she should be an expert on everything."

His attempts to lift her spirits fell flat. She looked up at him and studied his face for several seconds.

"Maybe."

She turned to Wes and bundled the baby back into her arms, cradling him and rocking him back and forth on the seat.

Something was definitely wrong. He could feel it. This was not the same woman he'd driven to church only hours earlier. Had someone said something to upset her? He'd been right beside her the entire time.

He knew that women often went through a period of

depression after childbirth. Perhaps she suffered from that.

"Oh! Oh, no!"

Barrett raised the baby from her lap, where a huge wet spot adorned her skirts. Two glistening drops fell from the soaked blanket.

"Oh, God, I can't take this."

She shoved the baby back into Wes's arms and grabbed her cape. Fussing agitatedly with her wrap, she finally bunched it up, buried her face in the dark wool, and sobbed uncontrollably.

Chapter 5

BARRETT DRIED HER eyes and allowed herself the momentary lapse of composure. After all, when someone finds herself dropped into a foreign time by a meddlesome angel, into a body with leaky breasts, and into responsibility for an even leakier baby, a tear or two can be expected. But now her spine had its starch back, and her anger simmered just below the surface of her skin. Being shoved into a whole new life was something she didn't plan to take sitting down. She had never allowed others to make her decisions for her, and she had never tolerated heavy-handed maneuvers.

She didn't plan to start now.

As soon as Chase pulled the horse to a stop in front of the neat little farmhouse, Barrett knew what she would do, and she didn't waste a minute in doing it. Chase leaped from the wagon while Wes climbed down with Adam. Barrett grabbed an armful of skirts, yanked them above her knees, and bounded to the ground, ignoring Chase's wide-eyed shock.

She quickly made a mental note never to "bound"

from anything again, as her tender groin, flabby stomach, and throbbing breasts sent spasms of pain skimming along every nerve in her body. But it was either jump from the wagon or chance a surge of sexual lightning from contact with Chaser's outstretched hand. Dealing with the pain was safer.

Refusing to give in to her sore, aching body, she shook out her skirts and set off toward the woods at a brisk pace.

She actually put quite a distance between her husband and herself before the crunch of her footsteps in the dry grass of the yard was joined by Chase's shocked voice.

"Barrett! Where are you going?"

She ignored him.

"Barrett!"

She kept walking.

"Damn it, Barrett! For the love of reason, where the hell are you going? You've got a baby to feed!"

Barrett didn't turn, but waved one hand idly and lifted her head to shout behind her.

"*You* feed him! I'm leaving!"

Silence descended for a few seconds, then the angry cry of a newborn pierced the air. Chase's and Wes's voices were nothing more than distant murmurs by the time she entered the nearby woods. The moment she lost sight of the house she turned sharply to the left, leaving the well-worn path for a somewhat overgrown one. When her gown and cloak caught on the thick, clinging vegetation, she gathered them into a wad above her knees and stormed on.

"Thinks he can zap me here and just run my life for me! *Nobody* tells me what I need! Open my heart, indeed!" Barrett raged as she forged ahead, yanking her clothing higher and slapping at branches that weren't in her way. "I'll show him! Angel! Ha! More like demon spirit from hell! Let's see how he explains to the Man Upstairs that his 'assignment' is out in the woods, refusing to go back, starving for food, and freezing to death in the next cold snap! We'll see just how fast he sends me home!"

Barrett turned sharply again, stomping deeper and deeper into the woods, getting farther away from a path with each passing second.

She didn't have any idea how long she'd walked or how far she'd gone. The deeper into the woods she went, the colder the air became. Stopping to rearrange her armful of skirts and cloak, she took a moment to look around.

No sign of Chase, which surprised her. She hadn't expected him to give up so easily. She wasn't the least disappointed, though, that he hadn't bothered to come after her. He probably wouldn't even miss her except when that baby of his needed feeding.

She forged on, with no clue now as to where she was or how to get back. Ah, yes. This would show hell's angel.

Just when her feet started to really ache in those torture chambers these people called boots, she broke through a stand of trees to face a breathtaking sight.

"Oh! Bear Club Creek," Barrett breathed, recognizing the narrow, shallow body of water. How many times had Nana collected her grandchildren, kicking and screaming, from their computers, televisions, and video games to bring them to this creek for a picnic

feast or horseback riding. Nana would slide the ever-
present book from Barrett's hands, even after they'd
gotten to the picnic site, and teasingly tell her to get her
nose out of the book and join in.

"Life's passing you by, punkin. Loosen up a little and
live it for a change."

She could almost hear Nana's voice on the wind as it
sifted through the leafless tree branches. Barrett blinked
away the unexpected blur in her view of the sparkling,
rock-strewn water. Funny thing, the picnics. She'd always had fun after Nana dragged her away from her
books.

A little sadness took the edge off her anger, and she
sank to a fallen log to catch her breath.

The ache in her breasts, which she'd been too angry to
notice since starting this journey, throbbed now with ferocious, burning pain. The semi-dried rings on her
bodice blossomed again into even bigger circles, drench-
ing the fabric while, underneath, warm liquid trickled
down her skin to her midriff. Her breasts, straining
against the front buttons of her gown, felt as if they'd
turned into downsized bowling balls.

She hunched her shoulders, trying to make herself
smaller, less engorged. A whimper broke from her throat
as each throb intensified the pain.

Desperate, unable now even to rest her arms at her
sides, she flung her cloak from her shoulders and clawed
at the buttons beneath her neck. Frantically she plucked
at each round, stupid, impossibly tiny button, fumbling
until she lost her temper and yanked the edges apart,
spraying the last of the buttons everywhere. Even *that*
action resulted in searing agony. With thumb and index

finger she slowly loosened the ribbon holding her thin chemise, trying desperately not to touch the ultrasensitive skin beneath. With the ribbon undone, she gently peeled the sodden garment from her skin.

Needle-thin streams of watery, translucent milk shot in a dozen directions from each nipple, showering her skirts, the log she sat on, the dead grass at her feet, her hair. Barrett watched the fountainlike display with slightly amused awe. She had never known they did *that*! But, oh, how blessedly wonderful to have the pain, the throbbing, swelling pressure relieved. She leaned forward, allowing the milk to flow until the last of the streams turned to glistening droplets. Her breasts still felt marble-hard, but the burning ache had thankfully subsided.

When a twig snapped behind her she started violently before a viselike grip on her arms hauled her to her feet.

"Why the hell did you run off like that?" Chase roared as he yanked her over the log and spun her around. "Have you completely lost your . . ."

His tirade stopped a split second after his gaze dropped and his eyes locked on her breasts. Barrett attempted to cover herself, but his ironclad grip on her elbows made the gesture impossible.

He stood as still as if he'd been dipped in liquid nitrogen, staring at all that exposed flesh still damp from the impromptu milk bath. He looked mesmerized. His only movement, only sign of life was when he swallowed—hard—and his Adam's apple rose and fell in his tanned, muscular neck.

Keenly aware of the heat of his hands on her arms, Barrett wished he would let her go so she could pull the edges of her bodice together and hide herself from his eyes. Why hadn't she fought him? With her training she could break his hold and have him begging for mercy in any number of painful ways. She'd held her own in self-defense skills when she moved to Chicago. Even taught a few classes.

But she didn't want to break this hold. She let herself relax a bit, let the anger drain from her and be replaced with a warm, honeyed languor. A staccato heartbeat pulsed on her arms where Chase's hands held her, and she realized it didn't match the thrumming beat in her ears.

The thought of his heart racing as he looked at her sent hot tingles exploding like fireworks through her. She allowed her arms to relax in his grip and raised her gaze to his face.

He hadn't moved, hadn't shifted his gaze. As he stared, one white, translucent pearl formed at the peak of her breast and hovered there, shimmering. Trancelike, he released one arm, then raised his hand slowly, ever so slowly, to catch the drop of milk on the tip of his index finger.

The moment his finger touched her skin, Barrett felt as if she'd been hit with a stun gun. Every instinct in her body screamed not to jerk away from his touch. She stood quietly, outwardly calm while inside, fiery rings of electricity pinwheeled through her veins. Though the chill air of the woods cooled her skin, her blood smoldered, threatening to burst into flame.

Chase looked with awe at the droplet moistening his finger, then hesitantly lifted his hand and brought the glistening bead to his mouth. As he closed his lips on the milk-coated finger, he raised gentle, wonder-filled eyes to meet Barrett's. Another shiver threatened to wrack her body, and again she suppressed it while he studied her as though seeing her for the first time.

He lowered his finger from his lips—lowered it in un-hurried leisure, only to touch her once more. To touch her with the softness of a fluttering butterfly as he filled his palm with her. He freed her other arm, raising heated fingertips to her cheek, his thumb grazing the lips she'd nervously moistened with a flick of her darting tongue.

Her every nerve, every sense heightened, she could feel the calluses on his hand, hear his breath so shallow it was almost nonexistent, feel the heat of his entire body radiating through their clothes. His scent—woodsy, leathery, all male—invaded her brain, swirled through her blood, and skipped along with her sporadic heart-beat.

He was going to kiss her. She knew he was going to kiss her, and she could barely wait to feel his lips on hers. Their eyes remained locked as he lowered his head, as her bones melted, as her blood turned to warm, drug-ging cognac in her veins. She didn't consciously close her eyes, but when his lips touched hers she waited, breathless, for fireworks to flash against the darkness of her lids.

She waited.

And waited.

And waited.

His lips, all but closed, touched hers, moving so slightly she couldn't be sure he'd moved at all. He just stood there, the dry kiss about as exciting as watching a guy wait for the fish to bite.

Finally, thank God, he lifted his head, looking unchar-
acteristically restrained.

Barrett ached for the kiss she'd expected. She felt let
down, cheated. Her sore body, her throbbing breasts, her
helplessness and rage at Mr. Gideon—all joined with her
disappointed, surging hormones, leaving her ready to
scream.

"You call that a kiss?" she managed to croak with obvious disgust.

Chase's head snapped back as if she'd slapped him. A
deep, livid red tainted his skin and a vein pulsed at his
temple. He looked at her with that all-too-familiar
loathing in his eyes.

"No," he said as he grabbed her shoulders, "I call *this*
a kiss."

Pulling her hard against his chest, he claimed her lips
with his, moist, demanding, grinding . . . and igniting a
kaleidoscope of Roman candles when his tongue sought
and found hers.

Barrett's body molded to his with a will of its own.
His arms slid around her, pulling her ever closer. Her
arms circled his waist to press palms and fingers against
his back.

Chase kissed her until her knees buckled, until her
mind swam drunkenly. He kissed her nearly breathless,
and deepened the kiss with every movement of his head.

Her breasts pressed against the soft buckskin of his
jacket, and she whimpered low in her throat. He dragged
her down until they knelt on the soft pine needles at their
feet, kissing her still, and then his head dipped to trail
kisses down her neck.

She felt tinglingly alive, aching in her deepest, most intimate regions.

His lips touched the hollow below her neck and milk surged again from her, unheeded, until Chaser's lips closed over her and captured the nectar in his mouth.

Barrett's head fell back as she went weak with want. She felt like a goddess being worshiped by a god. She savored the touch of his mouth on her skin. Luxuriated in the incandescent heat of his body. When his lips finally returned to hers he tasted even sweeter than before.

Barrett slid her hands along his sculptured back, dropped them to skim along his firm, buckskin-clad hips, then brought one hand around to brush inexpertly against the hard swell pressing into her belly.

Moaning low in his throat, Chase ground into her, pulling her toward the forest floor.

Then suddenly he pushed her away. He was on his feet, pacing, as she fought to pull air into her tortured lungs and tried to comprehend the reason behind his abrupt, unforeseen, *insulting* departure.

Maybe he'd stopped because they would have to wait six weeks to finish what they'd started here. She might be inexperienced when it came to consummating a relationship, but she wasn't completely innocent. Guys didn't take well to having to wait, especially if they'd done without for months.

She smiled up at his back, preparing to salve his ego and compliment his second kiss.

Before she could speak he turned to her, one cocky eyebrow raised, and said, *"That's* what I call a kiss."

Barrett felt as if he'd punched her in the solar plexus. She could see an underlying emotion hidden deep in his eyes, but she responded with injured pride to the smug, overwhelming conceit in his voice.

She forced herself to look bored, then shrugged.

"At least it was moderately better than the other one."

"Oh, and you would be the expert, wouldn't you? You, who laid so stiff and still on our wedding night that I feared you'd lapsed into a coma. That is, until I discovered the reason for your . . . lack of enthusiasm. Tell me, was your ennui out of some misplaced loyalty to my brother? Because if his interlude with you was even twice as exciting as mine, I fear he would have dozed off from boredom before completing the task. But then again, very probably your starving son is the fruit of his efforts."

Barrett sat back on her heels, concentrating on tying the soaked ribbons of her chemise to hide the hurt in her eyes. How could he be so vile only seconds after he'd shown her such an exquisite slice of heaven? Obviously Elizabeth had slept with Chase's brother, and there was undoubtedly a question as to Adam's parentage. But why had she done it? And when?

And did Mr. Gideon really expect her to find happiness with a man who thought his wife had given birth to his brother's child?

She diligently fastened the few remaining buttons on her bodice. She felt naked, helpless, accused before judge and jury of a crime she hadn't committed. Her emotions raw, her hurt feelings stinging inside her heart, she couldn't believe he could share what they'd just shared and then look at her with such revulsion.

That's what I get for opening my heart. Go to hell, Mr. Gideon.

She fumbled for the locket, which had somehow worked its way around to trail down her back. She squeezed her eyes closed, flicked the thing open with her fingernail, and prayed that she would open her eyes to the sight of *anything* in 1997.

Nothing. Only Chase glaring down at her.

She rose to her feet, knocked a few dead leaves and pine needles from her skirts, whisked her cloak off the log, then turned and headed deeper into the woods.

"Home is this way, Barrett."

"Go to hell."

"I'm already there," he bellowed.

She stepped around an unmelted pile of snow and continued on her way.

"Don't anger me further, Barrett." But his warning feel on deaf ears.

Her cloak snagged a clinging branch and she tugged to free it. But wait! Why did she need a cloak? The sooner she put herself in danger of freezing, the sooner "Clarence" would have to send her home. She left the cloak tangled in the briars and marched on.

Suddenly Chase grabbed her wrist and spun her around. How the devil did he move through the woods without making a sound?

"You're going home with me, Barrett."

"In your dreams."

He forced her toward the creek. "You have a hungry son to feed. When he's weaned you can disappear and good riddance to you. But the boy stays here. He's my blood, whether son or nephew. And you will be a mother to him until he no longer needs you."

Barrett dug in her heels and dragged both of them to a

stop. With a flick of her arm she broke free, leaving Chase staring at his empty hand and nursing a throbbing thumb.

Aikido had been her favorite martial art.

"I'm not going anywhere with you. I'm not going to be your private milk cow, nursing your son—or you—whenever you have a taste for breast milk!"

She glared at him, willing him to believe she'd hated those glorious moments.

"You need have no fear that I will ever desire to taste any part of you again. And if I had a choice, neither would your son. But you are going home with me if I have to throw you over my shoulder and carry you back."

Barrett bestowed an acid smile upon him. Wouldn't it be fun to take him on? The big, bad man forcing the weak, helpless woman. What she wouldn't give to see his expression when she pinned him to the ground with a handful of "family jewels," a thumb pressed deep in his throat. But right now the effort would cost her more than the reward. She still felt weak from the difficult birth, and her breasts, as hard and swollen and painful as they still were, would only get in the way.

Ah, well. In another life, perhaps. Or another time.

"If you force me I will only run away. Will you always be there to watch me? Will Wes? Do you plan to chain me to the wall so I can't run? Take me back and I'll be gone the first time you leave my sight. I plan to go home, to *my* home, one way or another."

The wind picked up as she stared down her pseudo-husband. A few lonely snowflakes spun in an erratic dance on the breeze, and for the first time she realized that the earlier mild temperatures had dropped to near freezing.

She cocked her head up at Chase. Would he let her leave?

"You are an insane, self-centered twit," he said in answer to her challenging look.

Twit! He's calling me a twit?

"And *you* are a slobbering pig!" she retaliated.

"Inconsiderate prude!"

"Impotent wimp!"

"Bitch!"

"Bastard!"

"Slut!"

"Now now now, children! Lovers' spats should never descend into name-calling. Whatever the misunderstanding, I'm certain you can resolve it in a civil manner." Mr. Gideon strolled up beside them, pulling a pipe from his jacket and patting his pockets. He put the empty pipe between his teeth, looking for all the world as though he was accustomed to strolling deep into the woods and happening upon screaming couples. "Could I offer my help with the problem?"

Chase scanned the woods as if he expected others to appear from the dense copse of trees.

Barrett glared daggers at the dubious angel while the cold permeated her clothing and seeped into her bones.

"I'm sure you know *exactly* how to help. But I don't expect you to oblige."

Chase sucked in a startled breath. "Barrett!"

She ignored him. "But I *do* plan to force the issue. I'm leaving and going into the forest." With a smugness she didn't feel, she turned to walk away. "I'll see you when hypothermia sets in." Her teeth chattered with her last words and a little stab of satisfaction spiked through her. *That'll teach him.*

"Child, this serves no purpose."

Barrett spun on her heel and marched back to face down this hell's angel. She didn't stop until she was almost nose to nose with his little old man persona.

"It serves the purpose of getting me home!" She shot Chase a glance, expecting him to interfere, but he seemed to be moving in slow motion, yanking her cloak out of the bush's thorny grip. She turned back to her adversary and wanted to scream as he smiled around the stem of his pipe. "I don't know what you've done to him so he can't hear. And to tell you the truth, I don't care. I'm getting out of here, one way or another. If I die, have fun explaining that to your boss. Put *that* in your stupid empty pipe and smoke it!" Frosty puffs of air exploded from her lips as she punctuated her statement with a jab of her finger into his wool-clad chest. She was somewhat surprised that her finger actually made contact with something solid instead of poking right through him. After a final quick glance at Chase, she turned and headed out of the clearing.

Before she had taken five steps she realized something was terribly wrong. Her teeth had stopped chattering, the chill bumps smoothed from her skin. Warmth trickled through her veins, swirling unwanted heat to the very tips of her fingers and toes.

"I can make you warm. I can give you a full stomach, but," the voice behind her said, "I cannot send you back. Only you will have that power. And you know what you have to do to get it." She turned slowly back to face the man who was fast becoming her archnemesis. "Would you really rather die, Barrett, than live here and learn to love with this family who needs you?"

Barrett closed her eyes and sank to the ground in momentary defeat. When she looked up, snowflakes spun in the air around her, but they might have been dandelion fuzz in the warmth that surrounded her like an early-summer breeze.

Suddenly Chase was there beside her, kneeling, wrapping the cloak around her, making her feel as if he'd draped a hot electric blanket around her shoulders.

"I'm sorry, Reverend Gideon," Chase said as he stood and pulled the angel aside. "I don't know what's wrong with her. She's not been herself since the baby, wanting to be called Barrett, saying and doing things that make no sense."

Barrett looked up at the two men, a lethargy invading her limbs, a sense of hopelessness numbing her mind. Did he think she couldn't hear him? Did he even care—this man who supposedly needed her so?

"Don't worry, son. Childbirth and motherhood cause monumental changes in a woman's life, and some need special handling more than others. Humor her for a while, and don't dwell on the inconsequential."

Chase scrubbed his face with the palm of his hand, then pinched the bridge of his nose.

"I'll try, Reverend," he said with his head bowed.

"That's all one can ask for."

Barrett seethed, following Chase and the angel of doom at a distance as they wound their way back to the house. Don't dwell on the inconsequential? He had the nerve to refer to her reaction to this intolerable situation as inconsequential? Her mood swung from fiery, determined outrage to hopeless resignation. She lagged behind, purposely slowing a little more every time Chase shot a hateful, impatient glare over his shoulder.

Even before they neared the house, angry wails of hunger pierced the windows and broke into the frigid air. At the sound of the cries, Barrett's breasts again tingled ominously before engorging hard as rocks. She drilled Mr. Gideon with dagger looks as the throbbing grew in intensity.

The front door swung inward and Wes stepped onto the porch with a squirming, screaming handful. He wore a haggard expression of impatience and anger, the first Barrett had seen in this gentle man. His one look of censure spawned more guilt in her than all the words Chase or Mr. Gideon could have said.

Wes wasted no time in handing her the noisy bundle. Casting him a look as close to apologetic as she would allow, she breathed a deep sigh. "Might as well get your two cents' worth in too, Wes. Everybody else has." She cringed inwardly in anticipation of the expected tongue-lashing, but instead of lighting into her, he looked at her with the tiniest hint of tolerant amusement flickering in his clear, robin's-egg eyes.

"You picked yourself the wrong nickname. Shoulda been Brat instead of Barrett." Mild humor still lit his coffee-colored features. "Now feed that youngun before my eardrums get calluses."

Chase could not help but gape at this friendly little exchange. Had he actually heard Wes call Barrett a brat, and had she actually looked repentant instead of furious? Had Wes just told her to do something, and she was actually moving to do it? Without reminding him of his status or refusing to cooperate at all?

"Oh, no!" Barrett exclaimed.

Ah, so the true colors are about to show.

"Adam's soaking wet! Again!" she declared, amazingly with no hint of anger. She held the baby at arm's length, as if offering up a soggy gift to the gods.

"Yep." Wes's lips curled upward in a devilish smile. "Reverend, I got some fresh apple cider out in the kitchen. Care to wet your whistle with it while you're here?"

The minister jumped at the offer, following Wes into the house and back to the kitchen. Barrett stood just inside the door, looking helpless as she watched Wes disappear into the other room. Finally, she turned back to Chase.

"He's wet," she informed him needlessly.

Chase stepped inside and kicked the door shut, quirking an impatient eyebrow at her. "So change him."

"I can't change him!"

Oh, for the love of Pete.

"Why not?"

"I've never changed a baby! I have no idea what to do. Besides, it's disgusting."

Chase scrubbed his palm across his eyes. "I can guarantee it will be even more disgusting if you don't."

Barrett pushed the red-faced, squirming, screaming baby into Chase's chest. "You do it."

He heard his jaw pop when his teeth ground together. "Barrett, go change your son so you can feed him." Then he added twice as loud, "So he'll stop his infernal screaming!"

He watched his wife yank the baby back to her breast, then wince before moving to the side of the mattress. Tomorrow he would put the bed back into their room, now that she'd ended her lying-in.

Barrett moved to lay Adam, dripping diaper and all, on the quilt that Chase's mother had painstakingly made for his wedding.

"Here!" Chase barked and snatched up a piece of oilskin. "Put this under him. Unless you've a desire to change the bedding as well."

"Oh," she squeaked, as if the thought had never occurred to her. She fumbled with the sheet of oilskin with one hand, botching the job, until Chase grabbed it from her and smoothed it across the quilt. With a look that he hoped conveyed even a modicum of his long-suffering, he turned to build up the fire.

What in Sam Hill had gotten into the woman? Had some evil twin come and taken his wife's place on the day of Adam's birth? A couple of hard jabs at the logs with the poker vented some of his pent-up frustration. He stirred the fire with so much force he nearly put it out. When the chunks of coal he loaded on finally blazed into a steady flame, he rose to his feet and knocked the coal dust from his hands.

Adam's screams had not diminished one whit, though Barrett had had time to change a dozen diapers. Every earsplitting, reverberating cry shot through Chase's nerves like fingernails on a slate.

"For the love of heaven, will you do something about that . . ." Chase roared above the din, but his words died in his throat when he turned to face his wife.

Barrett stood over the baby, trying to look down with

her head turned away and her nostrils pinched, attempting to remove the safety pin using only the tips of her thumbs and forefingers. Miraculously the pin popped open and she gingerly slid the thing from the diaper, but then, unbelievably, she tried to remove the sodden cloth by hooking it with her fingernail.

Chase walked, trancelike, to stand beside his bizarre wife while she performed this most unusual ritual.

"Dare I ask what you are doing?" he inquired above the latest cry.

She stopped her questionable activity and gifted him with a look of pure exasperation.

"I'm playing a piano concerto. What does it *look* like I'm doing?"

"Oh, for the love of . . . Here. Let me show you how to do that." He moved in, gently grabbed Adam's ankles between his fingers, then pulled the soaked cloth from beneath the angry baby, dropping the diaper with a wet *splat* onto the edge of the oilskin. Feeling smug, he expertly wrung out a washrag over the ever-present basin and turned back, just as a yellow stream shot skyward from between those scrawny, flailing legs, arcing with exquisite timing to splash off his unsuspecting wife's forehead.

Barrett screamed and jumped away, batting ineffectually at the impromptu shower. Grabbing a handful of skirts, she plastered them to her face, yelling, "Ick, ick, ick," in her failed attempts to dodge the liquid barrage.

The briefest flash of horror flickered in Chase's mind at what his perfect wife's reaction would be to a faceful of piss.

Then he laughed.

He laughed as he had not laughed in years . . . maybe in his entire life. The baby continued to scream, Barrett continued muttering her muffled "Ick!" and Chase doubled over, gasping for breath, tears streaming from his eyes. Wes and Reverend Gideon's curious faces appeared in the doorway before the Reverend silently hooked Wes's shoulder and pulled him back into the kitchen with a smile.

Weak with laughter, Chase pulled a handkerchief out of his pocket and mopped tears from his face, belatedly thinking to offer the square to his damp wife. After one feeble attempt to hand her the handkerchief, he sobered just a little at the sight of her shaking shoulders, her face still buried in a handful of skirts while muted, feminine whimpers mingled with the baby's cries. Before he could think of his first consoling word, she dropped her hands, threw back her head, and gilded the air with the most delightful laugh he'd ever heard.

The breath caught in his throat at the sight and sound of his wife's astonishing reaction. Charmed against his will, he felt the mirth rising in him again, exploding with hers in equally helpless laughter.

When he finally caught his breath enough to release his aching ribs, he tardily tossed a diaper over the source of the gusher, then had to wipe away more tears when Barrett piped up, "Oh, now you check the aim, after the gun's been fired."

It took Adam's furious screams to finally sober them both. Chase moved back to the business at hand, a little guilty at enjoying such a good laugh during the baby's discomfort but fighting down a lingering chuckle nonetheless. Barrett sniffed and dabbed at her eyes.

"Here now, here now," Chase murmured, calming the baby. "You've every right to be angry. But dinner will be nicer if both participants are dry." The last words cracked with an uncontrollable chuckle. Barrett stunned him again with a blind punch to his arm as she busily rinsed lather from her face.

Adam's cries subsided to pitiful fussing when Chase again bent to his task, thoughts of his wife's uncharacteristic behavior shimmering in his head. He swabbed thoroughly at the rosy little bottom, but when he plucked the protective barricade from young Adam's lap, he found himself fighting down a rising flush of heat.

Apparently newborn baby boys were just as prone to the . . . ungovernable reflexes that plagued males throughout time. Chase flicked a glance at Barrett, only to see her hand slow in its scrubbing, then drop away from her face.

Damn. How could the sight of a baby's willy embarrass a husband in front of his wife? *It can if that man and wife are strangers.*

Chase weighed the possibility of whipping the diaper on in record-breaking time, but a few patches of red erupting on the tender skin persuaded him to finish the job, uncomfortable though it might be.

Resigned, he opened the washcloth and set to work bathing the inflamed area, acutely aware of Barrett studying his every move. She leaned a little closer. Chase fought to ignore a *zing* that shifted his stomach.

"Now, see?" he almost barked in an effort to pull his stomach back down where it belonged. "You're going to have to actually touch him in order to take care of him."

Barrett made no comment. She simply watched Chase's hands with more attention than he thought was called for. She stood so close he could feel her warmth, could smell the faint scent of milk that clung to her bodice and the lye soap she'd washed her face with.

She smelled heavenly.

Chapter 6

BARRETT TRIED NOT to swallow past the tension in her throat, because she knew it would come out a gulp if she did. She kept her eyes trained on the strong, muscular hands skimming so gently over the baby's skin. The same hands that had so recently touched her own bare flesh.

"Now." Chase's voice pulled her thoughts away from warm lips, fragrant pine needles in the forest, and calloused palms. "Just fold this like this . . . and then again . . . then put it under him like this . . . now gather up the three corners and fasten them with a pin . . . and *ta-da*."

He gave a "nothing up my sleeve" flourish that seemed to Barrett more relieved than triumphant. She pulled in a deep breath and finally dragged her gaze to meet his.

Something had changed between them. She didn't know exactly what, or when, or even how long the change might last, but for the first time since waking in this time, she felt him look at her. Really look at her.

It turned her knees to butter.

The hungry scream slapped her back to reality. Chase scooped Adam up just a tad too quickly, shoving the noisy infant into her arms just as the sound of carriage wheels and jangling harnesses stopped in front of the house.

Before Chase could remove the soiled diaper, the door swung inward and the face of the little brown-wren woman from church appeared around it.

"Yoo-hoo! Oh, good. I didn't think you'd be out visiting so soon, but then I never guessed you'd be out of bed just four days after your ordeal either. I brought you some supper, though I know it won't come close to your own cooking, Elizabeth." The woman named Carrie bustled into the house, a huge basket that looked like it weighed more than she did swinging on her arm.

"Manna from heaven, Carrie, since we've been eating Wes's cooking for the last few days," Chase quipped. Barrett started to remind him that the cooking had been just fine, but the words died in her throat when he bestowed a smile on their visitor that Barrett grudgingly admitted would have sent her to her knees if he'd ever turned it on her. "Let me take that to the kitchen. I was just going to get the Reverend and show him the new milk cow. It'll give you ladies time to fuss over the baby in peace." He lifted the basket, pulling in a deep, appreciative sniff before disappearing through the door, exclaiming dramatically, "Wes! Real food!"

"My soul, this little fellow has a temper on him, doesn't he?" Carrie chimed with what seemed close to uncomfortable enthusiasm as she turned back to Barrett.

Barrett sank into a chair opposite her visitor. Almost

immediately Adam's crying subsided in anticipation of lunch. "Please, have a seat. He's hungry."

She flicked open what buttons were left on her bodice with one hand.

Carrie's eyes drifted to the dozen or so places where buttons were missing.

Great. How do I explain this?

"Oh. Well . . . these . . . ahhh . . . I was out . . . You see, I got so . . ."

Adam saved her from further stammering with an ear-piercing reminder that he was waiting to eat. Barrett thankfully concentrated on opening her chemise. The moment air hit her breast, milk shot in a dozen directions, glancing off her face and sprinkling her gown. She felt a giggle rising as she pressed the baby to her. *Beats the heck out of the last facial I got.* Adam locked onto his target with unfailing accuracy, creating a much-welcomed silence in the room.

She adjusted the baby's position and tried to relax back into the chair. Carrie remained quiet as Barrett racked her brain for something to talk about. Was this woman a good friend or just a friendly neighbor?

"It started out to be a beautiful day, didn't it?" she ventured lamely. Carrie blinked and dragged her eyes away from the baby.

"Oh, my, yes. Even if it didn't last long, it was refreshing to have such a mild day." Carrie's gaze dropped back to the baby. "Was the birthing terribly difficult? I couldn't believe my eyes when I saw you at church already."

Barrett knew the custom was to stay in bed for a good

two weeks after delivery, and she also knew it was the worst thing in the world for a speedy recovery.

"Well, I feel fine. There's really no reason to stay in bed if I'm not sick, is there? And childbirth isn't an illness."

A shadow of something flickered in Carrie's eyes, but she only gave a preoccupied nod, still spellbound by the baby. Adam made little swallowing noises in his throat as he struggled to keep up with all that milk. His tiny fingers clutched the edge of her chemise while the heel of his hand kneaded her swollen breast.

"Is it as wonderful as it seems?" Carrie's voice was almost a whisper.

Barrett studied the face of the woman across from her. *So that's it.* She felt a surge of unexpected sympathy.

This was the face her mother had described so many times across the dinner table. The face of a woman desperate to have a baby, praying every month that her period wouldn't come, devastated when it did. Barrett had never seen such yearning in a person's eyes. Or such fathomless sadness as Carrie watched every tiny movement Adam made. This was what her mother had meant when she said some women grew so desperate for a baby that she feared for their sanity. And the nineteenth century was a time when a woman was defined by her children and her home. A woman was viewed as less than whole if she failed to have children—even if the fault lay with her husband.

Barrett gentled her voice when she answered.

"It's exhausting, and confusing," she admitted. "And *painful*," she added with a little laugh. But was it wonderful? If she had married Andrew and had his baby, would it have been wonderful?

"Oh, but Elizabeth, you and Chase have created a new life. And even now you're giving him nourishment with your own milk. That has to overshadow all the exhaustion and the pain. That has to be the most magnificent feeling in the world."

For the first time Barrett looked at nursing this baby not as a chore demanded by some nightmare husband, but as the miracle that Carrie saw it as.

Still, somewhere in the back of her mind she felt as if she'd been cheated, or that she, herself, was cheating. She hadn't conceived this baby. She hadn't carried it for nine months. It hadn't been her body that delivered this tiny human being, and it wasn't her breast from which he drew sustenance now. She just inhabited this body, taking credit, or blame, that wasn't hers. It was like being complimented on a beautiful dress and not admitting that it was borrowed. She wanted no part of it.

"Tom and I are still hoping," Carrie said dreamily, then snapped to attention and swatted at the air. "But I don't need to tell *you*, do I? My soul, I've cried on your shoulder often enough!"

So Carrie had been a close friend to Elizabeth. And that look on her face, that hint of desperation in her sad, kitten-gray eyes, told Barrett that she and her husband had been "hoping" for longer than any woman should have to.

Carrie's eyes followed every minute movement of the baby with undisguised, pitiful longing. Guilt ribboned through Barrett's conscience as she burped little Adam, then switched him to her other breast. She'd never wanted a child, never taken the time to even contemplate the possibility, and she'd been zapped into instant motherhood against her will. Carrie would never understand that mentality. She would probably hate Barrett if she knew.

Feeling awkward and at a loss for words, she followed Carrie's gaze to Adam's tiny face.

He ate with the gusto of a little pig, smacking and swallowing, his lips and chin coated with translucent milk that bubbled at the corners of his mouth. As Barrett watched, his face turned a bright lobster red, and soon an embarrassing rumble vibrated the diaper beneath Barrett's hand.

"Oh!" She forced an uncomfortable laugh and darted a flustered look at Carrie, who beamed with gentle amusement. When another ominous rumble boomed, Barrett jerked her hand away from the offending area. "Oooooh! Gross!" she cried. "This is worse than getting soaked." She gaped at the dark yellow substance coating her palm. "It looks like Grey Poupon! Ugh!" She held her hand up and looked at it through the corner of her eye, trying to keep her nose upwind.

Carrie giggled and plucked a fresh diaper from a stack near the baby's basket.

"I daresay it looks more yellow than gray. Here, use this while I get you a washrag."

She disappeared into the kitchen while Barrett fought down the gag reflex that rose in her throat. She carefully wiped every vestige of the disgusting stuff off her palm, then systematically scrubbed each and every finger. Amazing. The stuff had a tangy smell, but *not* the one she expected. But it was still repulsive. Carrie reappeared with a wet washrag and handed it to Barrett.

"Umm," Carrie murmured when she saw the diaper Barrett had used, "I meant for you to put that under the baby."

Barrett's gaze dropped to her lap as the realization struck her. "Oh! Yuck!"

A veritable puddle of Grey Poupon spread on her skirts beneath Adam.

Holding him aloft, one tiny, smeared leg kicking happily from the troublesome gap in the blanket, she tried to will the mustard-colored glop from seeping through her skirts. She glared in the direction of the kitchen. This was all the fault of that angel of doom!

Carrie misread the look. "The men went out to the barn to see that new dairy cow. Here, let me have him while you get out of your skirt."

The little wren woman expertly whipped a thin blanket around the worst of the mess, then took Adam out of Barrett's arms. Barrett didn't waste a minute in gingerly gathering up her skirts and making a beeline for the bedroom.

She slammed the door behind her with more force than necessary, considering the act she should be putting on for Carrie. But, damn it, she'd had just about all she could take today—being yanked out of a cozy bed before the crack of dawn; riding to and from church in a wagon that rattled her teeth; confronting the fact that she wasn't going to wake from this nightmare and having her plans to get home foiled; strapping on this blankety-blank corset just to be able to get into something with more color than a tub of wallpaper paste; and finding that she'd landed in a twilight zone as a human bull's-eye for everything that squirted.

She tore off the repulsive skirt, then yanked off the already unbuttoned bodice. Wadding the yards of fabric into a tight ball, she dropped it on the floor, making sure the "mustard" was all on the inside. The corset came off next. Barrett took a heavenly minute to breathe deep and dig at the red imprints of stays on her midriff before slipping into the drab gray dress she'd worn the day before.

She couldn't let herself think. If she did, she would surely go mad. Picking up the wad of contaminated material, she threw open the bedroom door and marched back into the parlor. With the skill of Michael Jordan going for a slam dunk, she shot the bundle of dark-green wool straight into the roaring fire.

"Elizabeth!" Carrie squeaked.

"*Barrett!*" Chase roared as he and the other men stepped into the parlor.

Barrett nearly jumped out of her skin, spinning around and grabbing the mantel with one hand and her heart with the other.

"*What?*" she barked back. What in the world had she done to deserve being screamed at?

"What in the name of God—pardon me, Reverend—Barrett, *what* do you think you're doing?" Chase's voice now was only marginally quieter than his initial roar had been.

"I'm burning that dress," she answered in a tone that didn't need the words "you idiot" tacked on to get her message across.

"*Why?*"

"Because," she stated deliberately so this slow-witted

man might understand, "it was covered in . . . baby feces!"

Chase, as well as everyone else in the room, gaped at her. "Have you ever heard of laundering—"

"And half the buttons on the bodice were missing. Besides, you can't wash baby poop out of wool!"

"You could have at least tried!" Chase bellowed. "You could have sewn on more buttons! Even if the dress was ruined, you could have cut it up in pieces and used it for quilting squares! Good Lord, Elizabeth, did you lose your mind when you gave birth to that child?"

Like a jagged rock against a delicate piece of glass, his words shattered the fragile truce that had fallen between them.

"I haven't lost anything I came here with," she gritted through clenched teeth. "And for the last time, don't call me Elizabeth! Call me Barrett, or 'hey, you,' for all I care, but don't ever call me Elizabeth again!"

"Hell! Elizabeth. Barrett. Next thing I know you'll be telling me your last name is Browning!"

"No," she answered in an escalating yell, "that's my brother!"

Chase's mouth worked, opening and closing, but he visibly checked a dozen retorts that wanted voicing. Finally, without uttering another word, he did an about-face and marched out of the room.

The only sound for several seconds was that of Chase's steps thumping to the back door. Moments later Wes and Mr. Gideon discreetly followed. Carrie resumed the cleanup job she'd started on Adam, casting a hesitant look at Barrett through lowered lashes.

"You . . . you want to be called Barrett?"

Barrett leveled a look toward the back door that would have rendered Mr. Gideon dead and buried had he not already been an angel.

"Yes."

"But your name is Elizabeth Marie—"

"My first name is Barrett."

Carrie blinked several times, her mouth a silent "O" as she absorbed this information and finished dressing Adam.

"I've always hated being called Elizabeth," she stated in all honesty. Not that many people mistook her for her sister after they got to know them.

Carrie was obviously uncomfortable with having been a witness to the scene with Chase, so Barrett plastered on a bright smile and changed the subject. "So, you brought food? How about a snack?"

For just the briefest of moments, Carrie stared at Barrett as if she were a two-legged horse. Barrett ignored the look, moving to the kitchen, deliberately leaving Carrie to bring a contented, gurgling Adam with her. Carrie followed, cooing to the baby, dreamily rubbing her cheek against the dark feathery down on his head. Just as Barrett flipped open the top of the picnic basket a sharp rap sounded at the door.

Just what she needed. More company.

She craned her neck to see if Chase was near enough to hear the knock, then flicked a glance at Carrie, who sank onto a kitchen chair, so absorbed with the baby that Barrett couldn't be sure she'd even heard.

The knock fired again, more insistent this time, and Carrie looked up from her baby-gazing.

"Oh. Would you like for me to get that?"

"No. You take care of Adam. I'll get it." She'd have to start facing all the strangers sooner or later anyway.

She opened the front door to three of those strangers—three women of assorted sizes and shapes bearing platters and baskets. The one with her knuckles raised to rap again stood nearly six feet tall, her iron-gray hair pulled back at the base of her skull in a knot so tight that it looked painful. Her face wore a no-nonsense expression, and her skin was corrugated with wrinkles. An ugly brown bonnet hugged her head like a helmet.

A crepe-hanger, Barrett thought. That was what Nana had called people who found fault with everything and everybody.

The second woman looked to be in her late thirties, obviously the daughter of the crepe-hanger. She seemed to be in a perpetual cringe, like a dog or child who'd been yelled at too often. Her hair was scraped back, disappearing beneath a bonnet not quite as dark brown but just as ugly as her mother's.

The third visitor, Barrett realized, was a girl of about fifteen. She had to be the cringer's daughter, with the same pale blue eyes of the others, but that was where the similarity ended. Her hair, the color of ripened wheat, fell gracefully from where it was caught up at the back of her head, and a long green ribbon that matched her dress decorated the curls. She radiated exuberance, with her cheeks dusted pink by the cold and her eyes sparkling with curiosity. Barely controlled energy made her shift from one foot to the other.

"Ahem," the crepe-hanger barked.

"Oh." Barrett swung the door wide. "Come in."

"Margaret. Ann. Come along." The older woman

marched past Barrett with all the confidence of a drill sergeant who knew the troops would follow. The cringer, indeed, followed like a dog taught to heel, but the bouncy teenager handed a covered dish to Barrett and gushed.

"Oh, Mrs. Alston, you look so fetching! Why, if my hair looked like that I'd never pull it back in that ugly old bun you always wear." The girl's hand flew to her mouth and she gaped, mortified, before Barrett laughed and waved her into the house. What was left of the bun when Barrett finally got around to tackling her hair after Adam's birth had been none too flattering.

"Hello, Ann," Carrie called as Barrett and the girl entered the kitchen.

So Margaret must be the cringer.

Ann "oohed" over the baby, gently pulling away the blanket to get a good look at his contented, sleeping face. "He's just the most beautiful baby I've ever seen. Can I hold him?"

Carrie reluctantly gave the baby up but hovered nearby like a mother hen.

"If you ask me, he's not got enough blankets on. The child will catch his death," the crepe-hanger declared.

"My soul, Beatrice. Would *you* catch your death if we wrapped you up in two or three blankets?" Carrie won a glare for that piece of logic.

Margaret hadn't uttered a word, as far as Barrett knew, and didn't look as if she was about to add to Carrie's observation.

Beatrice turned to Barrett. "And you, Elizabeth Alston, are liable to find yourself barren, or worse, since you saw fit to end your lying-in so early. I always thought you had better sense than that. If you ask me, you'd do well to get back in that bed for another week."

Barrett's hackles rose at the name as well as the self-righteous lecture from this idiot woman.

"First of all, I'm not sick, so why should I stay in bed? And second, I prefer to be called Barrett."

She could almost hear the necks popping as three heads jerked around to look at her.

"But Mrs. Alston, isn't your name—"

"My first name is Barrett. I've always hated being called Elizabeth, so from now on, if you don't mind . . ." she let the statement trail off.

"Well, I never in all my living days ever heard of such a thing. What does Chase Alston think about this?"

"Oh, he's already calling her Barrett," Carrie volunteered, then shrank away just a bit under Beatrice's glare.

"I don't see anything wrong with it. It's her name." Margaret spoke for the first time in a timid, barely audible voice.

Beatrice gifted her with the same look she'd given Carrie.

"Would anyone like some tea? Carrie and I were just about to have a snack."

The ladies settled around the table, passing an oblivious Adam from lap to lap while Barrett tried to figure out how to make tea. How did they make it without tea bags? Coffee probably would have been easier to figure out.

"Let's see. Where did I put that . . ." she said as she searched for nothing in particular, stalling for time.

"Are you looking for the tea ball? It's there on the shelf next to the canister."

A tea ball. Of course. She could have kissed Carrie.

Now if only she'd given a hint as to how much tea to use.

While the questionable tea steeped, Barrett found plates and Carrie sliced the pumpkin pie she'd brought. With the first cup of the dark black beverage poured, Barrett, as well as all the ladies around the table, visibly stifled a shudder at their first sip.

Beatrice not so discreetly shoved her cup and saucer away. "I think perhaps you should go back to brewing your tea as you used to, young lady."

Barrett simply shrugged, and a flurry of topics swirled in the air as the others tried to smooth over Beatrice's less-than-tactful comment.

Barrett's mind reeled with the conversations about canning food, the latest quilt pattern somebody named Bessie was working on, recipes for everything from pumpkin pie to lye soap. She got advice without asking for it on what to do for colic, whooping cough, diaper rash, and weaning Adam from the breast. All of which seemed like a foreign language to her, considering that her usual conversations revolved around marketing, company projections, sales, profit margins, and trips to the four corners of the globe.

Again, she felt the urge to wrap her hands around Mr. Gideon's throat and squeeze the life out of him.

"We noticed *she* was in the congregation today. Could that be the reason you left the childbed so early?"

Barrett blinked and pulled her thoughts away from killing her guardian angel.

"She?"

Beatrice's lips puckered in disgust. "You know. *Her.*"

"Her?"

"The Widow Long," Margaret all but whispered across the table.

Barrett stopped herself from repeating the name.

"Why should the Widow . . . Mrs. Long being in church make me leave—"

"How long do you intend to deny that the woman has set her cap for your husband, Elizabeth?" Beatrice's mouth pursed with such fine lines she looked like she had a comb across her lip.

"Call me Barrett," she said out of habit. "And if another woman is after Chase, that's my problem, isn't it?"

The crepe-hanger sucked in her breath in a dramatic gasp.

"Well, I never in all my living days ever—"

"I appreciate your concern. I didn't mean to be rude." Best not to make any enemies until she knew what she was dealing with. "But honestly, everything is fine here. Chase and I are very much in love." She nearly choked on those last words.

"Yes. We are. And that's a sentiment a loving husband never gets tired of hearing. Right, Barrett, darling?"

She raised her eyes to see the husband in question stomp the snow off his boots at the back door and grace the ladies around the table with a smile that could have charmed the habit off a nun.

All he'd heard was, "Chase and I are very much in love." He looked at his wife and wondered what the conversation had been that led to such a spurious declaration.

A becoming peach colored her cheeks, but instead of the characteristic meekness he'd lived with for months, Barrett responded by rolling her eyes at him while the other ladies looked his way. Not one to back down from a challenge—and he knew a challenge when he saw one—he strode across the kitchen, leaned over his wife's shoulder, and planted a loud kiss on her cheek. He wasn't prepared for the jolt of sheer lust that ricocheted through him like a bullet off a canyon wall. And this woman, this wife who had not touched him intimately nor wanted him to touch her since their wedding night, leaned her head back against the front of his trousers, tilted her face up to his, and sent his stomach rocking with a brilliant smile. A smile that never quite made it to her eyes.

A smile that said, "Touché."

But had this been a fencing match, he was not sure who would have been awarded the touch.

He forced himself to step away calmly, as if his wife leaned her head against his fly like this every day.

Beatrice Ord looked at them both as if she'd just come across them naked in the churchyard at high noon. Margaret Keller suddenly found the toes of her matronly shoes infinitely interesting, and Ann Keller continued to watch with avid curiosity, with the ever-present hint of infatuation in her eyes that always made Chase uncomfortable. Only Carrie, poor, desperate Carrie, noticed nothing as she nuzzled the tip of her nose against the top of Adam's head, her finger tracing a gentle path along his tiny, angelic cheek.

Beatrice lurched from her chair. "Margaret. Ann. It's time we got home," she bugled, jerking on her pristine white gloves.

Adam jerked, stiff-limbed, at the loud command, while Margaret flinched and slid noiselessly from her chair. Ann continued to gaze up at Chase until Beatrice yanked the collar of her dress and nearly dragged her out of her seat at the table. Even Carrie came out of her trance with the baby and was soon hustled into her cloak by the indomitable Beatrice. Within moments Chase and Barrett stood alone at the front door watching the two wagons disappear down the road.

He turned to look at his wife as she lifted her gaze to his and looked him straight in the eye.

This was not the woman he had married.

Adam's early-morning squirming only halfway roused Barrett from a coma-like sleep. If her luck held, she could squeeze another ten minutes in before he realized he was hungry.

She curled her knees into the warmer part of the covers and skootched tighter against the pillows at her back. As that misty, deliciously relaxed state right before sleep overtook her, a hand readjusted itself on her ribs, coming to rest limply against her breast.

She sighed and snuggled closer, luxuriating in the shared warmth of the bed. The arm curled tighter around her, dragging her closer. A knee propped itself on her hip.

With jarring clarity, she realized precisely what she was backed up against. Suddenly the sleepy cobwebs of her mind cleared like a patch of fog in gale-force winds.

She wasn't snuggled against a pile of pillows at all, but a warm, firm body that curled around hers like two spoons nestled in a velvet-lined drawer.

Chase was in bed with her!

Her first instinct was to roll over and literally kick him out. How dare he? Granted, he'd slept there that first night, but he hadn't been back since then. She'd just assumed . . .

Apparently she'd assumed wrong.

The sense of comfort that his casually draped arm created stirred Barrett in ways she didn't want to think about. Using her thumb and forefinger, she gently tried to lift his hand so she could roll away from the maddeningly warm peaks and valleys of his hard body. But his arm curled tighter, pulling her closer still, until she lay nearly underneath him, his legs intertwined with hers, his cheek resting against the top of her head.

Now what?

For some reason, she didn't want to chance waking him by forcing herself out of his embrace. Not for a minute did she believe that her reluctance had anything to do with the way her body seemed to fit so perfectly against his. Nor the way her blood seemed to hum with tension while her bones and muscles melted from his heat. She simply didn't want to wake him. That was all.

She could tell from his breathing that he truly was asleep.

And she knew, without a doubt, the exact moment he woke.

The layers of sleep lifted from Chase's exhausted mind. Nights of trying to sleep through Wes's shingle-rattling snore had left him nearly dizzy with fatigue. When he'd finally gone to turn in at his brother's cottage the night before, Wes's snore was already resonating through the tiny home they'd all originally shared, piercing the air with an unearthly noise that would have brought a lesser built house down around their ears.

Chase had turned and walked the fifty or so yards home in the frigid hours after midnight, crept through the back door, then slipped out of his clothes and under the covers to fall immediately asleep at the edge of the feather mattress.

He was definitely not at the edge anymore.

Barrett lay nearly beneath him, his legs tangled with hers, his arms wrapped tightly around her. The feather bed surrounded them like a huge, fluffy nest.

She must surely still be asleep. She would never lie so contentedly if she had awakened with his body draped around hers as it was. At least Elizabeth wouldn't.

How odd, that he should think of his wife as two separate people. But since Adam's birth she seemed to be a different woman from the one he'd married. And while he lay there in the still of the morning with his arms wrapped around her, her warm, feminine scent teasing his senses, he finally admitted to himself that he much preferred this wife. Even when she called him an impotent wimp, whatever a wimp was. Even when she was walking away from him, yapping about hypo-something-or-other, making no sense and being rude to the reverend. This fiery, emotional side of her stirred feelings in him that he'd spent months forcing from his mind and heart. In fact, she stirred feelings he'd never felt before, for Elizabeth or any other woman.

He should release her before she had a chance to wake and shrink from his touch. But, God help him, the feel of this woman in his arms, of Barrett in his arms, was a balm to his soul. He reveled in the euphoria of the warm feminine contact against his affection-starved body. He savored the long-buried lurch of desire rippling through his stomach and chest and every appendage of his body. He had no need to act on the desire. Just to hold her, just to pretend for a moment that their marriage was good and the baby squirming in his basket was his own, created both an incredible sense of peace and a longing to make the fantasy a reality.

He lay quietly for a few minutes, willing Adam to stop his squirming and wondering why he suddenly wanted to hold his wife.

If she were awake, would she compare the way he held her to the way his brother had held her? If he ever made love to her again, would she be thinking of Aidan? Comparing him to Aidan? Would he be as good as Aidan?

The squirming in the basket turned into more-insistent fussing. When Barrett stirred and rolled over, Chase reluctantly released her, feeling unaccountably empty with her no longer in his arms.

When she scooted to the edge of the bed and sat up, he expected her to bend over the basket and tend to Adam's needs. Instead she turned and caught Chase watching her, her clear-eyed gaze telegraphing the message that she'd been awake all along.

Steam rose into the chilly air in thick white clouds from the laundry tub as Barrett tried to figure out what to do next. She used her forearm to push a straggling tendril of hair from her eyes, then had to wipe her hands on her apron and retie her ponytail when it flopped against her shoulder.

It was bad enough to have a mountain of laundry looming above her, with nothing more than a couple of tubs and a washboard to wash with, but dealing with all this hair trailing to her waist was getting the best of her. She was used to poker-straight, chin-length, blunt-cut hair, tucked behind her ears if it got in her way. For two cents she would take a pair of scissors and hack off a couple of feet of these unruly chestnut ringlets.

Come to think of it, she didn't need the two cents.

Without giving the matter a second thought, Barrett marched across the winter-dead grass, through the back door, and straight to a sewing kit in the corner of the living room. There had to be scissors in there. If not, she'd use a knife.

Just as she'd expected, Elizabeth had every spool of thread and every button neatly organized. Good grief, was she doomed to compete with perfect Elizabeths her entire life?

Not anymore. Starting from that moment, she competed with no one.

After plucking the scissors from their padded nest in the sewing kit, Barrett quickly checked the sleeping Adam, then headed for the kitchen. The shaving mirror on the wall reflected a face that was still a stranger to her, but when she lifted the scissors and chopped off a huge handful of hair at shoulder length, so did the reflection.

Lord, that felt good.

She grabbed another handful and chewed away at the thickness. Strand after strand piled up at her feet until at last the thick, curly mass on her head fell in a soft cloud to dust the tops of her shoulders. The first thing she did was tuck one side behind her ear.

"Hello?"

Barrett jumped and spun toward the back door at the sound of the feminine voice, sending up a little thank-you that she hadn't had the scissors pointed at an eye or something.

The head and shoulders of a stunningly beautiful woman appeared in the doorway. She looked at Barrett's hair and at the chestnut pile on the floor, then blinked twice.

"Oh. Come in. I was just . . . cutting my hair."

"My, yes. I see that." The beauty glided into the kitchen with a basket on her arm. A little boy of perhaps three or four followed her in, holding the back of her skirts in his fist. She placed the basket on the table and reached around for the child.

"Sam and I saw the laundry started, so we came around to the back." She looked Barrett up and down. "Surely you aren't the one doing it. My goodness, you should still be abed."

Barrett scooped up the mass of hair on the floor, self-conscious in the shadow of this woman. She dumped the loose curls in the ash can, then dusted her hands on her skirts.

"Well, I started it. I feel fine. I *have* noticed that I tire a little easier, but the laundry needed doing, and Wes has so much else to do, and of course Chase is busy all the time . . ." She was babbling. "Could I offer you some tea?"

The beautiful creature smiled. "Only if you sit down and let me make it." She guided Barrett to a chair and pressed her into it. "Would you mind helping Sam with his coat?" she asked as she peeled off her gloves, along with her own coat, then set about filling the tea ball with tea leaves.

Barrett paid particularly close attention to the process, remembering the toxic sludge she'd made the day before. Little Sam presented himself to her, and she quickly slipped his coat off as she watched the tea-making.

For the next thirty minutes or so she had a very enjoyable visit with the nameless woman and her quiet little boy. They "oohed" over the sleeping Adam, laughed when he smiled in his sleep, chatted about children and childbirth and how it was always so different from what one expected. When Barrett mentioned how sick she was of the dull colors in her wardrobe, the woman offered to help her dye some of her dresses.

Barrett found herself relaxed for the first time since arriving in this time.

As she sipped her tea, she watched Sam climb onto his mother's lap and plop a thumb into his mouth. His glossy honey-colored hair was the exact shade of his mother's. But where her features were fine and delicate, his showed hints that his father was a big man.

"I really must go before Sam falls asleep. We walked over here, and I don't believe I could carry him far, he's gotten so big."

Barrett rose and helped them into their coats, sorry to

see them go. "I'm not anxious to get back to the laundry,
but I can't ask Wes to do it anymore. I swear, he must
have washed diapers every day, the way Adam runs
through them."

The woman turned to Barrett. "He dirties that many?"
she asked, concern etched in her voice.

"Well, no. Most are just wet, but—"

"Surely you don't wash the wet ones."

Barrett just blinked at her. She'd already found out the
hard way that she couldn't *burn* them.

"Why, you just hang the wet ones in the sun and use
them again. My goodness, *no one* washes wet diapers
every day. You'd never get anything else done."

Barrett stifled a grimace at the thought. She could
have lived her whole life without that tidbit of knowledge.

As she walked them back the way they had come, trying to figure out how to keep clean diapers on the child,
she thanked the woman again for the basket of food. She
wished Chase or Wes would show up and give an iden-
tity to her visitors before they left.

"I'm sorry I couldn't get here sooner." The woman
turned, her hand resting lovingly on Sam's shoulder, and
smiled at Barrett. "Now that you're up and about, you'll
be coming to the barn raising with Chase, won't you?"

"Barn raising?"

"Yes. Friday night. Perhaps Chase didn't tell you,
what with Adam's birth. Our barn burned last week."

"Oh. I'm sorry."

"We managed to get the livestock out, so it wasn't a
total loss." A hint of pain flickered for a moment in her
beautiful blue-gray eyes, then it was gone.

"A barn raising Friday night. I'm looking forward to it." Barrett hoped her smile looked sincere. What in the world went on at a barn raising, besides the obvious? Would something be expected of her? Would she have to bring something to eat? God help them all. Power lunches, cocktail parties, catered dinners—those she knew how to do. But not food for a barn raising!

"I'll see you and Chase on Friday then." With a final wave the woman took Sam's hand in hers and the two of them set off down the road.

Dreading it, Barrett returned to the laundry tubs. It didn't take a genius to figure out how to use a washboard, and with every bumpy plunge into the now-tepid water, she wished fervently that it was the head of Mr. Gideon in her hands instead of a soggy diaper.

At long last, after several trips to check on Adam and finally stopping to nurse him, dozens of snowy diapers fluttered on the lines in the backyard. With the last one hung up to dry, Barrett flopped onto a wooden bench to rest before dumping the water. She twisted the kinks out of her back, rubbed the back of her neck, and cursed Mr. Gideon all over again.

A rustle low in the bushes across the yard caught her attention. Another rustle, closer this time, had her wondering what kind of animals ran wild around there. She had a sudden vivid memory of the gun leaning next to the front door.

Just as she prepared to bolt for the back door, a black and brown and white Border collie trotted out of the bushes. He stopped when he saw her and tucked his tail, as if to slink away.

"Ohhh. Hi, there, fella." Barrett patted her skirts. "Come here."

The dog gave her a wary look, his ears pinned back in indecision.

"C'mon," she coaxed.

The little collie cautiously edged sideways toward her, ready to bound away at the first unwelcome sign. As he got closer, his ears pricked up and he stopped and sniffed the breeze. His tail made a couple of hesitant swishes in the air, and he moved forward a few more steps. Finally, after slinking the last few feet, he sniffed the back of Barrett's hand suspiciously.

She knew she'd won him over when his tail went into a wagging frenzy as she scratched behind his ears.

"Oh, my. What a baby you are! Who do you belong to? Hmmm?"

He looked up at her with adoration in his big brown eyes.

Too bad I can't win Chase over as easily as I can this little dog.

Now where had that thought come from? The very idea that it had crossed her mind at all irritated her no end. She'd spent the whole day actively *not* thinking about what being in Chase's arms did to her and *not* thinking about the cartwheels her stomach had done that morning when she'd turned to find him looking at her.

She spent another few minutes scratching at the furry ears and pushing away thoughts of Chase, until the dog wiggled its way onto the ground and presented his belly. She found the spot that made his hind leg pump, and she laughed out loud at his sappy state of euphoria.

"You're just a spoiled baby, you know that? Who's spoiled you like this?"

The sound of Adam coming out of his nap drifted through the door she'd left cracked open. With a sigh she patted the little dog, rose and dumped the wash and rinse water from the tubs, then turned back to the house. The little collie followed at her heels, a black and brown and white shadow, until she got to the door.

"Go home now, little fella," she said through the screen door. He looked up at her and whined, barked once, and then whined again as he scratched at the door.

"Oh, all right. I guess you know a soft touch when you see one. But only for a little while."

To her surprise, he refused to come in when she pushed the door open, hovering instead in indecision with his nose almost, but not quite, across the threshold. He looked up at her, ears pinned back as before.

"Well, come on, if you're coming," she invited. He perked up at this, took a few halting steps through the door, and when whatever reaction he expected didn't come, he trotted farther in, making himself immediately at home by thoroughly sniffing everything he could get his nose close to.

Barrett washed her hands and dashed into the parlor, scooping up a now indignant Adam. The little dog studiously inventoried the baby while Barrett changed the diaper—something, she reflected, at which she'd already become an expert.

In minutes she had Adam, freshly changed and sweet-smelling, cuddled in the wooden rocker in front of the fire, greedily trying to keep up with her milk flow.

The dog finished his survey of the room, then returned

to grovel for more attention at Barrett's side. She smiled and buried her fingers in the fur between his ears, laughing at the worshipful look on his face.

How odd to experience such a surge of warmth just by laying a hand on an animal. Peaceful. That's what it was.

She relaxed and let her head fall back against the rocker. When had she ever been so exhausted? And it not much past three o'clock.

A log in the fireplace burned through and fell, stoking the fire temporarily and blanketing Barrett with a welcome heat. Muscles unkinked and she felt her mind drifting.

Who was the beautiful woman who'd come visiting with her little boy? Why had she had those flashes of unbearable sadness in her eyes? How could Barrett get the information out of Chase without making him even more convinced that she'd lost her mind?

At the back door Chase yanked off his muddy boots with the help of the bootjack, eager to get inside to dinner, hoping Barrett had fixed a lot, no matter what it was. He stepped into the house and breathed deeply, expecting his mouth to water at the delicious smells of supper cooking.

Nothing.

His irritated survey of the kitchen revealed breakfast dishes in the sink under the pump, a strange picnic basket on the table, and not so much as a single pot simmering on the stove. Hell, she hadn't ever *started* supper. What the hell had she been doing? It had never taken her all day to do the laundry before.

He'd skipped lunch, not wanting to chance another

awkward situation after the rather disturbing way they'd awakened that morning. But now hunger gnawed at his stomach, overriding any hesitation he might have had about being around his wife. In his stocking feet he marched into the parlor in search of her, determined to find out what was so important that she couldn't bother to put on at least a pot of beans.

Never, in his wildest dreams, could he have imagined the sight he encountered.

Barrett slept soundly in the rocking chair next to the fire, where the bed had been until only this morning, when he and Wes had moved it back into the bedroom. Adam slept in the crook of her arm, and a carelessly flung diaper covered the open bodice of her gown. But the most amazing thing—one he would never have believed if he hadn't seen it with his own eyes—was the sight of Bo sound asleep on the ottoman next to the chair, sprawled on his back, with Barrett's hand draped lovingly across the center of his furry belly. Elizabeth had never even touched Bo. In fact, up until now she'd forbidden him to enter the house. And Bo had disliked Elizabeth on sight, pinning his ears back and all but baring his teeth whenever she got near him.

There he went, thinking of his wife as two separate people again.

Something deep inside him lurched with an ache both pleasant and painful at the homey picture before him. A wife, a child, a dog, all in peaceful repose. This single moment, this one brief vision, was everything Chase had ever pictured as a family, everything he'd ever hoped his family life would be.

Careful not to make any noise, he returned to the

kitchen, tossed his jacket on a chair, and started rummaging. With all the food the ladies had brought the day before, he should be able to put together something for them to eat.

He dug into the picnic basket on the table and found a ham baked in brown-sugar glaze, a fluffy loaf of fresh bread, and a perfectly baked pumpkin pie with a golden-brown crust. The pie tipped him off as to the owner of the basket. He was more than a little surprised that she'd come here.

A loud growl of hunger pulled his thoughts back to eating, and he took a jar of canned green beans from one of the shelves of preserved foods. The sight of the perfectly arranged jars reminded him of the uncharacteristic pile of dishes in the sink. Before today, he couldn't for the life of him remember ever seeing even one unwashed dish left to linger.

"Need some help?"

Chase turned and raised his eyes to meet the sleepy gaze of his wife. Instead of the flustered apology he expected for not having his dinner ready, she tossed him a casual smile and sauntered into the kitchen, her gown rumpled, her apron stained, her hair a soft halo framing her . . .

Her hair!

"Barrett!"

She started so violently she bounced off the doorjamb. All sleep evaporated from her eyes and she yelled back, "What?"

"Your hair!"

She raked her fingers through it. "What about it?"

He couldn't believe his ears. Or his eyes. "You cut it."

She rolled her eyes heavenward and slumped back against the door frame. "Good grief! I thought maybe it was on fire."

"Why did you cut it?"

She reached up and pulled one springy ringlet straight. "It kept getting in my way. Don't you like it?"

He expected her to react in her old self-conscious, apologetic manner, but her attitude conveyed complete disinterest as to whether or not he approved of her hair.

Without waiting for him to answer, she strolled into the kitchen, picked up a knife, and took a deep, appreciative sniff of the loaf of bread on the table.

"Mmmm. Fresh-baked bread. And look at that ham. Where'd it come from?"

He quirked a brow at her. "It was in the basket Genevieve brought. I recognized her pumpkin pie. I assume she brought it herself, didn't she?"

"Genevieve?" Barrett turned and gave him a confused look, as if she didn't know the name. Chase bristled at her continued refusal to like the woman.

"For pity's sake, Barrett, she's a widow with a small child. Why do you insist on withholding your friendship—"

"A widow?" She stiffened. "The Widow Long?" All her earlier signs of softness turned to hard edges. A flash of something akin to hurt flickered in her eyes before she turned back to the table and began hacking the bread into thick slices.

"Didn't Genevieve bring it?"

"She brought it." Barrett bit off the words as if they tasted bitter in her mouth.

Now what had he done? For the life of him, he couldn't

figure out this new side of his wife. It was almost as if someone else inhabited her body. But, damn, he liked this side better, even when she stiffened up for no reason. He liked this wife who left washtubs upturned in the yard instead of hanging them in their place in the shed. He wanted to touch this wife who stood at the table in a hopelessly wrinkled gown, her apron covered with mysterious smudges and smears while she mutilated a fresh loaf of bread and sent crumbs and chunks hurtling to the floor with complete unconcern. He wanted to bury his fingers in the mass of curls that now kissed her shoulders and see if they felt as silky as they looked. As silky as he remembered them to be. With sudden clarity he relived the heat of her body as it had snuggled against him that morning.

As if sensing his gaze on her, she turned and looked him straight in the eye.

"What?"

Irritated at himself and the hopeless direction of his thoughts, he casually lifted his coat from the ladder-back chair and made certain it covered his unfortunately timed reaction.

"Nothing. Just call me when supper's ready."

He turned to make his escape from the kitchen.

"Excuse me?" Her words were more of a command to stop than a begging for pardon. "Weren't you just about to fix something to eat?"

Slowly he swiveled back to her. "You were asleep and I didn't want to wake you."

"Oh, so now that the little woman's awake, it's her duty to cook up some vittles for her man?" Her voice slipped sarcastically from cultured to the heavy accent of a backwoodsman.

All he could do was gawk.

"You know, I've had one hell of a day," she continued. "I've hauled water and scrubbed clothes and used muscles I didn't even know I had. And do you have any idea how pleasant a steaming tub of dirty diapers smells? I'm every bit as hungry as you are, and twice as tired, so if you don't mind, I'd like a little help fixing something to eat." She turned back to hacking at the bread. "I'd like to see *you* function on three hours' sleep a night, stuck in a situation you know nothing about, fumbling through the day, wondering when you're going to say or do something wrong . . ."

Barrett muttered more to herself than to Chase, but he heard her nonetheless. He never dreamed his capable wife felt so unprepared and insecure in her motherhood.

"Will Wes be eating with us too?" she asked. Chase heard the threat of unshed tears quivering in her voice. His pang of sympathy toward her surprised him.

"No." Tossing his coat aside, he went back into the kitchen and picked up the jar of green beans. "He went into town for supplies." The pot he wanted for the beans was still dirty in the sink, so he had to wash it before putting them on to heat. Barrett didn't seem to notice.

He peeled and sliced a couple of apples to stew, but they didn't look right when he got them in the pan. "What do I do next with these?"

Barrett turned her attention away from her new task of slicing the ham, or perhaps "shredding" was a more appropriate word.

"What?"

"The apples." He pointed at the stove. "What do you put in them?"

"How should I . . . ummm . . . cinnamon and sugar?"

What an odd response.

"How much?"

She turned back to mangling the ham and shrugged. " 'Til it looks right."

"Don't you use nutmeg and allspice too? I remember you telling Carrie just last month—"

Her head dropped to her chest for a moment, then she laid the carving knife aside and turned to him.

"Do we really need the apples? Haven't we got enough stuff to eat with all the food those people brought yesterday?"

Chase decided to shut up and just get the food on the table. Maybe he should talk to Dr. Logan about Barrett's bizarre behavior. As much as he disliked the man, maybe the old quack could shed some light on whether or not this was normal for a woman after childbirth.

Silence reigned at the supper table that night as Chase alternated between watching his wife, trying to figure her out, and stabbing at the tasteless, half-cooked apples on his plate, disgusted with himself for even being curious about her. When would he learn?

Barrett picked at the mountainous sandwich of shredded ham and sliced cheese she'd made for them. That was another odd little bit of behavior on her part. Up until a few days ago, she wouldn't have dreamed of having anything less than a huge cooked meal for dinner. She didn't even approve of fixing sandwiches for lunch. And she'd never wasted a bite of food, though obviously most of what covered her plate tonight would remain un-eaten.

From the parlor Adam drew her attention before she could take another bite. His contented cooing, Chase knew, was just a warning that he would be wanting his own supper soon, and he would tolerate no delays.

Seconds after the cooing started, Bo appeared in the kitchen to announce the fact that the baby needed atten-tion. His skittering toenails clicked on the floor while his soft, wide eyes sought out first Chase and then Barrett.

Chase dropped his hand to the top of Bo's head, giv-ing his perky ears a good scratching, waiting for Barrett to tell him to get that nasty dog out of her kitchen.

It never happened.

Instead she picked up what was left of her sandwich and waved it at Bo in offering. And the little traitor left Chase like he was a bad case of fleas, groveling at Bar-rett's feet until she tossed him the sandwich, which he caught in midair and swallowed in one bite.

"Why the change of heart?" Chase wondered aloud.

"What?"

He lifted his gaze to hers. "With Bo. You've never let him in before. You've certainly never fed him food off your plate."

Barrett buried all ten fingers in the collie's fur and rubbed it affectionately. "Maybe I never got to know him before." She smiled into the collie's eyes and continued to rub. "No. Maybe I never realized what a baby you are. Yes, you are. You're just a big baby. Oh, my, you like that, don't you?"

Chase could not believe his ears. Or his eyes. Was his wife engaged in baby-talk with his dog? Was she actually allowing Bo to lick her cheek, her happy expression as euphoric as Bo's?

Adam gave forth a few intermittent fussing noises, warning that his patience was almost at an end.

Barrett sighed. "There he goes again, Bo. I think he's jealous of us, don't you?" she said cryptically. With one last sigh she rose, washed her hands under the pump, then disappeared into the parlor, the traitor trotting at her heels.

Chase sat in stunned silence, listening to the sounds of Adam being changed and fed, trying to figure out if someone who looked exactly like his wife had come and taken her place. He looked around the kitchen at the pots and pans in the sink, the plates and serving dishes still on the table, and a pair of Barrett's boots with mud still clinging to the soles sitting by the back door.

Without thinking, without really knowing why, he found himself cleaning up the kitchen, washing and drying the dishes, then filling the bathing tub in the corner with hot water from the reservoir in the stove.

With the air above the tub wafting with curling wisps of steam, he tossed the drying cloth over his shoulder and stepped into the parlor.

Barrett sat in the rocker, her eyelids drooping with fatigue, Bo draped like a limp rag across one of her feet. Chase's stomach knotted at the homey sight.

"I've filled the tub. I thought perhaps you'd like to go first. That is . . . if it's safe for you . . . it's only been a few . . ."

Barrett lit up like a lightning bug. Before he could finish his sentence she had upended Bo and tucked Adam back into his basket. In a flurry of wrinkled skirts, she disappeared into their bedroom, reappearing seconds later with an armful of clean clothes and towels and soap.

"I'm fine. A bath will be heavenly. Gosh, I feel like I haven't bathed in weeks. You can only feel so clean using a washcloth and a basin of water." She scurried into the kitchen, almost tripping over Bo. A moment later she poked her head back into the parlor. "You're staying in there, right?"

He shoved his hands in his pockets and stifled a flash of irritation. "I wouldn't have it any other way."

Apparently taking him at his word, she disappeared again.

Chase dropped into the rocker and listened to the sound of shoes clattering to the floor, the swish and rustle of layers of clothing coming off. There were several moments of quiet before he heard the unmistakable sound of her body sinking into the water and then a sigh of utter contentment.

Little jolts of heat skipped through his veins, like rocks across a pond. He tried unsuccessfully to wipe her image from his mind. He rocked harder and tried to ignore the musical sound of water splashing against her body, tried not to hear the odd little tune she happily hummed. But when some flowery feminine scent drifted in from the steam of the bathwater, he sprang from the chair and lurched out the front door into a blast of mind-clearing frigid air.

Chapter 7

"YOU LOOK LIKE somebody tied a knot in your tail, little brother. That youngun of yours keeping you up?"

Wes reined in the horses in front of his cottage, then jumped to the ground. Chase unfolded himself from the top step, where he'd been watching his breath plume into the morning air, waiting for Wes to return from town.

"You have a minute to talk?" Chase asked as he hefted a sack of flour onto his shoulder.

"Spit it out. Something's been eatin' at you for months. Worse since your boy arrived."

"He might not be my boy."

Wes laid down the bag of oats he'd just picked up. He took the sack of flour from Chase and shoved him down onto the step.

"Sit. What do you mean the boy might not be yours? Are you blind? He's got Alston written all over him. Why, he looks just like you and Aidan did when you were born. I was old enough to remember—"

"He might be Aidan's."

"Huh?"

Chase might have laughed at Wes's expression, but the knot of misery in his stomach killed any laughter in him.

"What do you mean, he might be Aidan's? You think your brother—"

"She wasn't a virgin, Wes. She didn't tell me. I found out the hard way, on our wedding night. I think I scared her, I got so mad, and she told me it was Aidan who got to her first. And just the week before. Don't you see? Adam was born eight and a half months after we got married. How early was he? Two weeks, or one?"

"Why would she do such a thing?" Wes flopped onto the step below Chase. "She don't strike me as the loose type of woman. What'd she tell you?"

"Nothing. She said it happened once, and it was a mistake, and she'd spend the rest of her life making it up to me. Then she refused to speak of it again."

"Holy Moses, Chase, why didn't you tell me this before? Damn, this explains a lot."

"You think I like admitting that my own brother cuckolded me a week before my wedding?"

"What'd Aidan say about all this? I know he's always been jealous of everything you've ever had, but surely he wouldn't stoop—"

"I haven't talked to Aidan. We left Richmond right after the wedding, remember? We spent our wedding night on the train. Hell, we were in West Virginia before I got his name out of her. She begged me to leave it alone. If I'd known she was going to tell me two months later that she thought she was pregnant, I'd have caught the next train home and beat the hell out of the bastard."

"You ain't gonna take all this out on the youngun, are you? It ain't his fault."

Chase slid an irritated glance at Wes. "What do you take me for? Of course not. Besides, he's my blood, even if he is my nephew."

"Yeah, and he might be your son. A son you didn't even bother to build a cradle for. Now it makes sense, you bullheaded jackass."

Chase couldn't argue with him there. He made his mind up right then and there that Adam would be in his own handmade cradle within a week.

Wes shook his head in denial while he dug through his coat pocket and pulled out a long, thin cheroot.

"Last one. Wanna share it?"

Chase nodded, wondering how much more to tell. Wes bit the end off the rolled tobacco, dragged a match down his pant leg, then puffed at the flame until blue smoke wreathed his head.

Chase took the cheroot and pulled a deep breath into his lungs. He'd rather have been downing a stiff draught of whiskey, to numb his brain and body from his next words.

"I haven't touched her since that night."

Wes's blue eyes widened in disbelief.

"What're you saying?"

"I'm saying I haven't touched my wife since our wedding night." A vivid image of Barrett in the woods, and him very much touching her, flashed in his mind. As well as waking curled up against her just the morning before. But Wes knew what he meant.

"Lord a mercy, Chase, you mean—"

"Yeah!" Chase stood and grabbed the bag of flour again. "That's exactly what I mean."

Several seconds of silence ticked away in that awkward moment.

"Well, hell, little brother," Wes finally boomed and slapped Chase on the back. "You been nine months without a woman, you know what you need?"

"A woman?" Chase bit back a grin at his buffoon half brother.

"Hell, no. You need for me to whup some of that sass out of you."

Before Chase could duck Wes had him in a headlock. The flour landed back in the wagon as Chase threw himself to the ground, his fall cushioned by his well-padded brother.

"Oh, now you ain't playin' fair." Wes rolled on the thawing ground, taking Chase with him, but Chase flipped around and landed on Wes's chest with an *oof*.

"You're gonna pay for that, big brother."

Barrett watched Chase and Wes wrestle in a cloud of dust like a couple of little boys at play. Her throat tightened at the sibling camaraderie. What would it feel like to be in the middle of a tussle like that? She'd never in her life roughhoused with anyone, but it sure looked like fun.

Bo trotted to the back door to view the goings-on. With an indignant yelp he nosed open the screen door and flew across the yard in a blur of multicolored fur to the two tumbling bodies.

He circled the men, yipping at them, darting in to pull at their clothes, darting out again to bark some more.

Barrett thought he was trying to break up the fight until Chase hooked an arm around the dog's fluffy neck and pulled him into the middle of the fray.

Barrett leaned her head against the screen door, the corners of her mouth curving into a rueful smile as she felt a twinge of sadness. It warmed her heart to see such devotion among those three males, so much the little boys no matter what their age—or species. But she also felt like a fifth wheel.

Forever the fifth wheel.

A staccato rap at the front door pulled her musings away from the playful scuffle. When she opened the door, Carrie bustled in, nearly quivering with excitement, but before she could utter a word she stopped dead in her tracks.

"Oh, my soul, your hair!"

Barrett's hands immediately flew up to flatten the springy ringlets to her head.

"You don't like it?"

"Well, my . . . that is, it's such a shock. Well, of course I like it." She circled Barrett, viewing the hairstyle from all angles. "It's just so unlike you to do something like that, cutting your hair off and all."

Barrett could see Carrie was uncomfortable with the "shocking" side of Elizabeth.

"What's that you've got?" she asked in an attempt to change the subject.

"Look!" Carrie held out a ragged catalog as if it were a priceless artifact. "Mother finally sent it!" She dropped onto the sofa, squirmed to make room for Barrett, then patted the seat beside her, all the while throwing an occasional covert glance at the questionable hairstyle. "Come and sit! You've been as anxious as I have!"

Barrett sat down beside Carrie and eyed the beat-up cover of an 1887 Bloomingdale Brothers Fall and Winter mail-order catalog.

"What do you want to look at first?" Carrie bubbled with excitement. "My soul, there's so much to choose from!"

Barrett found herself spellbound as they leafed through the dog-eared catalog. She'd never seen anything like it. Everything from wedding gowns—or bridal suits, as they were referred to—to window shades. There was also jewelry, salad dressing, guns, hairpieces, drapery rods, hosiery.

"Good grief, look at the size of those legs!" Barrett blurted out, then giggled. The hosiery drawings of hefty legs from chunky midthigh to prim, pointed toes were definite contrasts to all the wasp-waisted corsets and hourglass figures drawn throughout the rest of the book.

Her gaze roamed back to the dress department and the clothing descriptions.

"Look at these dresses! This one's cashmere and only $16.75."

"Only? My soul, Elizabeth, where would you wear such a fancy dress?"

"Barrett," she corrected absentmindedly, enthralled at the novelty of the catalog. "Omigosh! Look! Rubber pants! And they're only a quarter. I can get rubber pants for Adam. No more puddles on my lap! No more changing his sheets every time he wakes up. You don't mind if I order these, do you?"

"Of course not, you goose." Carrie patted her arm

with such warmth that Barrett felt an unexpected hot sting of tears. Good grief, she must be on that hormonal, postpartum roller coaster she'd always heard about.

The two of them scanned the catalog pages together with intermittent bursts of laughter from Barrett over some of the ridiculous advertisements. She loved the electric hair restorers guaranteed to end baldness, and corsets that promised to bend so that shoes could be buttoned easily.

When they turned back to the dresses, Barrett read the description of colors with longing.

"Look at all the colors they offer. What I wouldn't give . . ." She made a split-second decision. "Carrie, do you know how to dye fabric?"

Carrie squinted at her with a wrinkled nose. "Of course. Don't you recall helping me dye that bolt of cotton pale yellow for my kitchen curtains?"

Barrett bypassed the question.

"Would you help me dye some of my dresses?"

"Why, my soul, yes. But why do you want to dye them?"

"Oh, I am so *sick* of those drab colors. If I have to wear nondescript oatmeal blah much longer, I think I'll scream."

"Well, goodness, El . . . Barrett, why don't you just get out all those dresses in your trousseau and wear those? I never did understand why you packed them away and never wore them. They're absolutely enchanting."

"My trousseau?" This was news to Barrett. She'd never found any other clothes. In fact, her armoire was a barren wasteland when it came to colors. "Now, let's see. Where did I pack those dresses?" She tapped her lips with her fingertip and tried to look like she was thinking.

"In the chest in the attic. My soul, did having a baby affect your memory?"

Barrett sighed over how close to the truth Carrie had come. She was just about to suggest that they go in search of the dresses, since she had no idea how to get to the attic, when Adam squealed with his usual impeccable timing.

Carrie's eyes lit up with joy, and before Barrett could rise from the sofa the little wren of a woman flew across the room, nearly rubbing her hands together in anticipation of holding the baby.

"Wes, do you know where the door to the attic is?" Barrett had searched the whole darned house after Carrie left, and there wasn't a sign of a staircase. She couldn't remember seeing one at the bed-and-breakfast either.

" 'Scuse me?" Wes stepped into the kitchen, swung the bag of potatoes off his shoulder, and dropped the sack of flour he had tucked under his arm onto the scarred wooden table. A big smear of dirt from his scuffle with Chase adorned the right shoulder of his shirt, as well as both knees of his trousers. "You want to know where the attic stairs are?"

Barrett scrunched up her face and tried to look forgetful.

"Uh-huh."

"They're right where they've always been."

"And that would be . . ."

"Somethin' botherin' you, brat?" Wes had taken to

calling her that since the day she'd gone off into the woods in search of hypothermia. She found the nickname endearing rather than insulting.

He looked at her with concern now, waiting for her to answer. She unconsciously wrung her hands for a moment, then motioned for him to sit.

"I don't know exactly how to say this, Wes." She craned her neck and looked outside. "First of all, where's Chase?"

Wes glanced behind him and shrugged. "Still doin' the milkin', I reckon. What's on your mind?"

She sank to the chair opposite him and placed her hands over his on the table. How in the world could she possibly word this and still sound sane?

"I have a confession, but it's going to sound crazy. Will you hear me out?"

He studied her for a moment with those incongruous blue eyes of his before he nodded.

"Well . . . I'm not the same person I was before Adam was born."

Wes threw back his head and sent his deep laughter bouncing off the ceiling of the kitchen.

Barrett stiffened. A vision of Browning laughing at her flashed through her mind before she shoved it away.

"You ain't telling me nothin' new, brat."

"Why do you say that? Do you think I've changed all that much?" She hadn't thought she'd been so obviously different from Elizabeth.

"Well, now, I think you and I both know the answer—"

"That's just it, Wes. I don't." She scooted to the edge of the ladder-back chair and squeezed his hands. "Would you believe me if I told you I don't remember anything before Adam's birth? I don't know where you and Chase came from. I don't remember any of the names of Chase's friends. And I certainly don't remember how to get to the stupid attic. I literally woke up with Chase delivering the baby and you holding me down. That's my first memory."

She searched his face, waiting for him to laugh again, but he just studied her, his features unreadable.

"Why ain't you tellin' this to Chase?"

Barrett sighed and shook her head. "He'd never believe me. For some reason, he has a really bad opinion of me. I don't know. I guess I just felt like you'd be more understanding." She watched for any sign of his openness to be shuttered in his eyes. "Do you believe me?" she finally asked.

He blew out a long breath and patted her hands.

"I believe you. Can't say I understand it. But you sure ain't the woman you used to be."

Barrett cringed. "Is that good or bad?"

"That's a compliment, far as I'm concerned. But don't you think you should have Doc Logan look at you?" Wes looked everywhere but at Barrett, then concentrated on knocking the dirt off the knees of his trousers. "You ain't having problems, are you?"

Barrett smiled, touched by his discomfort. Though obviously ill at ease with the topic, he still cared enough to voice his concerns. The thought struck her how different his worried gaze was from the clinical, diagnostic glimmer that would have been evident in the eyes of any of her family members.

"No. I'm perfectly fine, other than this memory problem. And I'm sure even *that* will resolve itself soon. Now" —she patted his hand and stood— "show me how to get to the stupid attic."

Shaking his head, Wes heaved himself out of the chair, then clomped over to the tiny pantry and threw open the door. Barrett followed, completely confused now.

Without a word, he slid a large crock on the back shelf to the side, reached in, and turned a very ordinary-looking doorknob.

"Why, it's just a plain old door with shelves on it," she said as the door swung open on well-oiled hinges.

"What'd you expect?"

"I don't know." Barrett laughed. "But nothing so exotic as a hidden stairway."

"It ain't hidden on purpose. It just took up less space here." He handed her a kerosene lamp from one of the shelves on the wall, fished a match out of his pocket, then dragged it along his denim-clad leg. The flare of the match against the soaked wick lit the dark stairwell and the dried herbs hanging along the wall. Without asking, he took the lamp from her and waved her up the stairs. "You tell me what you need and I'll carry it down."

Barrett gathered her skirts and headed up the stairs with Wes right behind her. As the yellow light illuminated the chilly attic, Barrett realized the place was as spotless as the rest of the house. Good grief! Elizabeth needed to get a life.

At the top of the stairs she stopped and scanned the room for the trunk. It shouldn't be hard to find in all this meticulous organization.

A huge leather trunk sat nestled between small stacks

of wooden crates. She tried to contain her excitement as she dropped to her knees in front of the trunk and fumbled with the latch. Her breath exploded in frosty clouds when the lid fell open.

The contents obviously belonged to Chase, but a different Chase than the one she'd come to know. The leather chest brimmed with elegant clothing; suits of fine wool as soft as cashmere; silk ties and cravats in a rainbow of colors; shirts of linen and lawn and other expensive fabrics she couldn't begin to name. A small black box on top held a set of solid-gold shirt studs and cuff links set with diamonds. Handmade shoes and a pair of riding boots still held a mirror-finish shine.

"Wes," she said glancing over her shoulder at her towering brother-in-law, "what *is* all this?"

"That's Chaser's trunk. You don't recognize that suit on top? He married you in it."

An icy-hot tingle skipped across her neck. He'd married Elizabeth in an exquisitely tailored suit expensive enough to feed a family for a year. The studs and cuff links alone could pay for a home twice the size of the one they lived in.

"Is Chase wealthy?" she asked as she ran her hands over the wedding suit.

Wes didn't answer right away, but Barrett didn't notice. She continued to smooth the lapels of the suit, wondering what it would have felt like to stand beside Chase, to watch him as he looked into her eyes and promised to take care of her. How ironic that for a moment she was jealous of the very woman whose body she inhabited.

"Chaser ain't wealthy, but his family is."

Barrett had forgotten she'd asked a question.

"His family's wealthy? Where do they live? Why did he leave?"

Wes raised a brow at her. "You don't remember?"

"The first thing I remember is you holding me down and Chase on the other end of me."

His blue eyes narrowed for the briefest of moments, then he propped his left hip against a wooden crate and started tying knots in a stray piece of rope.

"We're all from Virginia. Richmond. Chaser's one of the Virginia Alstons."

That piece of news meant nothing to her.

"He left because his brother—"

"Aidan?" She wasn't even sure if Chase had more than one brother.

"Yeah. Aidan. He and Chaser butted heads a lot. Aidan always wanted what Chaser had, even though Chaser was younger." Wes seemed to study her a moment for some type of reaction. "Little brother decided to come to Ohio and try his hand at farming when the Reconstruction laws didn't agree with him."

Reconstruction. From the Civil War? History had never been her strong suit.

"Is my family wealthy? Did I know Chase long before we got married?"

Wes shook his head, as if he couldn't believe he was having this conversation.

"Your daddy died in the war, before you was born. In '62 if I ain't mistaken. Your mama made dresses for Miss Patricia, Chaser's mama, but she made a good enough livin'. That's how you two met. You was helpin' your ma."

"Did we love each other?" Barrett nearly whispered the question, not sure how she wanted Wes to answer. He squirmed and finished tying an intricate knot.

"I 'spose. It ain't somethin' me and Chaser talked over. Little brother keeps his cards close to his chest." He tossed the rope aside and shoved away from the crate. "I've got to finish unloadin' the wagon. You find what you want and I'll bring it down when I'm through."

He was halfway down the stairs before Barrett called out, "Wes!" When he turned, she grinned gratefully. "Thanks for believing me."

He smiled a tolerant, brilliantly white smile and scratched the back of his head.

"It'd be hard not to, brat."

With one final swing Chase sank the last nail into the last board of Genevieve's new barn. Tired but satisfied, he dragged his shirtsleeve across his forehead, the grit of sawdust scratching his skin.

He looked up, blinked some chilly sweat from his eyes, and watched the Widow Long make her way with a tray of cider through the dozen or so men. Beautiful, serene, smiling with warmth, she still had that air of sadness about her that had come to be her constant companion since Samuel's death.

Samuel Long had been one lucky devil.

By the time she reached Chase she had one glass of cider left.

"Can I tempt you?"

He grinned and took the offered glass. Genevieve reached up and gently removed something from his lashes.

"Sawdust," she said with that serene smile. "You're covered in it. Why don't you go to the house and get cleaned up? I've enough heated water for all the men. Besides, the ladies should be arriving any minute now."

Chase joined the others in the bedroom set aside for them, peeling off his dirty, sweaty shirt and sluicing the blessedly warm water over his arms and chest, soaping up from his forehead clear to his waist.

Barn raising could be a smelly business.

Once he'd rinsed away the soap and freshened up as much as he could without a thorough dunking, he slipped into the set of clean clothes he'd brought.

Lord, had he ever been so tired? The last thing he wanted to do was spend the evening trying to keep a safe distance from Barrett without stirring up gossip. He still hadn't cooled off from those visions of her in the bath, and that had been days ago.

The sound of wagons bumping up the rutted road drew the men's attention. The noise heralded women and an abundance of food, both of which were high on every man's list right now. The room cleared in no time, leaving Chase alone, wearily shoving his feet into his boots and wishing he was on his way home to a soft bed and a good night's sleep.

He'd not slept well the past few nights, and then there'd been all his work to do that morning before leaving for Genevieve's. Besides, his back ached, his shoulders throbbed, and there had to be a pound of sawdust stuck to the insides of his eyelids.

"Chase, come along." Genevieve quipped with excitement as she scurried past the door. "We're going to have dancing in the barn."

Well, that's just fine and dandy, he thought, with equal parts exhaustion and dread. But at least his wife wouldn't be expecting him to dance with her. She'd sworn off that activity when she'd taken to wearing boring day gowns and ugly topknots.

With a sigh of resignation he plowed his damp hair into place with his fingers and trudged into the bustle of the parlor.

Wives brought husbands heaping plates of food from the kitchen. Misbehaving children got reprimands from any adult who happened to witness the misdeed. A group of men in the corner were having another good laugh over Bill Myers's accidentally nailing Harley Griffen's trouser leg to the wall.

All these people milling around and working their way out to the barn, and not a sign of his wife anywhere. Maybe she'd decided not to come after all, considering how touchy she'd been about Genevieve during the pregnancy with Adam.

Well, he'd spend a little time at the barn dance, then slip out and get to bed early.

Genevieve appeared again with a plateful of food and shoved it into his hands with a teasing smile.

"Here. You've got to keep up your strength. I expect at least a couple of good dances out of you before Elizabeth drags you home."

The comment wasn't meant to be vindictive. Everyone knew his wife frowned on such "frivolous" entertainment. The irony of it all was, before their wedding night, she could dance the soles right off her slippers. And had done so more than once. Had done so on their wedding day.

Chase pushed the memory of that time from his mind.

"Thanks for the food, Gen. We'll work in a dance or two." He hesitated before continuing. "Ahhh, by the way, it seems my wife prefers to be called Barrett now."

"She what?"

"Don't ask me why, but she gets pretty testy when someone calls her Elizabeth."

"Well, of course, I'll try to remember . . ." When Gen's voice trailed off, Chase turned to follow the direction of her gaze.

Beatrice Ord watched them from across the room like a vulture waiting for its victim to die. Not until Armistead Ord shoved his empty plate toward his wife did she turn her suspicious glare away.

"Looks like we're going to be fodder at the next quilting bee," Genevieve stated, then shrugged. "I'd best check in the kitchen, anyway. I've got an apple pie baking."

His favorite.

When she left Chase alone he wandered out to the barn with the others, following the plucking twang of fiddles tuning up.

There was still no sign of Barrett when the first dance started. He tucked himself away in a warm corner on a bale of hay, calculating exactly how long he had to stay before he could make his excuses and leave. His eyelids felt like lead, every muscle ached like a bad tooth, and his entire body cried out for sleep.

He leaned his head back against a new, fragrant, freshly cut timber wall and stared off into space. With his body so tired, his mind so numb, he didn't even realize he was staring at his wife as she made her way through the crowd looking for him.

Or maybe he just hadn't recognized her.

Barrett Alston threaded through friends and neighbors lining the dance floor, leaving quite a few of them gaping as she passed. She nodded every now and then at someone and craned her neck as she searched the crowd.

Heavenly days, this woman couldn't possibly be his wife.

Her hair, as it had done since that day she'd cut it, haloed her face in dark, fluffy ringlets begging to be touched. Her gray eyes sparkled as if she couldn't wait to join the fun. From her trousseau, she wore a gown of sapphire blue that turned her skin to flawless porcelain.

He couldn't drag his gaze away from her. All of a sudden the ache left his muscles and traveled south. The thought of sleep no longer beckoned him. His mind, wide awake now, spun at the sight of his wife.

He pushed away from his dark corner and stood just as Barrett found him. When his gaze met hers, Chase nearly staggered from the white-hot jolt that pulsed through his body.

An air of excitement lit her eyes and heightened her color to a becoming dewy glow. As she made her way to him, she pulled off her elbow-length matching cape and did a quick spin to show off her dress. Her brilliant smile hit him in the chest like a fist.

He swallowed hard and wished he had something to wet his suddenly dry throat. Hell, he wished he had a whole damn bottle of whiskey. The only thing that would get him through this night would be to numb his senses because, God knew, nothing else about him was going to be numb. Not with Barrett looking the way she did.

"Do you like it?" she asked in a breathless voice when she finally reached him.

"Yes, it's . . . yes. I like it." He'd liked it when she'd worn it to catch the train on their wedding day. But to mention that would surely dim the exquisite light in her eyes. "Where's Adam?"

"He's in the house with the other children. Some of the older ladies are going to watch him."

They fell into an awkward silence, watching the dancers, and when the ragtag musicians struck up another song, Chase nearly gaped when Barrett started tapping her toe to the music. He wondered where her usual disapproval had gone as she watched the dancers with avid interest. When the next song started, she actually swayed to the music. After she bobbed in time through the third tune, people started to stare even more openly than they had been.

Well, he could either ignore her or take a chance of ruining her mood by asking her to dance.

"Would you care to dance?" he asked, deciding to follow the request with a bow worthy of his upbringing.

She gave him an embarrassed shake of her head, then stunned him by saying, "Oh, I wouldn't dare! I don't know any of these dances."

On the contrary—she could probably teach every person there a thing or two. Before she'd given up having fun and started scraping her hair into that despised bun, before the wedding night that had changed them both, Elizabeth had been as light on her feet as she was lighthearted. He hadn't realized how much he'd missed that side of her.

With more than a little reluctance, considering his present physical state, he pulled her into the double lines of dancers in spite of her protests. Much to his surprise, though the square dance was simple, she studiously watched the others go through their steps. When the time came for her and Chase to come together in the center, she made every deliberate move just half a second after Chase.

If he didn't know what a dream she could be on the dance floor, he'd have sworn she didn't know how to dance. Within minutes, though, she relaxed somewhat, stopped concentrating so hard on her feet, and enjoyed the dance. But he wished for her studied concentration back when her body seemed to move in an unconscious invitation. Nothing blatant, nothing he could even be sure anyone else would notice, but enough of a playful, sultry change in her to wreak havoc with unwanted urges already far too close to the surface. Urges already stifled far too long. He was damned tempted to give in to those urges.

When the spirited song ended, the musicians went straight into "Aura Lee." No one left the dance floor as every couple came together for the sentimental waltz so popular during the war. The song had always been one of Elizabeth's favorites. Chase sent a furtive glance around the barn while Barrett stood with uncertainty, watching folks move onto the dance floor in droves. If Chase took Barrett off the floor now, they would be the only couple to leave. There was nothing for it but to dance again.

When he took her hand and laid his palm on her waist with a sigh of resignation, it occurred to him that this was the first time he'd purposely put his arms around his wife since their wedding night. Images of the recent morning in their bed crept into his memory, but he sent them back to where they belonged, to reside with the urges that he kept under lock and key.

Barrett seemed much more at ease with the waltz, but she still didn't dance at all like Elizabeth.

There he went again! Why did he continue to refer to his wife as if she were two separate people? Probably because, though Elizabeth had waltzed as if she were on a cloud, she'd never, ever, even after their betrothal, danced so close that Chase could feel every contour of her body. Which meant, no doubt, that Barrett could feel every contour of his.

As they turned around the dance floor, her skirts swirled around and between his legs. The common, everyday movement of the fabric took on a painfully intimate feel as her skirts dragged against his trousers.

He thought the song would never end, and at the same time part of him didn't want it to, as he tried to hold her at arm's length and keep her skirts from mating with his legs. The warmth of her radiated through his palms all the way to the center of his soul. Her clean, flowery scent drifted from the cloud of silky-soft ringlets that bobbed just beneath his nose.

The mingling aroma of fresh sawdust would never smell quite the same to him again.

She sang along to the music in a sweet, almost inaudible voice, but instead of the words to "Aura Lee," she sang something about loving her tender, loving her true, and never letting her go.

He couldn't recall his wife ever singing, other than the hymns she knew by heart, and then only in church. Now she was making up her own romantic lyrics to her favorite song?

When the melody finally, blessedly ended, Barrett stayed in his arms for the briefest of seconds, glancing up at him with a bewitching smile before stepping away. Her smile rippled through him like a summer breeze through wind chimes, reminding him that he needed something to moisten his throat. Preferably something harder than cider. Something that would dull his senses fast.

"Alston, could I steal your wife away for a dance?" Tom Davis strolled up with Carrie on his arm, looking as if he expected Barrett to turn him down. Any other night Chase would have expected her to decline as well. But tonight she radiated with life, and Chase found himself less than willing to share her.

"Only if Carrie will suffer through one with me."

"My soul, I suppose I could force myself. You being such a terrible dancer and all." Carrie grinned up at Chase as he led her into the dance. He glanced back just as Barrett spun away into the crowd with Tom. Could that have been a look of regret in her eyes just before she disappeared into the throng?

"Motherhood seems to be agreeing with Eliz . . . Barrett. My word, I just can't get used to calling her Barrett. But she even seems a different person, doesn't she? Why, she's never looked lovelier."

Carrie babbled on, and Chase nodded every now and

then as he watched the crowd for a glimpse of his wife.
He watched through the rest of that dance with Carrie,
and through two more, alone, at the edge of the dancers.
A glimpse was all he got. Glimpses of her laughing, fan-
ning herself, spinning arm in arm with yet another partner.

"Chase, come over here and play one of them Virginia
reels for us." Willard Ivors waved him toward the musicians, pulling his attention away from the search for his
wife. He'd rather be dancing the reel with Barrett than
playing it, but Willard wasn't about to be swayed.

Someone stuck a fiddle in Chase's hands when he
stepped up to the musicians. After settling his chin on
the chin rest and adjusting the pad against his shoulder,
he pulled the bow across the strings a few times to test
the tone, more from second nature than from caring
about the sound.

When he'd learned to play, it had been in the music
room of Woodchase, his family estate, and his music
teacher had called the instrument a violin instead of a
fiddle. Chase liked the fiddle better.

Just as he played the first notes of the reel, he caught
sight of a wide-eyed Barrett at the edge of the crowd,
looking up at him with what seemed a mixture of surprise
and . . . could that be pride? He could credit neither of
those looks, but before he could study her closer, Abner
Bailey presented his portly body, and she was off again
into the mass of other dancers.

"Let's give 'em another waltz before we take a wet-
the-whistle break," Willard yelled over the music. "How
'bout the 'Blue Danube' when we finish the reel?"

Everyone nodded. At least then Chase could try and

catch Barrett alone. Maybe they'd duck out and go home then. He couldn't say that watching his wife dance with other men made for an entertaining evening.

As the musicians ended the lively reel and began the sedate waltz, Chase saw Barrett thank Abner and step away, shaking her head when her partner obviously asked for another dance. She strolled to the edge of the crowded floor, turning down Carl Raye, and then Alec Montry along the way.

Chase watched every move Barrett made, every smile as she declined an invitation, every wispy curl moving in the breeze as she fanned herself, every dart of her tongue as she moistened her lips.

And she watched him.

Her eyes, all smoky gray, sparkled as she watched him. Two other suitors came up and invited her to dance, and she turned them down without ever taking her gaze from Chase's.

He never had gotten that drink he needed so badly, and now his throat made the desert seem like swampland. He had to concentrate on the music to remember to keep playing, and when a half smile curved Barrett's lips, he forgot to play altogether. Without another thought, he shoved his fiddle into the nearest pair of hands, then parted the crowd as he strode across the barn, stopping only when he stood in front of his wife.

Wordlessly, he slipped his arms around her waist and swirled her into the swarm of dancers. They'd never once broken eye contact. She never once glanced away with an uncomfortable frown. She met his stare, matched his heat, and that in itself sent ribbons of fire licking through his veins. Without thinking, he reached up and sifted his fingers through the loose, silky, spirally curls that now barely touched her shoulders.

God, he wanted to kiss her. She looked so soft, and happy, and . . . kissable.

He stopped dancing, right there in the middle of the floor, and ran his fingers through her hair until he cradled her head in the palms of his hands. Suddenly he didn't know whether he wanted to kiss her or break her neck.

How dare she?

How dare she show up looking like the wife he'd always dreamed of, smiling, full of life? Glowing? How dare she make herself so appealing that for the first time since their wedding he wished devoutly that he could find some reason—*any* reason—to forgive her for sleeping with his brother?

She continued to look up at him. No fear. No shame. In fact, he detected a hint of mischief in her eyes.

Her lips parted. She leaned closer. He could feel her breath warm against his skin, almost feel her mouth on his.

"Chase," she whispered, "the dance is over."

Chapter 8

Barrett couldn't for the life of her figure out what she'd done to tick Chase off. One minute they'd been dancing, the next he looked like he was going to kiss her, then the next he looked ready to kill her. She'd thought she was doing him a favor by pointing out that the music had stopped. For pity's sake, people were starting to gawk.

The wagon hit another rut in the road, jarring Barrett's teeth and sending her gaze back to Adam in his basket. He slept through it like a champ.

"I didn't see Wes there tonight. He helped build the barn, didn't he? Why didn't he stay to celebrate?"

Chase stared over the horse's back for several seconds, the reins dangling from his fingers, his forearms propped on his thighs. He finally shot a disgusted glance in her direction before going back to studying the road.

"He's just trying to live a quiet life, like he always has since those threats against him when we first moved here. Being the only Negro for miles around isn't easy. Besides, would *you* have danced with him?" Then before she could answer, he continued, "You know as well as I that he's not comfortable in those types of gatherings. You yourself have gone out of your way before to make sure he felt that way."

Barrett's mouth dropped open to protest, but she stopped herself. It didn't take a rocket scientist to figure out from Wes's comments that Elizabeth hadn't been his biggest fan.

"Did you see Margaret Keller tonight?" Barrett decided to change the subject. "She had a big bruise on her cheekbone. She looked like hell."

Chase's neck all but cracked when he jerked his head around at the word "hell." So. Elizabeth hadn't been one to bandy profanities about. Oh, well.

"Yes," he finally said. "I guess Miller got drunk again."

Barrett couldn't believe her ears. Chase's tone had been no more outraged than if he'd said, "Ah, yes, the weatherman's predicting rain again."

"You mean he beats her?"

Chase kept a stoic watch over the horse's back, down the dark ribbon of moonlit road. "Barrett, we've known since the first month we moved here."

She couldn't believe this.

"And nobody does anything about it?"

"He's her husband. That's a family matter between the two of them."

"Oh!" Barrett had to stop herself from going for the man's throat. "Until he kills her. Or will that be chalked up to an unfortunate accident? What happens if you get the urge to beat the daylights out of me someday? You'd better kill me, because I won't take it sitting down!" The thought erupted in her mind that maybe he'd already beaten Elizabeth.

"Barrett, you know I would never do anything . . . for Pete's sake, calm down. You'll wake the baby." He grabbed her arm and shook it, but Adam had already let out his first yelp of outrage at their noisy exchange.

Barrett jerked her arm free of his grasp, yanked her cape tighter around her, and jiggled the basket to quiet Adam.

"Now see what you've done?"

"Me?" Chase choked out. "I'm not the one who—"

"There, there, Adam. Daddy's sorry he yelled and woke you up. Shhh, shhh." Barrett ignored Chase and took Adam out of his basket when he refused to be quieted.

She felt the now-familiar tingle that always preceded the release of her milk.

Well, just great. Now she would have to nurse him again, even if he wasn't hungry, or else she'd never get to sleep with her aching breasts, let alone be able to sleep on her stomach. And since it couldn't be much past ten o'clock, he would probably wake up at three, starving and ready to play.

Men!

When the wagon bumped the last few feet to the barn, she scrambled off the seat before Chase had a chance to help her. Shooting a parting glare over her shoulder, she marched across the moon-silvered yard.

The house vibrated when she slammed the back door behind her. Bo jumped from his coma by the stove and peered at her through bleary eyes as she stomped toward the bedroom.

"Sorry, Bo," she said over her shoulder, then turned her attention back to Adam as she propped him on a pillow. "Okay, little fella. Let Mommy get out of these clothes and you can have all the . . ."

She'd called herself "Mommy."

A strange, warm wave of . . . something . . . pleasant rippled through her.

Adam didn't let the warmth and wonder settle for too long before he reminded her what mommies were for.

"Okay, okay, okay!" She yanked off her bodice, shivering in the cold air of their room. "Why the heck they didn't put fireplaces in the bedrooms of these old farmhouses—Okay! I'm coming." Barrett peeled off her remaining clothes in record time, aimed the pile of them toward the rocking chair, and yanked the scratchy nightgown on. "What I wouldn't give for a big bottle of Downy. Okay! Here I am! Dinner is served."

Adam's little mouth frantically searched the nightgown until Barrett pulled the fabric out of the way for him. She settled into the feather mattress and adjusted the covers over them.

"Gee, are you that hungry or are you just mad because you had to wait? You've got a little temper on you, you know that?" Barrett stroked the dark, fuzzy down of his head with the back of her finger while he ignored her in favor of more interesting things.

She loved the little swallowing noises he made as he tried to keep up with her milk. And she loved watching his tiny little hand open and close against her breast.

Was this what a mother felt like? Had her cool, clinical mother ever watched her babies nurse with this same sense of warm, tingling awe?

Barrett snorted herself back to reality. Her mother had
barely stopped her medical practice long enough to deliver, and certainly never to nurse. The one who had fed
the Overbrook babies with warmth and love had been
Nana.

She refused to let herself dwell on her grandmother.

Chase came in long after Adam had fallen back to
sleep. Barrett watched his silhouette step to the door, the
black of his body outlined by the flickering orange from
the low fire in the parlor. He surveyed the pile of clothes
that had almost made it to the rocker. With a shake of his
head he walked over and scooped them up, shook them
out, then draped them neatly over the back of the chair.
He left the room and returned with Adam's basket,
placed it on Barrett's side of the bed, then gently took
Adam from her arms and put him in his bed.

Barrett knew Chase thought she was asleep. The dim
white light of the moon turned everything to shades of
light and dark gray, and the head of the bed stood in the
deepest part of the shadows. She watched through par-
tially slitted eyes while Chase peeled off his shirt, then
sat on the rocker and yanked off his boots. He grabbed
both boots and placed them by the armoire, then hung
his shirt on a peg on the wall. Only Barrett's eyes moved
as she followed his progress around the room.

He stood at the foot of the bed, bathed in the dim,
frosty light from the window. His suspenders hung limp
around both sides of his hips as he reached over his
head, grabbed a handful of his long-underwear shirt and
dragged it over his head the same way men would do
one hundred years later.

Barrett took her time surveying the body she'd been

waking up next to, trying her best not to let the sight affect her, and failing miserably. What was it about the play of shadows across a finely muscled torso that could turn a girl's insides to honey? If guys knew exactly what went on in the female brain at the sight of a well-toned stomach, they'd all be in line to buy an *Abs of Steel* video.

Before she could move on and ponder the exquisite artwork of his shoulders, he plowed both hands through his hair and presented his back.

Not a bad score there, either.

She'd just allowed her appreciative gaze to dip to his trim waist when his trousers slid from their resting place on his hips to pool on the floor. The bottom half of his long underwear went with them.

The tiniest catch of her breath was enough to have Chase spinning around, unfortunately, and peering at her face. She scrunched her eyes closed and willed herself not to move a muscle. She willed herself to forget that brief glimpse of Chase as well.

It seemed like an eternity before she felt his side of the bed sag and the covers lift as he climbed in.

Good grief, had he pulled some clothes back on or was he still buck naked? She was afraid to move, for fear she might accidentally touch . . . something. She didn't want to take any chances of keeping him awake.

She lay as still as a corpse. Her nose itched. Her leg itched. A place below her right shoulder blade itched.

This was going to be a long night.

She'd never been so relaxed. Every muscle in her body seemed to melt right into the mattress, and the blankets were tucked around her like a warm cocoon. She could tell through her closed eyes that dawn had already crept over the windowsill. She hadn't slept so well since—

She catapulted from the bed, bringing half the covers and dragging a sleeping Chase with her.

"What the . . ." Chase mumbled, then landed on his feet beside her when he saw her hovering over the baby's basket. "What's the matter?"

She shushed him, then laid her palm gently against Adam's warm back. His tiny rib cage rose and fell just as it should.

"Oh, thank God." Barrett flopped onto the edge of the bed, her hand to her heart. "He's never slept this late. I was afraid . . ."

"You're sure he's all right?" Chase scratched the back of his head with one hand and held a blanket around him, Barrett noticed with mixed emotions, with the other.

"Well, he looks fine. He's not feverish. He's breathing. Who do I look like? Dr. Spock?" Once she thought about it, she wasn't even sure if Dr. Spock was an M.D. Good grief, could anyone be any less prepared for motherhood?

"Dr. who?"

"Oh" —she waved away Chase's question,— "forget it. I was thinking out loud. He's okay."

When Chase grabbed his trousers from the foot of the bed Barrett jumped up and headed for the door, scooping up her robe and slippers along the way. Much as she'd like to hang around and watch the blanket drop, she didn't think her willpower was up to the test.

Wes appeared at the back door just minutes after Barrett put on a pot of coffee. At least she'd mastered coffee. Anything edible was a different matter, and they'd finished off the last of the canned goods and covered dishes the neighbors had brought. As she opened the door for Wes and to let Bo out, she idly wondered how long they could survive on the canned and dried food that Elizabeth had preserved.

"Mornin', brat." Wes pulled off his cap and wiped his feet as he came through the door. Barrett wondered if he even realized her called her Brat now, so easily did the name roll off his tongue.

"Hi, Wes. We missed you last night at the barn dance."

His only response was a calm smile and a slight shake of his head.

"Chaser up yet?"

Barrett pointed toward the bedroom. "Getting dressed. Barge in if you want to. Change a diaper. Bathe a baby."

His calm smile broadened a little as he plodded toward the bedroom door.

Barrett turned her attention back to breakfast. Oh, what she wouldn't give for some Pop-Tarts, frozen waffles, *any* kind of cereal. Wait a minute. Eggs! She could do eggs.

Tying her robe tighter around her waist, she slipped through the back door in the direction of the chicken coop.

"All right, girls," she said as she approached the wary-looking hens, "nothing personal here, but your eggs are part of the food chain." She'd managed to gather quite a few in the fold of her robe before one of the old biddies decided to fight back.

"Okay, okay. Fair enough. I'm a lover, not a fighter, anyway."

"Good morning, Barrett."

She nearly scrambled the eggs right then and there when she backed out of the chicken coop and almost stepped on Mr. Gideon.

"You know, you have a way of showing up at the most inopportune times," she said, not bothering to hide her irritation while she checked for cracked eggs.

"There are those who would argue that point with you," he replied with his usual calm.

"I've been wanting to talk to you anyway—"

"I know. That's why I'm here."

She ignored his interruption. "Because I've been thinking, and I have a few questions that need answers."

"Ask away, child. I'll answer what I can."

Barrett narrowed her eyes at him. He seemed entirely too agreeable.

"If I'm inhabiting Elizabeth Alston's body, what happened to Elizabeth? She's definitely not in here with me."

"Elizabeth died in childbirth."

He might as well have slapped her. She hadn't expected him to answer, let alone answer with such bone-jarring honesty.

"She's dead?" she repeated, more to allow the information to sink in than to affirm his statement.

"Yes. She had neither the constitution nor the will to live that you do."

"All right." She pushed the thought of Elizabeth away for the moment. "If she's dead, and I'm in her body, what happened to my body in 1997?"

"Well, that depends."

"On what?"

"On whether or not you go back."

Barrett stiffened all over.

"What do you mean, whether or not I go back? There's no question there, Clarence. The minute this stupid locket cooperates, I'm outta here."

He stuck his ubiquitous empty pipe between his teeth and patted the air for her to calm down.

"Yes. Yes, yes, child. I know. But one never knows what the future will bring. If, by chance, you decide to stay behind, I thought you'd want to know what would happen to your body."

"Well." Barrett calmed down. She guessed it wouldn't hurt to know. Or would it? She asked anyway. "What's my body doing now?"

Mr. Gideon pulled a deep drag off his empty pipe. "Nothing, actually."

"Nothing . . ."

"The future is a relative thing, child. And time has a way of standing still in the future, if we need it to. If you decide to go back, you'll wake up at the inn the morning after you arrived there."

"Will I remember being here?" She bet she knew the answer to that one.

"Yes."

"Yes?" Wrong answer.

"Repetition is a wonderful thing in learning, isn't it? Yes. You'll remember everything. Chase, Wes, Adam, Carrie, Bo. Every minute. Every thing."

That one left her speechless for a moment.

"And if I *don't* go back?"

"Your body will be found by me at the inn. You will

have died of an abdominal aortic aneurysm. That's somewhat like an aneurysm in the brain, only it happens in the stomach."

Barrett felt as if someone had just kicked her in the stomach. She sank down onto the stump Chase used for chopping wood.

"I'll die?"

"Your body will die. Your spirit is here, very much alive. But you humans put too much stock in this life business. If you only knew what was waiting . . . but"— he held up a hand—"that's another sermon."

Barrett wasn't listening anyway.

She would die if she didn't go back. Literally.

She was honest enough with herself to admit that, once or twice, in just brief flashes, and usually when she was with Adam, she'd wondered what it would be like to stay. But if she stayed, her body in the future would die. Her life there would cease to exist. It wasn't much of one, she knew, but it was hers. She'd worked hard to get where she was at FutureTech. She would never see her family again.

"If I go back, what happens to Elizabeth's body?"

"She dies."

"She dies. I die. Elizabeth's already dead! Don't you have any better ideas of how to deal with this than death?"

Mr. Gideon simply shrugged. "That's life," he stated calmly.

Barrett sat there on the stump, her teeth chattering in the icy morning, her mind spinning. She looked up at Mr. Gideon.

"You're not going to make it easy for me, are you?"

He smiled and placed his hand on her shoulder. Warmth spread throughout her body at his touch.

"Very little in life that's worth having comes easy."

She didn't know how long she sat there staring into space, mulling over the information Mr. Gideon had imparted.

"You got a hungry youngun in here, brat."

Barrett blinked herself back to the present. Mr. Gideon was nowhere in sight and Wes's head disappeared back into the house before she could answer him.

With a lot less bounce to her step, she got up, adjusted the eggs, and started back across the yard.

As she walked she raised her face to the sky and said, "Thank you, Mr. Guardian Angel, for taking my simple, uncomplicated, quiet life and dropping me into an impossible situation. With guardian angels like you, who needs hell?"

Barrett hoped this was the right house. Wes, in his unquestioning, long-suffering way, had given her directions. Ever since she'd told him that she couldn't remember anything before Adam's birth, he'd watched her with the expression of a man waiting to hear the punch line to a joke.

Barrett's arms ached from carrying Adam in his basket and the baking dish she planned to return to Margaret Keller. Her feet ached from what seemed like a ten-mile hike, but Wes swore it was no more than half a mile.

The small, immaculate white clapboard house with the dark-green shutters matched Wes's description exactly. Stepping up onto the pristine porch, Barrett reflected on how, if she could find a broom, she might sweep her own porch someday. Come to think of it, she thought she remembered seeing a broom in the pantry next to the stairs.

Before she could raise her knuckles to knock, the dark-green door swung inward and Margaret peered out at her.

"Elizabeth. Oh. What a surprise."

Clearly not a pleasant one. For once Barrett let being called Elizabeth slide.

"Hi, Margaret. I brought your baking dish back." Margaret just stood there, looking uncomfortable. Barrett set Adam's basket on the porch floor, then offered the dish to the woman in the shadows. Did she really think Barrett couldn't see the bruise? "I've put some biscuits in it. They aren't very good, but my Nan—my grandmother always said, 'Never return a dish empty.' Actually," she babbled on, "these are the second batch. The first batch came out looking like charcoal briquettes." Too late, Barrett wondered if Margaret would know what charcoal briquettes were.

Finally the woman opened the door a little wider, wiped her hands on her apron, then took the dish from Barrett.

"Thank you. I'm sure they're wonderful. Everyone knows what a good cook you are."

Barrett could have groaned out loud.

"Well, don't expect too much." She flapped her hands toward the biscuits. "New recipe," she added lamely.

One of those long, uncomfortable silences fell between them as Margaret stood in the shadows and Barrett stood on the porch, nodding like an idiot.

She wondered if things could get any more tense.

"Could I get a glass of water from you before I head back? I'm kind of—"

"Oh! Of course." Margaret's head darted out of the shadows for a second. She looked up and down the road in both directions. "How rude of me. Come in and sit down." She swung the door open, picking up Adam's basket and hauling him in like a drug dealer snatching a delivery. Barrett had to virtually jump through the door before it closed behind her.

She didn't know if Elizabeth had ever been in the house, so she tried not to look around with too much curiosity as she followed her hostess to the kitchen. The place looked normal enough.

They walked through a neat little parlor—almost too neat—with a bazillion doilies covering tabletops, chair backs, hanging over the mantel. Every little knickknack sat on its own little doily. A nightmare to dust, Barrett thought with uncharacteristic domesticity. But there wasn't a speck of dust in sight.

She caught a glimpse of a bedroom through an open door. She would have laid odds she could bounce a quarter off the bedspread.

The kitchen was no different. Pots and pans hung in perfect rows across the wall. Windows sparkled. The wooden floor gleamed with recent waxing.

Good grief, what a sterile place.

"Let me get some fresh water. I'll be right back." When Margaret snatched up a bucket and scurried out the back door, Barrett realized there wasn't even a pump for water in the kitchen.

Within minutes Margaret presented Barrett with a glass of fresh water, clean and clear except for the tiny specks of fiber from the well rope floating lazily through it.

The icy water had a metallic taste that reminded Barrett of the iron drops that Nana used to give her and Elizabeth and Browning.

Margaret didn't join her in a glass of water, nor did she sit down to visit. Instead she bustled about, straightening things that were already straight, polishing things that were already gleaming, wiping off the already spotless surface of the table.

"How's Ann?" Barrett ventured.

"Oh, fine. She's in school today." The nervous polishing continued.

"And your mother?"

"Irascible as ever."

Barrett didn't try to stifle her grin. The small talk wasn't working, though. Time to say what she came here to say.

"That's a pretty nasty bruise on your cheek."

The polishing stopped, then started again.

"Oh. Wasn't that clumsy of me, walking into the door the way I did?"

Barrett shook her head. For some reason, she'd expected something a little more creative.

"I guess that excuse has been used since the invention of the door. But it's as good a one as any. Better than the truth, huh?"

The polishing, which had slowed with Barrett's first words, stopped completely.

"The truth?" Margaret's back was to her, but Barrett could visualize the desperately innocent look on Margaret's face. They all wore it at least once.

"Yeah. Blaming a door for your bruises is better than saying, 'My husband beats the crap out of me.'"

Margaret spun around, her hands clutched together at her breast, a bright, plastic smile pasted on her face.

"Oh, no! You've misunderstood. I really did walk into a door. I got up in the night to check on Ann, and—"

"And you walked into the door. Yeah, right. Look, Margaret, when I was in college, I minored in family counseling. My—"

"You went to college? Why, Elizabeth, I didn't know that about you. How interesting. Where did you go?"

"I'm not changing the subject. My last two years I worked in a shelter for abused women. I can help you deal with this, but you have to want to help yourself."

Margaret went back to polishing. "You're wrong. Why, my Miller is the salt of the earth. He would sooner cut off his hand than strike me." She stopped scrubbing the table and looked Barrett in the eye, defying her to challenge the statement.

Barrett had heard that one before. Strangely, there were still lots of bruised faces, but she'd never seen one amputation.

"Well, I guess I was wrong, then." Barrett gave her a level stare. "I apologize." She stood, tucked the blankets tighter around Adam, and hooked the basket on her arm. She started for the door, then turned back to meet Margaret's gaze. "One interesting thing I learned, working with those women whose husbands knocked them around like punching bags, is that so many of them thought they deserved it. Some didn't leave because they didn't think they could do any better. Then there were the ones who were afraid to leave. Afraid of what their husbands would do if they caught them."

Margaret's gaze flickered for only a moment.

"People hear about a wife being beaten and say, 'Why doesn't she get out of there? Just leave the guy?' Do you know the reason?"

Margaret gave her an innocent, minuscule shake of her head.

"Because by the time he gets around to beating her, he's got her convinced that she's a worthless, invisible piece of nothing. Can you believe they convince their wives they deserve it? Imagine that. Deserving a beating because you ironed a wrinkle into his shirt. Deserving a beating because you forgot to dust the top of the door-jamb."

Margaret wet her lips and swallowed as Barrett let her words sink in.

"Well, I'm sorry I kept you. I really didn't mean to stay so long."

Margaret just stood there, trying to bring her eyes up to meet Barrett's.

"Thanks for the water, and I really appreciate the food you and your mother brought. It was a lifesaver. But now I'd better get home before Adam wakes up. Patience isn't his strong point."

When she stepped out onto the porch she turned back

to Margaret one last time. "Stop by whenever you're near the house. And if you ever want to talk, I'll be there to listen."

She left before Margaret said another word. Maybe the biscuits weren't edible, but at least she'd given the woman some food for thought.

The next step was Margaret's.

Chapter 9

"YOU'RE GOING TO do what?" Chase stopped tossing chunks of coal into the wheelbarrow and gave Wes his full attention.

"You heard me. I been thinkin' about this for a long time, but the barn raisin' made up my mind." Wes bent over, grabbed a large piece of coal in each of his massive hands, then tossed them on top of the load. "It's about time I started a family."

Chase couldn't blame him. In fact, he'd wondered more than once if Wes ever got as lonely for a woman's touch as Chase did. Lately there had been times he'd ached for gentle fingers to stroke his cheek, straighten his tie, rub his shoulders after a hard day. Touches that had nothing to do with sex.

Of their own volition, his eyes flicked toward the back of the house where Barrett bent over a steaming tub of clothes. She straightened, one hand on the small of her back, the other swiping her forehead, brushing damp tendrils of chestnut curls out of her eyes. Using a short wooden pole, she scooped up several pairs of his trousers and dumped them into the rinse water.

Chase went back to loading the wheelbarrow, suddenly aware of the black grime of coal dust coating his pants legs.

"So when are you planning to leave?"

Wes threw on another handful of coal, then dusted his palms together. "Day after tomorrow. I figure I'll be back from Richmond before March."

March. That would leave him and Barrett alone together for more than a month. With no buffers. No one to communicate through. No one to ease the tension.

"And Rose is willing to leave Woodchase now?"

Wes nodded and scratched the back of his head through his wiry salt-and-pepper hair. "Says she is. I reckon she's missed me as much as I've missed her. She says Reconstruction ain't agreeing with anybody back there, anyway." He smiled that derisive half smile that always meant he was amused with himself. "'Course, that has nothin' to do with why she's willin' to marry me now."

"Of course not, big brother. You've simply overwhelmed her with your modest charm." Chase yanked up the handles of the wheelbarrow and started off toward the coal bin at the back of the house. "It's high time you two got married. How long have you been courting now?" he asked over his shoulder as Wes fell in behind him.

"Let's see." Wes did some mental calculations. "Must be close to twenty years."

"Criminy! Twenty years!" Chase stopped and set down the wheelbarrow. "You mean to tell me you've been sparking Rose since you were seventeen and you're just now asking her to marry you?"

Wes stooped and picked up a couple of pieces of coal that had fallen off the load. "Didn't want to rush into it." He smiled that amused, blue-eyed smile. " 'Sides, I asked her last year, before we left Richmond."

"Oh. Well. Glad to know you didn't wait too long."

Wes juggled the pieces of coal and whistled an off-key tune while he ignored his brother's wisecrack. Chase heaved up the wheelbarrow and continued on toward the bin.

"Chaser?"

With a mighty shove, Chase upended the coal into the bin.

"Yeah?"

"You ever think about making peace with your wife?"

Chase turned and glared at his brother, who forged ahead with the topic.

" 'Cause if you have, I'm thinkin' a good time to straighten things out would be while I'm gone. You wouldn't have to worry about me bargin' in on you all the time."

Chase looked away and almost released the bitter laugh that grew in his chest. They both knew Wes's presence had nothing to do with why he hadn't reconciled with his wife.

"She slept with Aidan, Wes. That boy in there might be my nephew."

"And he might be your son. Hell. He *is* your son, no matter who fathered him. You gonna spend the rest of your marriage makin' her pay? Or are you gonna divorce her?"

Chase blew out a frustrated sigh and shook his head. "You know I would never get a divorce."

"So you're just going to be miserable for the rest of your life, and make Barrett miserable, and eventually make the boy miserable. And he won't have no brothers or sisters to play with 'cause his daddy won't touch his ma." Wes poked Chase in the chest so hard he stumbled back a step. "And you want to touch her. I see it in your eyes every time you look at her."

Chase gritted his teeth, ready to deny the statement. But Wes was right. He wanted to touch her. He wanted to do more than touch her. But, God help him, more than that, he wanted her to touch him.

"It doesn't matter what I want. What's to keep her from being unfaithful again?"

"What caused her to be in the first place? Did you ever ask her?"

"Of course! She refused to talk about it."

"Yeah. Almost a year ago, right after it happened. Ask her again, you stubborn jackass. Find out why she did it or forget about why she did it. Either way, work it out, little brother, or you got one sorry life ahead of you."

Chase turned his back on his brother, picked up the wheelbarrow, and headed back to the coal pile.

Damn, he hated it when Wes was right.

"It seems strange, not having Wes here at dinner. He's only been gone since this morning, but I miss him already," Barrett said as she clanged around at the stove. Chase watched her from the corner of his eye. She seemed as uncomfortable as he was.

He peeled off his woolen shirt, then dragged the long-underwear shirt over his head. The icy water from the pump bit into his skin but cleared his head somewhat.

The sound of a metal ladle hitting the floor drew Chase's attention back to Barrett. She stood there, looking at him, her gaze sweeping from his shoulders to his waist. Suddenly she jumped, as if she'd just realized he was watching her.

"Here!" She snatched a teakettle from the back of the stove. "Let me warm up that water for you. It's as cold as ice."

She hurried across the floor, kicking the forgotten ladle and sending it spinning across the room to come to rest across the toe of Chase's boot. She burst out with a quick, nervous giggle completely uncharacteristic of the woman he'd married.

Chase retrieved the ladle and rinsed it off while Barrett poured the boiling water into the basin. He made quick work of sluicing the water over the rest of his upper body and donning a clean shirt. The last thing he needed right now was his wife dragging her gaze down his chest again. That first time had been enough to release a swarm of angry bees under his rib cage.

The shirt, he noticed as he worked his way down the buttons, had yet to be touched with the heat of an iron. Could she have missed that shirt in her ironing? It wasn't like his wife to overlook that kind of thing.

"Did you miss this one?" he asked.

"What?" She jumped and spun around to face him. Yes. She was definitely uncomfortable.

"The shirt. It's not ironed. Did you miss it when you ironed the others?"

Barrett blinked at him, then cocked an eyebrow and planted her hands on her hips.

"Do you have any idea how heavy that iron is? What kind of *work* is involved in heating the stupid thing up and then trying not to burn your hand while you use it? I'll live with a few wrinkles, thankyouverymuch, before I suffer third-degree burns."

She must be tired, Chase reasoned. She was upset about Wes leaving, and she'd had a hard day with Adam.

As if on cue, Adam's fussy whine drifted in from the bedroom. Barrett's shoulders slumped at the noise and her chin dropped to her chest. "I just fed him. He can't be hungry."

Chase held up his hand to stay her. "I'll get him. You put the meal on the table while I change him."

Bo hopped up from his rug by the fire and trotted ahead of Chase into the bedroom. The dog had appointed himself keeper of the baby, and anytime Adam let out a peep, he was right there, hovering over him like a hen with its only chick.

Chase threw a diaper onto his shoulder and leaned over the baby's bed.

"Come here, big fella. What are you so mad about?"

The squirming little bundle had kicked off his covers, and his tiny hands and pudgy legs flailed above the basket. He quieted immediately at the sound of Chase's voice.

"Oh, now that you have my attention, you quiet down, huh? You sure know how to get your way," Chase crooned as he picked the baby up and laid him on the oilskin to change his diaper. "But you're not so tough, you know that? You're not big enough to hurt anybody. No, you're not."

Adam stared at Chase in unblinking fascination while Chase expertly traded a wet diaper for a clean one. Once the diaper was securely pinned, the baby emitted quiet, contented gurgles, jerking every now and then as if something inside startled him. A little foot waved in the air under Chase's nose, and without thinking, Chase grabbed it and planted a loud kiss on the pink toes.

A smile that only an innocent angel could have smiled lit Adam's face at the touch of Chase's lips. And with that tiny, baby smile, an unexpected warmth, a ray of sunshine, entered Chase's soul and melted the block of ice around his heart that had kept him from loving this baby.

The smile left Chase's face as he looked at Adam, this child that he would raise. His son. He brought his index finger next to the tiny, waving hand, and Adam grasped the finger in his fist and held on as if he would never let go.

"You did it, didn't you, little fella? You've got my heart now just as surely as you've got my hand."

Adam held tight, smiling, making little baby noises until Chase reluctantly pried his finger free. The gentle moment, the unexpected tenderness surprised Chase and made him more than a little uncomfortable.

"Sorry to ruin your good time, big fella, but it's dinnertime for both of us. And I don't know about you, but I'm hungry enough to eat a whole cow."

He sniffed the air, expecting to smell at least part of that cow cooking, but the mouthwatering aromas he'd always taken for granted were woefully *not* perfuming the air.

Barrett wore a frown as she stood staring at the stove. She chewed on the side of her finger, picked up a salt shaker, and shook it with obvious uncertainty over one of the steaming pots. She grumbled something under her breath that sounded like, "Where's a good caterer when you need one?" Surely he hadn't heard her right.

"What?" she barked without looking at him. "Haven't you ever seen someone cooking?"

"Uhhh . . ." On second thought, Chase decided not to answer that question. "Could you hold Adam a minute? There's something in the barn I want to get."

He had transferred Adam and was halfway out the door before Barrett said, "Wait a minute! What are you—"

The door slammed behind him as he trudged across the frozen ground to the barn. Within minutes he shoved his way back into the house, his arms laden with his surprise.

Barrett set a bowl on the table, then spun around at the sound of the door opening.

"You know, it's hard enough to cook without holding a baby while I'm doing it. You could have put him . . ."

Her voice trailed off and her mouth dropped open.

"Oh, Chase." She dropped to her knees beside the brand-new cradle, running her fingers over the hand-carved spindles.

Chase watched her caress the wood, feeling unaccountably proud—and relieved—that she liked the infant bed.

With her head bent over the cradle, the baby in her

arms, she created a picture that Chase had longed to see since before their wedding.

She looked up at him in wonder. "Did you make this?"

"Yes." He nodded, surprised again at how pleased he was with her reaction.

"So that was the reason for all the hammering in the barn?"

Chase shrugged, uncomfortable at being found out.

When she started to rise, he held her arm and helped her up. Both of them stepped away quickly, breaking the contact that had sent little sparks of energy flying through the air.

"Well," Barrett was the first to speak, interrupting the humming silence, "let's see how he likes it."

"Yes." Chase nodded once, numbly. "I'll, uh, I'll get the basket."

Once the tiny mattress and bedclothes were transferred to the cradle, Barrett laid Adam in the center. He seemed dwarfed in it, compared to the basket he'd been sleeping in. When Barrett gently rocked him, Adam's eyes grew large and his uncontrolled waving stopped. Within a matter of seconds, his lids drooped, his little rosebud mouth grew slack.

"Wow," Barrett whispered and looked up at Chase with a melting smile. "You should have built this weeks ago."

Her voice held no censure, but Chase felt about as small as Adam. She was right. He *should* have built it weeks ago.

"Well, let's eat before he wakes up again. Here." She

handed Chase a couple of plates with silverware on top. "Set the table while I get the stuff off the stove."

Chase stood there for a minute, staring at the plates in his hands. Even when he'd offered to help before, Elizabeth had never let him. With a shrug, he went to work setting the table, deciding that women in general were hard enough to figure out, let alone new mothers.

"Here's the salt and pepper. We need some butter and some napkins."

Chase did as he was ordered, amused at her bossiness, then waited until she set the last bowl on the table and seated herself before he sat down. She handed him a bowl of small, boiled potatoes.

"Are you forgetting grace?" he asked.

"What? Oh, grace. Sure. I forgot."

Chase said a quick prayer, then dug into the bowl of anemic-looking potatoes. A bowl of green beans came next, followed by a bowl of corn and then a bowl of stewed apples. His survey of the table revealed nothing but a sea of bowls.

"Where's the meat?"

"The meat?"

"Uhhh, yes."

"Well, this is a . . . vegetarian meal."

Chase scrubbed his eyes with the palm of his hand, then pinched the bridge of his nose as he looked heavenward. All right. She was nervous, what with Wes being gone. And she certainly hadn't been herself lately. He would eat the . . . vegetarian meal and not complain about the lack of meat.

A knock at the front door interrupted their silent meal. Bo sprang to attention from his post beside Adam as Chase rose to answer the door. As usual, Bo self-importantly trotted ahead. It occurred to Chase as he walked through the parlor how easily Bo had taken to living in the house and how easily Barrett had accepted it. Indeed, she had encouraged it.

When the door swung inward, the intrepid, vicious watchdog all but leaped for joy at the sight of little Sam and Genevieve.

"Genevieve. Come in." Chase stepped away, and the two visitors wiped their feet before scurrying in from the cold.

"Chase, I'm so sorry. I know I've probably interrupted your supper."

"Don't worry about that," Chase reassured her, the thought of the lackluster meal definitely *not* calling him back to the table. "Is there a problem?"

"I was on my way back from the quilting society and— by the way, we've missed Eliz . . . Bar . . . your wife there."

"Think of me as Barrett." The wife in question strolled into the room. "It's good to see you again, Genevieve. Come in and have a cup of coffee. Tea, maybe?"

"Oh, no, thank you. I just stopped by to see if Chase could fix a couple of things at the house. One of my doors is sticking, and a branch fell and broke a window in my bedroom. I have it covered up now, but I can still feel the cold air coming in."

Chase leaned over and scratched Bo's head. "Of course. Would tomorrow be soon enough?"

"Oh, yes. I hate to bother you, but I haven't any idea at all how to fix that window. Samuel always did those things." Genevieve's voice caught on the last word. An almost tangible sadness filled her eyes.

Chase wondered what it would be like to love someone that much. To *be* loved that much. He glanced at Barrett and wondered if he would at least reach a sense of peace with her at some point.

Barrett crossed the room and took Genevieve's hands in hers. "It's no trouble. Don't you worry at all. Chase will be over first thing in the morning. Now, won't you stay and have some coffee?"

Genevieve blinked away the excess moisture shimmering in her eyes and shook her head.

"Thank you, but Sam is starting to tire, and I need to get him home and into bed."

After their company left, Chase helped Barrett clean up the kitchen. He still puzzled over the strange un-Elizabeth-like meal. In fact, everything about his wife was getting less and less like the woman he'd married. She'd even given up wearing those hated drab gowns and started wearing more things from her trousseau. The only time she wore the homely dresses now was when she did laundry.

Chase dried the last plate and turned to give it to Barrett. The plate slid out of her wet hands and crashed to the floor, breaking into sharp shards and splinters.

"Oh, great." Barrett stooped to pick up the mess, and Chase knelt to help her. "Ow! Damn, that hurts." She grabbed her wrist and held her hand out to Chase. "Get it out! Ow! Pull it out of there!"

Chase stared at her for a second, stunned by both her language and her reaction to the pain. When she'd sliced

her hand wide open a few months ago, she hadn't re-
acted this strongly.

A long, needlelike sliver of crockery protruded from
the center of her palm. Chase held her hand gently and
studied the splinter.

"Hold still. I don't want it to break off." He grasped
the bottom of the sliver and plucked it free. Barrett
sighed with relief and started to pull her hand back, but
Chase held it tight. "Let me make sure I got it all."

He reassured himself that nothing remained beneath
the skin, then lifted his gaze to tell her to clean it.

The words died in his throat.

Her head was bent over their joined hands, her hair
just inches from his face. The clean smell of whatever
she washed her hair with stirred up that swarm of bees
inside him again. She showed no sign of reclaiming her
hand, though he'd held it for far longer than he needed
to.

She knew he was looking at her. He could feel it, with
both of them kneeling there on the floor, her hand in his,
her silky hair so close.

He didn't remember planning to, but he found himself
leaning forward, just far enough to touch his cheek to
her hair. The soft curls caressed him like a lover's kiss.
He closed his eyes, blocking out the world and concentrating on the softness against his cheek, her delicious
scent that he drew into his lungs, the warmth of her radiating against his skin. Without thinking, he brought his
hand up and touched her hair, ever so gently, marveling
that the curls felt as wonderful as they looked. He sank
his fingers into the dark tendrils, cupping the back of her

head, his palm rubbing the base of her neck. An ache formed in his throat that wouldn't be swallowed away.

Barrett still knelt, her head still bowed so that her face remained hidden from him. He released her hand, a hand that now trembled slightly, and brought his own up to touch her chin, tilting her face up to his.

Her eyes remained lowered until, finally, she lifted her gaze, her soft gray eyes holding touches of desire and touches of fear. Chase caressed her cheek with the lightness of a feather, shaking his head slightly, trying to convey that she had nothing to fear. As she stared into his eyes, he watched her fear disappear.

He held her face in his hands, traced his thumb across her lower lip, felt her heartbeat thundering beneath his fingertips. She made a hesitant, timid movement toward him, and that permission was all he needed. His lips covered hers, gentle at first and then more insistent when the passion in him, so long banked, exploded at the touch of her lips against his. A tiny muffled sigh deep in her throat sent the flames roaring through his body like fire through a parched forest.

Barrett's hand found his face, her lips never leaving his. Her fingers caressed his jaw, behind his earlobes, along the tendon of his neck.

He felt like a man dying of thirst in the desert who had finally reached the water he must have. He could drink of her forever and never get his fill.

"Barrett," he moaned against her mouth. She clung to him, kneeling there, returning his kisses with mind-numbing fervor. "Why?" his voice rasped. "Why did you sleep with him?"

The fire left her kiss an instant before her lips left his.

He opened his eyes to see anger, hurt, and a dying passion reflected in hers.

The passion died in him as well, leaving behind an ache that would haunt him until he settled this question with his wife.

"Why did you sleep with him? Don't you see? Until we talk about it, until you tell me why you slept with my brother a week before the wedding, we can never resolve our marriage. We can never have a marriage like Genevieve and Samuel had. Like your parents. Or like mine. What we have now is no marriage at all."

Barrett's body still ached with the longing Chase's touch had ignited. Her lips still felt the pressure of his. She could still taste his kisses.

And she felt as if he'd sucker punched her in the stomach.

Elizabeth had slept with her brother-in-law just days before her wedding. Why? If she loved the brother, why did she marry Chase? If she didn't love him, why did she sleep with him?

And how could she ever answer that question for Chase?

She shouldn't have to answer it, damn it. Why did she have to clean up some other woman's mess? Why did she have to fall in love with a man whose kiss made her want to melt into his skin and who believed she was another woman?

Damn you, Mr. Gideon. You took my nice, safe, quiet life and turned it into a Movie of the Week. You want me to learn to love him, to open my heart, but even if he loves me back, he'll be loving another woman.

She looked at Chase, ready to tell him what he could do with his questions. But his eyes, those strange golden eyes, held a deep, genuine pain in them. He wanted to fix things. He didn't want to hate his wife for sleeping with another man.

The wind went out of her sails, the fire went out of her anger. She dropped her gaze and shook her head.

What could she tell him? She didn't know why Elizabeth had slept with . . . Aidan. If she could have Chase, why would she even have looked at another man? Why would any woman?

He waited. She could feel his eyes burning into her.

"Chase." She had to stop and clear her throat. Any explanation she could fabricate died before it ever reached her lips. She had never been good at lying. "Whatever E . . . whatever happened before the wedding, it's done, and nothing can change that. We need to start fresh. A clean slate. Put the past behind us and start over brand-new."

It sounded clichéd and lame, even to her. She lifted her gaze, begging with her eyes for forgiveness for something she hadn't done.

His hot amber stare pierced right to her soul.

That's fine, she thought. *Look at me. Look into my soul. See me for who I am—a woman who's never had sex with anyone, let alone with your brother. I'm not the woman you married. I'm not the woman you want so badly to love.*

Why did that thought cause such an ache in her chest?

"Do you love Aidan?" he asked tonelessly.

At last she could answer truthfully.

"No."

"*Did* you love him?"

"No."

"Then why?" he roared, jumping to his feet, leaving her kneeling there on the floor. He plowed both hands into his midnight hair and walked away from her. Crockery crunched into dust beneath his boots.

Barrett reached out automatically and rocked the cradle until Adam's squirming quieted.

She stood, the effort costing her more energy than she could have imagined.

"I don't *know* why."

He stood with his back to her, as if she hadn't spoken.

"Chase, look at me." She, too, crunched through the broken plate, heedless of the cuts to the floor.

He remained where he was, ignoring her existence, until she walked around in front of him, forcing him to look at her.

"I don't know why. I honestly don't know." She laid her hand gently on his arm. "If I could explain it to you, I would. But that woman doesn't exist anymore. I'm not the woman you married. Can't we start over, two people starting their lives together?"

His level glare dropped to the slender hand resting on his forearm. Barrett stepped back, giving him room to sulk, giving him time to think.

Giving him a look that apologized again for a sin she hadn't committed.

Chapter 10

"CHASE! CHASE, WAKE up. Something's wrong with Adam!"

Barrett shook Chase's shoulder in the thin gray light of dawn. He started to groan, then leaped from the bed, blinking blearily, his hair standing on end.

"What's wrong?"

"Adam's burning up with a fever." Barrett cupped the tiny head in her palm. "Get that thermometer Dr. Quack left."

Chase touched the sleeping infant's forehead with the back of his hand, then looked at her, his eyes narrowed. "What do you want it for? Do you know how to use one of those things?"

Barrett rolled her eyes. Mr. Hell's Angel had sent her to the Dark Ages.

"It doesn't take a medical degree to take a temperature. Now, where is it?"

Chase shrugged. "I don't know. You're the one who put it away. You said to let the quack come back and get it, if he was man enough to face you."

"Oh, yeah." Barrett remembered putting the thermometer and tongue depressors away, somewhere. But where? She flew to the dresser, yanking open drawers and tossing things into the air. Finally, the thermometer glistened up at her from a box filled with the tongue depressors, extra safety pins, a baby's hairbrush and comb, a rattler.

The thing seemed more fragile than modern thermometers. Did she dare chance taking the temperature rectally?

A memory of Nana flashed in her mind. Once, when Barrett had been so congested she couldn't breathe through her nose, Nana had taken her temperature under her arm.

Barrett rushed back to the cradle, pulled away the blankets and Adam's nightgown and placed the thermometer in his tiny armpit. She held his arm to his side while she waited for three minutes to pass.

"What are you doing?" Chase asked as he sank to the edge of the bed, his worried face hovering over the baby.

"I'm taking his temperature."

"But I thought you put it—"

"I don't want to take a chance of this breaking. This glass is more fragile than modern ones."

"But Dr. Logan used it. How much more modern do you need?"

Barrett clenched her teeth. "Trust me." Damn, she was sick of censoring her speech.

She withdrew the thermometer and held it up to the dim light from the window. Over 103 degrees. She closed her eyes and tried to remember what Nana'd said. Add a degree to it if it was under the arm. Was that right? Add it? Yeah, add it.

Fear swept through her at the thought. Over 104 degrees. How high was too high? Damn, now she wished she'd paid more attention at the dinner table.

"How high is it?"

Barrett had forgotten about Chase.

"More than 103. And adding a degree for being under the arm makes it over 104. I don't like it that high."

"I'll get Dr. Logan." He shoved his feet into his pants legs as he spoke.

"No! I won't have that quack touching Adam."

Chase yanked his pants to his waist and buttoned the fly halfway. He grabbed his undershirt and pulled it over his head.

"He may not be much of a doctor, but he's the closest one around."

"I don't care! He'll be sticking leeches on Adam, or cupping him." Barrett didn't even know if people still used cups or leeches in 1887, but she wasn't about to find out firsthand.

Chase ignored her, yanking on a heavy work shirt and tucking it into his pants. He pulled on his socks and boots, then marched to the kitchen, where his coat hung on a peg.

"I'll be back as soon as I can."

"I won't let him touch Adam," Barrett yelled at Chase's back as he swung the door open.

Snow tumbled into the kitchen from the snowdrift against the door. The snow stood in the yard at least two feet deep and was falling from the sky so densely that Barrett could barely see the barn, even in the growing light of morning.

"You can't go out in this. You can't leave me with a sick baby and take off into a blizzard."

Chase shut the door and peeled off his coat. Barrett rushed back to the bedroom, wringing her hands over the cradle and running every medical discussion she'd ever heard through her mind.

What she wouldn't do for a bottle of Tylenol now. Did aspirin exist in 1887?

"Chase!" She spun around to get him, but he was right behind her. "Do you have any medicine in the house? Aspirin? Anything for fever?"

He shook his head. "No. No one's been sick. There's just the laudanum Dr. Logan left when you cut your hand. I don't think you took any, did you?"

Laudanum wouldn't do.

Maybe if she nursed him his fever would come down. She pulled the covers off and lifted Adam from the cradle. He felt so fragile and limp. Was he limp from the fever or from sleep?

. . . *worried more about the fever if the patient is lethargic*, she heard her mother say.

"Adam, wake up, baby. Come on, punkin, time to eat. Come on, punkin. Wake up for Mommy." She jiggled the tiny bundle. His head bobbed slightly in sleep. Not a flicker of an eyelash heralded his waking.

"He won't wake up. How can I feed him if he won't wake up?" Somewhere in the back of her mind she remembered that newborns could sleep like they were in comas.

Beside her, Chase touched his finger to the corner of

Adam's mouth and tickled. While he tickled, he blew gently into the baby's face.

Adam squirmed, frowned at having his sleep disturbed, then turned his head and tried to nurse Chase's finger.

"You're brilliant," Barrett sighed, then bustled into the parlor, unbuttoning her nightgown on the way. She sank into the rocker in front of the fire, putting Adam to her breast on the way down.

Adam nursed, but not with his usual enthusiasm. Was his lack of interest from the fever or from being awakened to eat?

When she heard Chase coming from the bedroom, she grabbed a diaper from the edge of the sofa and draped it so that it covered her. She didn't know how modest or immodest Elizabeth had been, but Barrett wasn't ready to bare all in front of Chase. Even though he'd seen everything she had to offer the moment she'd arrived in this time.

Chase came in, plunging his fingers through his hair, then smoothing down the spikes. He dropped onto the sofa.

"How's he doing?"

"He's nursing. But not very strongly."

Silence fell between them. Chase got up, stirred some life back into the fire, then layered on chunks of coal and pieces of wood.

"How about some coffee? This could be a long day."

Barrett leaned her head against the chair back and sighed. "That would be wonderful."

While Chase made the coffee, Barrett racked her

brain, trying to remember anything, a snippet of conversation, an article in a magazine, anything that would tell her how to get Adam's fever down if it didn't break on its own.

The bark of some kind of tree had been used to reduce fevers in the old days. Was it sassafras? Willow? Willow sounded right. But that had a form of salicylic acid in it, didn't it? Which was in aspirin, which could cause Reye's syndrome.

Damn! For the first time in her life, she wished she had the medical expertise of her family members. But would they be any more capable than she, without their twentieth-century drugs and high-tech equipment? Medical school didn't have required courses in how medicine *used to be* practiced.

Chase reappeared with a cup of heavenly, steaming coffee, asked how Adam was doing, then disappeared back into the kitchen. He'd brought with him the scent of bacon cooking, and now Barrett's stomach rumbled, reminding her of the tasteless meal they'd had the night before. The first meal she'd cooked. Another reason to miss Wes. He'd volunteered to cook their meals until Barrett got back on her feet. She'd managed to get the offer extended until he left yesterday morning for Virginia.

Adam lost interest in nursing, so Barrett sat him up to burp him. He fussed, refused to burp, cried a whiny cry that was different from all the others she'd grown used to. He had his change-me cry, his feed-me cry, and his I'm-bored cry. But this was a new one in his repertoire.

And she didn't like the sound of it.

"Come on, punkin. Oh, I know. You're so mad. Yes, you are. You don't feel good, do you?"

Barrett crooned soothingly, laying Adam across her legs and rocking him back and forth. He continued to fuss, restless and squirming.

Chase came in and Barrett looked up at him, hoping he'd have some miraculous words of wisdom.

He traced his fingers along the fuzzy down of Adam's bobbing head and said, "I've got some breakfast on the table for you." Her stomach rumbled as if on cue. "I'll hold him while you eat."

Worried as she was, she didn't think she could eat, but she knew she would function better on a full stomach, so she transferred Adam into Chase's arms and rose to go to the kitchen.

"Will you come in and keep me company?"

Chase blinked a couple times, as if surprised by her request. Hadn't Elizabeth ever asked for her husband's company? He answered by plucking up the heavy wooden rocker in one hand, as if the chair were hollow, and carrying it into the kitchen.

The bacon and eggs tasted like food for the gods. She wolfed down half the meal before she noticed Chase watching her, then a sudden wave of self-consciousness struck her.

Adam continued to fuss, so Barrett justified finishing her breakfast quickly. Maybe if she tried to nurse him on the other breast, he'd quiet down enough to fall asleep. One thing she'd learned through dinnertime osmosis—sleep was best for anyone who was sick.

It wasn't until Chase put Adam back in her arms that she realized they hadn't spoken during her meal.

"Have you already eaten?" she asked, just to make conversation.

"No, I thought I'd hold Adam while you ate. He didn't sound like he was going to be content to lie in his crib."

Barrett couldn't believe how that small gesture touched her. He could have fixed his own breakfast and eaten first, or eaten when she did and let Adam cry while she jiggled him on her lap. Instead, he now stood at the stove, cracking his eggs into a frying pan, after making sure his wife and son were taken care of.

She sank into the rocker and made herself comfortable. If he could be that thoughtful, after being as angry as he was last night, the least she could do was keep him company. Unfortunately, she had no idea what to talk about.

"Do you think it'll snow long?" Good grief. Reduced to talking about the weather—and this from a woman who had schmoozed with CEOs all over the world.

"I don't know. Tom Davis tells me February and March can be pretty unpredictable."

"This is our first winter here?"

Chase looked up at her, the skillet of eggs forgotten.

"I mean . . . this is our first winter here." Nothing like stating the obvious to kill a conversation.

Chase finished cooking his eggs, piled them onto a plate with a dozen slices of bacon and at least four biscuits, and sat at the table facing Barrett. Clearly, he was struggling for a topic of conversation as well.

Adam helped out in his own little way by refusing to be pacified. He felt as warm as he had earlier, but at least now he was rooting around while he fussed, his little mouth in search of the only comfort she could give him.

He nursed better this time, and by the time Chase finished his breakfast, Adam had fallen back to sleep. She eased her way out of the chair and tiptoed into the bedroom, sliding him into the cradle without disturbing a hair on his fuzzy little head. He squirmed for a moment, but a few gentle rocks quieted him.

Barrett turned to the armoire and swung open the doors, sinking down onto the bed to gaze at the row of long, constricting, heavy, cumbersome dresses. Just the thought of putting one of those on again depressed her, no matter how pretty they were.

She was sick of those dresses. She was sick of everything here; doing laundry by hand, sitting by a fire to keep warm and having her face sweat and her back freeze, having to use a chamber pot, for Pete's sake. Having a husband who wanted to love her, yet blamed her for something she hadn't done.

"Thanks a lot, Clarence," Barrett said to the ceiling with more bitterness in her voice than she'd had in a long time.

"Did you say something?" Chase called from the kitchen.

Barrett stood up and moped to the door. "No. Just talking to . . . nobody."

Well, aren't we having a nice little pity party. Barrett could almost hear Nana's voice floating to her in the silence of the bedroom.

Well, hell, she had a right to be depressed. She missed her life in 1997. She missed telephones and radios. She missed Wilmot's Laundry Service, Take-Out Taxi, pizza. She missed lipstick and hairdryers and Jessica McClintock perfume and Colgate and Arrid Extra Dry. And she would *kill* for a tub of movie theater popcorn, a Snickers bar, and a Coke. She missed her jeans and sneakers and . . .

Her eyes drifted to Chase's side of the dresser. Without a second thought she pulled open the bottom drawer, plucked out the top pair of denim jeans, and held them up in front of her.

That could work.

Excited now, she rummaged through his other drawers and found a dark-green flannel shirt. She washed quickly and slipped into the jeans, donned the shirt over her camisole, then had to rummage again to find a belt. A little creative surgery with the seam ripper from the sewing basket put an extra notch in the belt that made it fit perfectly.

Darn, that felt good! She felt so free, so unencumbered, she could have twirled around for joy.

She found a pair of Chase's wool socks, put them on, then buttoned up Elizabeth's walking boots over the socks.

She closed her eyes and savored feeling almost normal.

When she entered the kitchen, Chase was nowhere in sight. At first she panicked, thinking he'd gone for the doctor after all, in two feet of snow and a blizzard outside. Then she heard the *scrape-shush, scrape-shush* of a snow shovel.

From the back door she could barely see Chase's bent form clearing a path from the house to the barn.

Snow already coated his dark clothing so that he was just a light gray shadow in the swirl of white.

She watched him for a few moments—his easy movements, his quiet strength. He stopped, yanked his collar tighter around his neck, rubbed his gloved hands together, then tucked them under his arms.

Barrett went to the bedroom, checked on Adam, then pulled a quilt from the top of the armoire. She dragged the heavy rocker back into the parlor by the fire, remembering as she struggled how Chase had lifted it like a toy. Unfolding the quilt, she draped it across the back of the chair so the fire could warm it.

One more thing from modern life to miss. If she had a clothes dryer, she could just pop the quilt in and have it nice and toasty for Chase when he came in.

The back door slammed and she heard him pulling his boots off and dropping them on the mat. A few seconds later she heard buttons clack against the wall when he hung his coat on the peg.

Barrett grabbed the quilt and held it closer to the fire. When she heard him coming from the kitchen, she stood by the sofa, the quilt in front of her.

"Come and sit down. I've got the quilt all warm to wrap around you."

Chase's stride faltered, but only for a second.

"Thank you," he said with a degree of uncertainty. His face retained its ruddy color from the icy winds of the snowstorm, and he sniffed while Barrett wrapped the quilt around him.

"I'll get you a cup of coffee. Or would you rather have tea?" she asked as he sank to the sofa. "Tea might be better to ward off a cold."

"Barrett!" Chase catapulted from the sofa, staring at her as if her head had just fallen off her shoulders and rolled across the floor.

"What?" she yelled back, her hand to her chest, trying to still her pounding heart.

"What in the name of heaven are you wearing?"

Barrett looked down and saw the jeans. They were so comfortable, she'd forgotten she had them on.

"Oh! Your jeans. Eli . . . *I* . . . didn't have any, so I had to borrow yours. You don't mind, do you?"

His bewildered gaze swept the length of her as he shook his head.

"No, but—"

"I was so sick of those heavy dresses. And I'm much warmer in these. Oh, I borrowed a shirt, too."

Chase had regained some of his composure. "Yes, I see that. As well as a belt." He quirked his eyebrow, then his bewildered look turned to a frown that carved deep vertical lines between his brows. "Barrett, this is so unlike you. Are you feeling ill? Perhaps you've caught Adam's fever. You know, it's been less than a month since your lying-in." As he spoke, he tried to put his palm on her forehead.

Barrett swatted his hand away and stepped back.

"I'm fine. Good grief, just because I put on a pair of pants in the privacy of this house doesn't make me delusional. Do you have a problem with me wearing pants?" She didn't care if she sounded belligerent.

"I never thought about it. I don't understand. You've never indicated before—"

"I told you last night, I'm not the Elizabeth you

married. So don't expect me to act the same way. And don't judge me by past actions."

Chase watched as the warmth and openness in Barrett's eyes cooled to a distant, icy challenge. He studied her for a few moments, and when she lifted her chin defiantly, he simply waved away the argument and sank to the sofa. She spun on her heel and marched to the kitchen.

Let her wear men's clothes, for all he cared. He'd never been a stickler for the ridiculous comings and goings of women's fashions. If she wanted to wear trousers in the privacy of their home, why not?

What worried him was why she wanted to wear trousers at all. This behavior was totally out of character for the woman he'd married. She'd been doing and saying odd things since the day of Adam's birth. She even spoke differently. Aside from the occasional profanity, which was in itself out of character, Barrett's speech patterns had become . . . different. Less formal, perhaps that might be the best way to describe it. But there was something more, something he couldn't put his finger on.

Could she have had a stroke during the birthing process? He'd heard of such things before, of women suffering from loss of speech or movement. She'd come so close to death that he'd thought she *was* dead, then she'd screamed, cursed, and stared at him wild-eyed, as if she hadn't known him.

But she had no impairments of speech or movement. Could she have suffered a mild seizure that affected her brain? Should he have Dr. Logan see her? Could he keep her from dumping a chamber pot on Logan's head if he did something she didn't agree with?

The woman in question entered the parlor, balancing a tray with a pot of tea and a plate of biscuits he knew would be rock-hard.

And that was another difference. Elizabeth had been a wonderful cook, the envy of every lady in the area. But suddenly she couldn't seem to boil water without burning the pan.

Barrett set the tray on the low table in front of the sofa. She poured a cup of tea, then glanced up at him through her lashes.

"I'm sorry I was so hateful a minute ago. I guess my hormones are out of whack, and Adam's being sick has me really stressed."

"Stressed?" There she went again. And what the devil were hormones?

"How do you take your tea?" she asked before he could come up with a suitable reply.

Her question caught him off guard. He reached out and touched her cheek until her gaze came up to meet his.

"I don't drink tea, Barrett. I never have."

Her eyes grew large for a moment, then she blinked her features back to normal.

"Oh. Yeah. I forgot."

She hadn't forgotten. He could read that in her eyes. She looked as if she'd never known.

"Well, then. I'll go make you some coffee." She was up and escaping to the kitchen in the space of a heart-beat.

He watched her go, the denim trousers so baggy they

fell in gathers around her hips. Tucked in, his huge green shirt all but swallowed her until the belt cinched it in around a ridiculously tiny waist, even for someone who'd just given birth.

He refused to think of how appealing she looked in his clothes. How his shirt and trousers were brushing against her skin. How his belt hugged her waist.

One thing was certain. This snow couldn't melt fast enough.

Barrett now had more than a nodding acquaintance with the phrase "sleep-deprived."

Adam had fussed all night long, coughing a congested, wheezing cough. When she wasn't rocking him, nursing him, or walking the floor with him, she was hovering over his bed, making sure he was still breathing.

Chase had slept through it like he was breathing ether.

She'd dragged the cradle into the kitchen after Chase had roused himself and gone out to milk the cows, and now she occasionally stepped on the curved rocker to keep Adam quiet while she tried to finish breakfast.

She felt almost giddy now, as if her head floated a foot or so above her body while she stood at the huge black stove, alternately burning bacon and taking it out of the pan when it was still half raw.

She'd dressed in Chase's jeans again, pulling out one of his soft flannel shirts that still held the essence of him even though it was freshly laundered. When she slipped into the shirt, she gave in to the urge to lift the fabric to her face and bury her nose in the collar, breathing deeply of the scent, stirring her senses, giving birth to urges best ignored, which she tried her best to do now.

Just getting out of those dresses and wearing a reasonable facsimile of modern comfort clothes put her in a brighter mood. She hummed a Billy Joel song while she labored over her first attempt at oatmeal. Adam slept fitfully, coughing every few minutes, then settling back to an exhausted sleep.

Chase stomped his way through the back door just as she pronounced the oatmeal ready. He brought with him a pail of milk, which Barrett still couldn't get used to drinking. Accustomed as she was to skim milk, the pure stuff straight from the cow, even when it was cold, went down like thick cream.

"Has it stopped snowing?" she asked as he slid out of his heavy coat and knitted muffler.

"All except a few stray flakes. I think the worst is over." He hung his things on the peg by the door before pulling off his boots.

Barrett smiled at his predictable routine. She'd noticed quite a while ago how meticulous he was about his belongings. He always wiped his feet before entering the house. Coats and clothing were never draped over chairs or left in an inside-out heap on the floor. Whenever he used a tool, he cleaned it and put it away immediately. As soon as a hinge creaked, he oiled it. The ax was sharpened after every use. If a drawer stuck, he rubbed soap on the sides before shutting it again.

"How's Adam?" he asked, as he knelt by the cradle to check for himself.

Barrett watched, her head still floating above her shoulders, as Chase repositioned the blanket where Adam had squirmed out from under it.

"His fever's not quite as high, but he's started coughing, and that worries me. If I had some way to give him water, I think it might help break up some of the congestion."

Chase craned his head up at her from his kneeling position by the cradle.

"Why can't you use the nursing bottles?"

"What nursing bottles?"

His expression never changed except for one raised eyebrow. He knelt there, staring up at her with that questioning look.

"What?" Barrett said after several unblinking seconds. She felt like a drugged insect under a microscope.

He finally rolled his eyes, pushed his palms against his knees to rise, and walked over to a cupboard by the sink. Reaching to the back of the top shelf, he pulled out six very odd-looking but very recognizable baby bottles, one at a time. When he finished, he turned and gave her that deadpan stare again.

"Well, how was I to know they were up there?" she asked, feeling as though her voice echoed inside her suspended head.

"Let's see." He contemplated the ceiling, as if searching for the answer to that puzzling question. "Perhaps because you put them there?"

"Well," she said, trying for complete nonchalance. "I forgot."

"Forgetting a lot of things lately, aren't you?" he said

as he dropped into his chair and bounced it up to the table. "Perhaps Dr. Logan should check you when he sees Adam."

Barrett slapped the steaming bowl of oatmeal on the table, then returned to the stove for the platter of bacon.

"Over my dead body," she stated on her return trip. She snatched the coffeepot off the stove and set it on an iron trivet on the table. Settling herself across from him, she sent him a challenging look that brooked no argument.

Chase didn't take the challenge. Instead, he harvested half a dozen pieces of bacon from the platter in the middle of the table, slowing in his enthusiasm to frown at the alternately charred, alternately limp slices as they dropped onto his plate. His gaze flickered toward her, but he said nothing. After ladling out a man-size portion of oatmeal, he handed the dish to Barrett, then doctored the hot cereal with butter, milk, and syrup.

Barrett allowed herself only a tiny bowl of oatmeal, trying in some misguided way to emphasize that she meant what she said about Dr. Logan.

Chase popped a black, crumbling piece of bacon into his mouth, then shoveled in a spoonful of oatmeal. After a few chews, his mouth stopped moving and his brows dipped into a comical V. He chewed tentatively a couple more times, then stopped and swallowed, his Adam's apple visibly forcing the food down his throat.

Barrett ignored these theatrics. So what if she wasn't the best cook in the world? How bad could she screw up oatmeal?

Her first bite lay on her tongue like freshly applied

drywall putty. Except that drywall putty tasted better. Flakes of half-cooked oatmeal stuck to her tongue and the roof of her mouth, even after she managed to swallow the gloppy mess.

Without raising her head, she slid her gaze to Chase, who'd been waiting patiently for her reaction.

A giggle rose in her throat, made all the more funny by her head swimming so many inches off her shoulders. A tiny laugh escaped into the quiet air of the kitchen, but when Chase's expression failed to show any appreciation of her humor, she rearranged her features into a serious, unblinking replica of his.

He rolled his eyes heavenward and pinched the bridge of his nose. Barrett did the same.

For some reason, she found this game highly entertaining. The giggles she'd managed to stifle bubbled up at his irritated look, breaking the silence, causing him to reach across the table and feel her forehead.

"Oh, for Pete's sake, I'm not sick," she said, backing away from the warmth of his palm, from the sudden, shattering desire that simple contact created. "I'm just slaphappy. I get that way when I give up sleeping."

Chase stood, then carried the oatmeal back to the stove, his wordless actions speaking volumes about his long-suffering life.

"Go and try to get some rest, Barrett. I'll finish cooking the oatmeal and you can eat when you wake up."

Barrett propped her chin in her palm and watched the muscles of his back move under his shirt as he dumped the hot cereal back into the pan. He turned when she made no move to get up, looking at her over his shoulder as he positioned the pan on the stove.

What would he do if she got up from the table right now and crossed the room to him? If she took the pan and dumped it in the sink? If she slowly unbuttoned his shirt, slid her hands around his waist, ran her palms along the warm contours of his chest and down the swell of his hips and thighs? What would he do if she guided his fingers to the buttons of her shirt, to the waistband of her borrowed jeans?

To the warm, aching body underneath?

Chase's gaze never left hers. He turned to fully face her, a forgotten spoon dangling from his fingertips. She looked at those strong masculine fingers, remembered how warm and gentle they'd been that day in the woods, willed him to drop that damn spoon and put his hands on her again.

Her breasts tingled, swelled, hardened, and then hot rivulets of milk spread in wet circles on her shirt and traced a warm path down her abdomen.

The spoon dropped from Chase's hand, landing with a dull thud on the rag rug. He moved, as if to come to her. Barrett pushed herself from the chair, her knees weak with anticipation.

A congested cough, then an angry cry rose from the cradle by the stove.

Chase blinked, as if he'd just awakened from a dream he didn't want to leave. Barrett dropped back into the chair, released a long, frustrated sigh, and silently recited every curse she'd ever heard.

*   *   *

She finished what she hoped was sterilizing the bottles, according to what she remembered from some old television show, dried them, then filled one with boiled water to cool for Adam. She walked around the kitchen, looking for something to do, checked on Adam in his cradle by the stove, then paced the floor again.

He'd slept better during the afternoon. His fever broke around noon and the congestion seemed to break up somewhat after she got some water into him. She'd gotten him back to sleep just minutes earlier.

Then she tried to take a nap, to catch up on all the sleep she'd lost during the night, but her body wouldn't cooperate. As light-headed and slaphappy as she was, she was simply too tired to fall asleep.

Chase had kept himself busy outside for the biggest part of the day. Even now Barrett could hear the rhythmic *thwack* of his ax splitting wood.

Bored and restless, Barrett pulled on a heavy coat, checked on Adam one more time, then slipped out the back door to see if she could help Chase outside.

The entire landscape looked as if it had been covered with a roll of thick white cotton. The eerie quiet of the muffling snow brought a sense of peace to Barrett's mind. There was something oddly soothing about the stillness surrounding her.

Chase worked steadily, breaking quarters of wood into kindling, then stacking it in that meticulous way of his. She crunched through the snow toward him, sinking clear to her knees. He didn't seem to hear her approach, he was concentrating so diligently on the task at hand. When she got within about ten feet of him, the sight of his broad back conjured up a devilish urge.

She scooped up two handfuls of snow and packed it into a nice firm ball. She took careful aim, hurled the snowball, then gasped in shock when it exploded against the back of his head.

Chase went still as a statue, his shoulders up around his ears. Barrett pried her hands away from her mouth and threw another one, this time hitting him squarely in the back.

He swung around then and ducked as another whizzed over his left shoulder.

"Barrett! What are you—"

He ducked again, this one almost parting his hair.

"What are you . . . ? Stop!"

She lobbed snowballs as fast as she could make them, laughing out loud whenever one hit her target.

Chase continued to dodge her grenades, shielding his head with his arms. When one exploded against his forehead, he grabbed a handful of snow himself.

"You're in for it now, dear wife."

Barrett blinked through tears of laughter, ducking with a yelp a split second before his missile hummed past her ear.

"Hey! No fair!" One of his snowballs burst against her chest like white fireworks. "Wait a minute! Time out! Flag on the play!" Another one hit her on a thigh.

She tried to turn and run as Chase waded toward her through the knee-deep snow, but when her body turned, her legs stayed put from the knees down. Off balance, she flailed about, felt herself falling, and turned her head just as another snowball landed with a wet *splat* above her ear.

She fell flat on her back, helpless with mirth, as Chase staggered toward her.

"Foul ball! No fair!" she gasped between giggles. Her body sank several inches until the snow cradled her like a giant featherbed.

Chase staggered nearer and Barrett struggled to get up, only to have her hands sink beneath her. Weak from laughing, she lay back and started pitching missiles of her own, scattering them like grapeshot so that he didn't even bother to dodge them.

"Oh, no! Help!" she cried in mock terror as he loomed over her. "Help!"

"Oh, I'll help," he told her with an evil, victorious laugh, then had to dodge another lob. He went down on his knees beside her, grabbing her hands and pinning them above her head before she could arm herself again.

Barrett closed her eyes and gave a token, playful struggle, then realized she had nothing to struggle against. He still held her hands, but no longer with force. She opened her eyes to his face hovering inches from her own. His hot amber stare seared into her, sending ribbons of heat ricocheting through her body. She returned his look, their erratic breath making two frosty clouds that mingled between them. Chase's hair fell across his forehead in wet spikes, an occasional drop of melted snow collecting on a tip, then dropping to his ruddy cheeks or into his sable lashes.

Barrett's gaze dropped to his lips, so close to hers. *Perfect lips,* she thought. Lips that were meant to spend a lifetime wreaking havoc on a woman's senses. One woman's senses.

Hers.

She would never know who moved first. Suddenly
his mouth covered hers, warm, moist, driving her back
into the cushion of snow even as she came up to meet
him. Then his arms found their way around her, pulling
her atop him as he rolled to his back.

Barrett's frozen fingers plunged into his hair, warming against his scalp, as she straddled him, denim
against denim, the low moan in his throat like a hot caress against her skin. When his icy hands found their
way inside her coat, he warmed his palms through the
layers of her clothes, but all she felt was the heat of his
lips on her, his demanding tongue first taking what he
wanted, then slowing to a languid, steamy pace that
gave back more than he'd taken. Lying there, coated in
snow, Barrett felt like an ice cream sundae with the
thick, hot fudge of sensations drizzling in swirls all
over her, rippling through her blood and melting the
frozen corners that had been so long in the shadows.

Chase rolled again, pinning her now beneath him as
a steady ache started low and grew, like a flower opening its petals. She'd never known such mindless, puls-
ing want. She ached for what she'd denied herself all
her life, both physically and emotionally. His tongue
found hers again, intensifying the ache, pulling a sigh
from her lungs, bringing again the milk she had so recently given Adam.

Chase raised his head, cradled her face in his damp,
icy palms.

"Can we make love, Barrett? Has it been long
enough?"

The heat of his request, the want in those hot golden

eyes nearly melted her and all the surrounding snow, until she realized what her answer must be.

It had only been a month. She still had traces of blood. Would he believe her?

All the heat drained from her, but the ache remained, deep in the pit of her soul. She took his hands away from her face and threaded her fingers through his.

"Maybe in a week," she whispered, meeting his gaze, watching his eyes close and his head drop. "Maybe less," she added hopefully.

He rolled off her and shook the melted snow from his hair like a dog. Barrett rose to her knees and leaned toward him until her lips covered his, until she straddled his lap and found that not everything about him had cooled.

"I promise you, Chaser," she whispered against his lips, deliberately adding the "*r*," "I want this as much as you do." As the heat in her flared again, she couldn't imagine wanting him more. "And I promise, you'll be the first to know when we can."

Adam's cries broke through the thick black fog of sleep that had taken so long to settle over Chase. He rolled over, dragged the pillow over his head and mumbled, "Barrett." When she didn't rouse herself, he lifted the pillow and groaned, "Barrett, Adam's hungry and I don't have the equipment to feed him."

Still no movement from her side of the bed. Was she already up and in the kitchen? He rolled over and stretched out his hand, encountering the firm contours of her body.

"Barrett?"

He raised up on his elbow, aiming his hand for the shoulder of her curvy silhouette. His hand encountered damp tendrils of hair plastered against skin so hot it had him leaping from the bed and fumbling for a match in the space of a heartbeat.

He turned up the wick to the lamp, holding the light over her while Adam's cries grew more insistent. She never moved a muscle. He brushed the damp, clinging hair away from her forehead and found her skin against his palm just as fevered as he'd feared.

Now what? A crying baby, an ill wife. Which one did he take care of first?

The baby. He knew what to do for Adam.

Setting the lamp down, he yanked on a pair of trousers and shoved his arms into the sleeves of the nearest shirt. The moment the flannel settled against his skin, he caught Barrett's scent drifting up to him. He ignored the feelings that stirred in his chest. He had a baby to feed, and Barrett's health was more important to him than the blood she heated with her mere scent.

"Shh. Shhh. You'll wake your mother," Chase whispered as he scooped Adam into his arms. Immediately another scent rose that overpowered the earlier, delicate essence.

Chase groaned, returned Adam to his cradle, then peeled away the layers of soiled fabric. The baby's cries became more indignant with each passing moment and each piece of clothing removed.

"Oh, for the love of . . ." Chase muttered at the sight of Adam's tiny body, liberally smeared with the contents of his diaper. After quickly assessing the best way to attack the problem, Chase hefted the cradle, with

Adam still in it, and carried it into the kitchen. Drawing hot water from the reservoir in the stove, he added some cold water, tested the temperature, then wrung out a cloth and picked a place to start wiping.

"How in the world did you get it on the bottom of your feet, boy?" he asked rhetorically as he unearthed patches of pink skin. Adam quieted with this undivided attention, gurgling happily, having the nerve to bestow a toothless smile as Chase diligently cleaned between impossibly small toes.

"Don't try making up for this mess you made. It's going to take much more than a smile," Chase informed the squirming baby, who gurgled again, then sneezed and blew a bubble out his nose.

"Ooooh. Insult to injury, son. Not the thing to do to impress people." Chase plucked a clean cloth from the stack beside the stove and wiped the nearly nonexistent nose before finishing the cleanup on the rest of the baby.

After drying, powdering, diapering, and dressing Adam, Chase tucked the baby into the crook of his arm and set about changing the cradle sheets as a bottle of milk heated on the stove. Once he had the sheets soaking, he checked on Barrett. She'd rolled over and kicked the covers off into a heap on the floor. He pulled them back onto the bed, tucked them around her, then checked her forehead, which felt as hot as ever. At least she'd moved. He felt more reassured than if she'd lain there as still as she had earlier. Sleep was probably what she needed most.

Adam didn't seem to mind the cow's milk, once he decided to try it. He took the whole bottle, then Chase tried to get a little water down him, but he was too busy cooing and kicking to be bothered with something he didn't want. Chase put him back into his cradle, carried the cradle back to the bedroom, peeled off his trousers and fell into bed, falling asleep to the sounds of a contented infant.

He couldn't have slept more than a few minutes when he blinked, rolled over, and tried to figure out what had awakened him. Then he felt the bed shaking.

"Barrett." He jostled her shoulder, realizing she'd curled herself into a tight little ball. "Barrett, wake up."

"So cold," she said, her eyes still closed. He couldn't be sure if she was even awake. "Can't get warm." Her teeth chattered and her body shook with chills.

Chase got up and pulled another quilt down from the top of the armoire. The added warmth did little to dispel her shaking. Barrett inched closer and closer to Chase, until he finally gave in and wrapped her in his arms, pulling her against his chest, sharing his body's warmth, the only barriers between them the thin, worn flannel of her nightgown and the bottom half of his long underwear.

Her hips nestled into the curve of his lap as he lay on his side, her trembling body generating more heat than she would ever realize. More heat than his sorely tested body wanted to feel.

Chase rose stiffly from the bed. The last few hours had felt more like a week. Barrett's shivering and restless squirming had kept him torn between worrying for his wife and reliving those aching moments in the snow.

Finally the shivering had stopped, but now Adam's

quiet rustling signaled Chase that he either had to get a bottle warming or try to wake Barrett so that she could nurse him. One look at her pale, exhausted face gave him his answer.

He pulled on his trousers, then found a shirt he was sure didn't have Barrett's scent lingering in the folds. Adam gurgled quietly while Chase rammed his feet into his socks and boots.

"Come on, little man," Chase said as he scooped the baby up into his arms. "Let's let your mother sleep."

He'd no sooner gotten Adam changed and a bottle ready when he heard noises coming from the bedroom. Sliding the odd-shaped nipple into the baby's greedy little mouth, Chase walked through the parlor to see what in the world Barrett was doing.

She'd kicked off her covers again, and her nightgown clung to every curve of her sweat-soaked body. Damp tendrils of curls stuck to her cheeks and neck, and she tossed and turned on the bed, trying to find a comfortable position, making the bed ropes squeak like they'd never been tightened.

Chase grabbed the covers with his free hand and pulled them back over her. She grasped them in her sleep and pulled them up to her chin. Seconds later she kicked them off again. Chase tossed them back over her, tucked them under the mattress, then wandered back into the parlor, trying to figure out how he could go for Dr. Logan, yet make sure Adam and Barrett stayed safe while he was gone. One glance out the parlor window, however, changed his mind. The snow hadn't melted at all. It would take hours to get to the doctor's office and then hours more to make it home again.

What should he do? Wake her and get some nourishment in her? Let her sleep and hope the fever would break? With no medicine in the house, his options were limited.

Adam finished off his bottle, then released a long, rumbling belch. Chase dragged his thoughts away from Barrett for a moment. For some strange reason he felt a ridiculous sense of pride at that burp. It was a man's burp.

I'm getting as slaphappy as Barrett, he thought, then blinked at using her odd word.

He laid Adam on the couch, pulled the rocker to the edge so he couldn't roll off, then went into the kitchen to fix himself some much-needed coffee. Next to the stove, Bo stood up, stretched his legs with a little bow, then trotted in to take up his post next to Adam.

When the coffee finished brewing, Chase poured a cup, savored the first few sips, then scooped Adam up on his way to the bedroom. Bo followed along at his heels.

He nearly choked on his next sip of coffee.

Barrett had kicked off her covers again, and they now lay in a heap at the foot of the bed . . . with her nightgown on top of them. All that covered her was her flimsy cotton drawers and a layer of perspiration.

Chase closed his eyes and shook his head, wondering what in the world he'd done to deserve such torture.

He set aside his coffee cup and put Adam back in his cradle. When he picked up Barrett's nightgown, his fingers encountered nothing but damp flannel. Pulling a fresh one from the dresser, he strode to her side of the bed, trying his best to remember that she was sick. Before he could even begin to dress her, she started shaking again.

"Chase," she moaned between suddenly chattering teeth. "Hold me, Chase. I'm so cold."

He hesitated, but then Barrett opened feverish, pleading eyes and stared at him, her teeth rattling in her head. When she curled into a tight, shivering ball, sympathy overrode good sense and he crawled onto the bed, gathered her into his arms and pulled her against the length of him while he tucked the covers around them.

He might have lain there for minutes or hours, but it felt like an eternity with her hot, bare skin against the length of his chest. Why hadn't he taken the time to button his shirt?

Adam squirmed in his cradle, making little smacking noises. Eventually he tired of behaving and started to fuss. Chase dropped one booted foot off the bed, felt for the rocker on the cradle, then stepped on it gently. Adam's full stomach, the pitch-black of the room, and the lazy rocking lulled him back to sleep before he had time to become too indignant.

When Barrett continued to shiver, he pulled her even closer and lifted his foot from the floor, draping his leg over hers and doubling the quilt on her side.

The clock ticked on the mantel in the parlor. Bo's toenails clicked against the wood floor as he paced worriedly from one side of the bed to the other. Finally he circled next to Chase and settled himself on the rug, his panting replaced by the snorting sounds of a dog grooming himself.

Barrett's shivering lessened somewhat, and much to Chase's relief he was able to distance himself from her a bit. But just as the gray haze of pre-dawn began to cast black morning shadows across the bedroom, she flung the covers off the bed, rolled to the floor, and made a dash for the pitcher and basin on the dresser, emptying the contents of her stomach into the china bowl.

Bo leaped to his feet with a yip, and resumed his pacing as Chase banged his shin against the footboard in his attempt to reach Barrett. Her shivering started up again, and when he finished cursing the bedpost he dragged the quilt off the bed and wrapped it around her just as her stomach gave forth with what remained of her dinner.

A sheen of sweat glistened on her forehead in the dim light as yet another round of heaves wracked her body. Chase snatched a handkerchief from a dresser drawer, plunged it into the pitcher of icy water, then draped it around her neck as he held her mussed ringlets from her face.

Barrett moaned, retched one more time, then staggered to the side of the bed, dropping facedown into the mattress with the quilt trailing behind her.

Chase tucked her back into bed, giving up on the idea of trying to maneuver her limp body into a clean nightgown. Once he had her covered up to her chin, he poured a glass of water, then dampened the handkerchief again.

"Here, sweetheart, do you want to rinse your mouth?"

He gently lifted her head, tipping the glass up to her feverish lips. Once she had taken a few hesitant sips, her head fell back onto the pillow and he used the handkerchief to smooth her hair away from her cheeks and wipe the beads of sweat from her forehead.

It was only while he was washing the basin Barrett had used that he realized he'd done something that he hadn't done since their wedding night.

He'd called her sweetheart.

Chapter 11

BARRETT FOUGHT TO sink back into the black oblivion of sleep, but her aching body dragged her to the surface and the bright sun of late morning held her there. She'd curled herself tightly around a pillow, and now she straightened, rolling to her back, groaning as every joint protested. When the last numbing vestiges of sleep left her, another pain besides the ache in her joints invaded her senses—excruciating, throbbing, burning with a fire she'd never before experienced.

Her breasts were hard as marble. Harder than the day her milk had come in. The slightest movement, even breathing, caused the piercing, burning throb to intensify.

She was in need of nursing Adam. Immediately. When was the last time she'd nursed him? Where *was* he? Where was Chase? She tried to prop herself up on her elbows, but when that proved too painful she inched to the side of the mattress, then ever so gently rolled off. As she stood, no matter how hesitantly, the pressure increased, and she wondered what kept her engorged, throbbing breasts from exploding.

That thought brought on the familiar tingle, and within seconds she and everything within three feet were being liberally sprayed with warm, needle-thin streams of milk.

Good grief, what had happened to her nightgown? She grabbed two diapers from a stack by the cradle and pressed them to her breasts, stanching the flow, remembering in a light-headed fog that she'd yanked off her damp nightgown earlier in an effort to cool off.

A fiery flush spread from her neck to her cheeks. Had she tossed her nightgown before or after she'd begged Chase to warm her?

The thought of Chase brought another memory. One of him holding back her hair while she deposited last night's dinner into the washbasin.

She closed her eyes and shook her head in denial. *Tell me he didn't hold my hair while I barfed.* Could there possibly be anything more gross to witness?

She would have to cringe over that thought later though, because she seriously doubted if her breasts could hold another drop of milk without bursting like two overfilled water balloons.

She found a clean nightgown at the foot of the bed and pulled it over her head. The whisper of the fabric across her breasts sent more pains shooting into her chest. Trying to walk without jiggling any part of her upper body, she went in search of Adam and Chase.

Stepping into the parlor, she stopped and smiled at the warm, touching scene that met her.

Chase sat in the rocker, his legs sprawled toward the fireplace, his head tilted back and to one side in sleep. Adam slept securely tucked in one arm, and draped

across the other half of Chase's lap, Bo slept, his pointy
snout lolling over Chase's other arm.

My men, Barrett thought, then blinked in surprise at
the possessive term. But the warm glow around her
heart remained, and she let the thought sink into her
mind and take root.

A week passed before the snow melted enough to travel,
and another week before Barrett and Adam were completely well. She'd had to put her foot down when Chase
started making noises about going for the doctor. After
much convincing, she'd finally talked him out of the
horrifying idea.

And that had been their only rough spot in the last two
weeks.

Barrett drew the last bucket of hot water from the
stove's reservoir and poured it into the nearly full tub. She
added a couple of drops of some oil she'd found, something light and flowery that had been pushed to the back
of one of Elizabeth's drawers. The scent swirled up with
the steam, delicate and feminine as it drifted through the
kitchen.

Chase had gone to make some repairs on Genevieve
Long's house, and Barrett, fighting a twinge of uncharacteristic jealousy, had decide to treat herself to a lazy
bath. With Adam exhausted from his playtime and
freshly fed, she should have all the time she needed to
pamper herself.

She pinned her hair up in loose curls, noticing, not for
the first time, that the corkscrew ringlets had relaxed
quite a bit since her first few weeks in this time. Her hair
looked darker too, almost back to the black of her 1997

self. She wondered if childbirth and hormones had anything to do with it.

Shrugging, she shimmied out of her robe, tossing it over a ladder-back chair, then sighed out loud with contentment as she slid into the steaming, fragrant bath.

As she soaked, her muscles melting in the blessed heat of the water, she thought about Chase. She marveled at how he'd changed from the cold, emotionless man who had delivered Adam. He smiled now, and teased her, and enjoyed it when she teased him. He'd roared with laughter when she told him an off-color joke, but not before gaping at her as though she'd grown a third eye.

Barrett ran the bar of soap up and down her legs and wondered what it would feel like for Chase to do that for her. She'd stopped bleeding just a couple of days after their encounter in the snow. Almost two weeks ago. Should she tell him? Would he ask her again? Just the thought sent delicious shivers dancing through her.

As she slid the soap over her arms and across her chest, her fingers encountered the delicate locket hanging from its fragile chain. She'd almost forgotten about it. She'd grown so used to wearing the necklace that she didn't feel it anymore. And after those first few weeks of checking to see if it would send her home, she'd finally stopped doing so.

She wedged her thumbnail into the groove to pop the locket open, then stopped herself. If she went back, would she disappear immediately, without seeing Chase again? Would she have a choice to go or stay? Did she even want to go back?

Barrett realized with sudden clarity that she'd been

happier here, with Chase and Adam and Wes and all the inconveniences, than she'd ever been in her own time. She felt needed and loved, and for the first time she admitted that she loved and needed these men in her life. Success in business and all that she'd worked so hard to achieve in the future paled beside what these people meant to her. Success meant nothing without someone to share it with.

The still-closed locket winked up at her, the golden glow of the lamp reflecting off it with a dull gleam. After several thoughtful seconds, she dropped the intricate heart back on her chest, sending a little prayer out to Mr. Gideon, apologizing for calling him an angel from hell.

The water cooled during her bout of reflection, and she hurriedly finished bathing. Just as she rose to get out of the tub, the back door opened and Chase barged in.

Barrett froze, torn between sinking back into the water or making a dash for the towel halfway across the room.

Chase froze as well, his gaze sweeping the length of her glistening body, watching rivulets of water as they zigzagged their way down her skin. Slowly he pushed the door shut behind him, then shrugged out of his coat, dangling it from his fingertips, his eyes never once leaving her.

Barrett fought the urge to cover herself. She'd never stood naked before a man, and this body, still showing the ravages of pregnancy and childbirth, did nothing to make the experience easier. But she stood there, the water cooling on her skin, her head high, her level gaze meeting his.

Chase searched her face, his odd golden eyes first

wide with shock, then narrowing with the heat of a man long denied. His coat fell to the floor at his feet. He took one step toward her and stopped, his hand reaching out, his eyes asking the question.

Barrett's outstretched arms answered him.

In a heartbeat Chase's lips were on hers, his hands sliding up her waist, around her back, down her hips. With every move of his head he deepened the kiss, his tongue finding hers, teasing her with knee-weakening finesse.

Barrett sighed, deep in her throat, and slipped her dripping arms around his neck, leaning her body into his, reveling in his warmth and the burning touch of his hands skimming over her flesh, the hard contours of his body pressed against hers. She breathed in his kisses, his breath, the scent that would forever be his.

Chase's lips never left hers as he bent and scooped her up into his arms. Water cascaded from her legs as he strode across the kitchen and parlor. At the bedroom door she shushed him, murmuring, "Adam," against his lips. With the stealth of a panther, he crossed the room, the only sound the tiny whimper in Barrett's throat as he continued his drugging kisses.

With one hand he jerked the heavy covers back, not waiting for them to flutter to rest before he lowered her to the snowy sheets.

Barrett grasped the collar of his shirt, staying him when he would have risen, pulling him back to her lips. He hovered over her, his mouth on hers, one hand on each side of her, inching closer until his thumbs caressed her skin.

A whirlwind of fire spun through her, growing outward, reaching every nerve in her body. Her mind swam with euphoria and all she could think was, *Don't stop. Please don't stop.*

Her fingers fumbled at the buttons of Chase's shirt. Frustrated, she yanked, sending the first few buttons clattering against the walls and floor. Chase rose impatiently, his hungry lips still on hers, and ripped the rest of the buttons free, pulling the shirt off his arms and tossing it in a wad over his shoulder.

He lowered himself slowly, oh, so slowly, until the heated flesh of his chest met hers, warming her, sending ripples of fire through her blood as he shivered at the full contact.

Barrett moaned, aching for something she had yet to know, wanting to prolong the exquisite torture yet fulfill the unknown need her body reached for.

Chase buried his head in her neck, trailing nibbling kisses from beneath her ear to her collarbone . . . and lower. She shivered, felt her eyes roll upward as her eyelids fluttered closed. Her breasts tingled, then filled at the contact, then warm rivulets of milk traced slow, lazy paths along her skin to the sheets.

Chase moaned and dragged his mouth back to hers, melting her bones like molten wax, exploring her body with his hands.

Finally he pulled away from her and stood, searing her with his gaze as he yanked at his belt and kicked off his boots.

Barrett watched, aching for him, wondering what to expect, wondering if she would know how to do this.

When his pants hit the floor, she sucked in her breath

at the sight of him. There were no dark shadows to hide in now as he lifted the sheets and slid into bed.

Without a word he gathered her into his arms. He rained gentle, sipping kisses on her lips, teasing her senses until she pulled him to her. Her tongue found his, and he breathed her name into her mouth, his very breath giving her new life, stirring her to the deepest parts of her soul.

"Chase," she whispered, and it proved to be his undoing. With a moan, he rolled atop her, pinning her with the length of his body, sending her mind reeling with his kisses as, at last, he slowly, exquisitely, took her to the heights of heaven, to the edge of the universe, to the center of paradise, then brought her back to earth in a spinning, undulating vortex of pure, mindless ecstasy.

Barrett lay folded in Chase's arms, her body limp, her thoughts nearly incoherent as she tried to find words for the sensations Chase had unleashed in her—words that were poor substitutes for even the least of what he'd done.

She rolled her head sideways and looked at her husband. Strange to think of him as *her* husband. She'd always before thought of him only as Elizabeth's. But Elizabeth was gone, and a fierce possessive surge roared to life in Barrett as she watched him sleep, his sable lashes innocently fanned across his cheeks, his angular jaw softened in relaxation.

Barrett's mind still swam, her body still tingled at all the magic Chase had worked upon her. Had she returned even a little of that magic? Had she given him even a fraction of the pleasure he'd bestowed upon her?

Chase rolled over and pulled her closer, his lips nibbling along the back of her neck.

"What are you thinking so hard about?" His voice hummed against the top of her shoulder.

Barrett closed her eyes and smiled, surprised at the glow of warmth his deep, teasing voice ignited. She turned in his arms, facing him.

"I'm wondering . . ." she faltered, then forced herself to go on, "I'm wondering if you got *half* as much pleasure from that as I did."

Chase's gaze flickered with surprise, then his eyes softened, the strange, dark gold barely visible in the darkening room. Several seconds passed as he studied her. Finally he smiled, then traced her lips with his finger.

"I thought more than once," he whispered, his breath precious against her face, "that a man is supposed to grow old and die *with* his wife, not *because* of her."

Chase watched a self-conscious, almost innocent smile spread across his wife's face. But what he'd said was true. She'd nearly devastated him, more than once. And he'd rejoiced in it, wedding his emotions with hers, sinking into the dizzying sensations and hovering there, never wanting to come up for air.

A voice he'd pushed to the corners of his mind, though, tried to make itself heard, vicious and hateful. Had she been this way with Aidan? Had she brought his brother to his knees with a mere sigh? Seared him with her touch? Been the wanton child of nature instead of the shriveled prune she'd been on their wedding night, when she'd lain there like a corpse and all but told him to pull her nightgown down and throw the sheets over her when he was done?

He shook his head and tightened his arms around her, rubbing his lips across the silk of her hair. He would have to put the past behind him if he ever expected to find any happiness. He would have to forgive her, stop wondering if she compared him to Aidan, stop picturing her in bed with his brother, naked, gasping at his touch as she'd gasped at Chase's . . .

Stifling a curse, he threw the sheets back and rolled out of bed.

"Chase?" Barrett sat up, dragging the sheet with her. "What's wrong?"

Chase looked at her worried face, framed by a mussed halo of loose curls dusting her shoulders.

He leaned over and kissed her, long and hard. Sliding his hand beneath the covers, he pressed her back against the pillows, pressed his body against hers, and kicked the sheets to the floor.

"Nothing," he murmured against her lips. "Absolutely nothing."

". . . if that mockingbird don't sing, Papa's gonna buy you a diamond ring. And if that diamond ring . . ."

Chase's voice trailed off and he held up a hand to listen. Barrett stopped singing as well, waiting while he turned his ears to the sound of a wagon pulling up the drive.

Chase had made the regrettable mistake of joining his voice with Barrett's during a desperate nocturnal attempt to sing a rambunctious Adam back to sleep. The tactic had worked, but the little dictator now expected the same treatment each time he had trouble nodding off.

Adam's eyes, just moments ago drooping in his losing battle to stay awake, popped open and looked around, his feathery, nearly nonexistent brows raised in surprise, as if asking what had happened to the music.

Barrett jiggled the baby while Chase went to the front door and looked out.

"It's Wes!" Chase rushed back to Barrett and pulled her off the sofa, guiding her to the door. She leaned into him when he slid his arm around her waist and pulled her close as they waited on the porch, still surprised at the physical jolt that rocked her every time he touched her.

Wes reined in the horses, threw on the brake, then leaped off the wagon. Without missing a beat, he reached for the woman beside him, a lovely, reed-thin woman with flawless caramel skin and glossy black hair pulled into a neat knot above her collar. He swung her down from her seat, planting a kiss on her lips as he set her on the ground.

This must be Rose. For some odd reason, Barrett was glad she'd decided to forgo wearing Chase's jeans and shirt today and had put on a gown for a change.

"Well, big brother, what kind of lies did you tell our Rosie to convince her to put up with you for the rest of her life?" Chase bounded off the porch, hugged Rose and gave her a loud, brotherly kiss, then wrapped Wes in the all-male, full-body press with two solid slaps against the back. Barrett smiled, and her eyes stung at the sibling affection. When was the last time her brother or sister had hugged her like that? With a sad, lonely lump in her throat, she realized they'd *never* hugged her like that. The most her family did—and she was guilty of it herself—was give hugs that barely made contact and air kisses somewhere close to a cheek.

"Brat, c'mere and let me see that boy." The next thing she knew, Wes had enveloped her in a ferocious bear hug, full of warmth and affection. She slid her free arm around his waist and squeezed gratefully, blinking back the stinging tears that such a small gesture elicited. Wes didn't seem to notice. He swept Adam from her arms and dangled him in the air.

"This youngun's grown a foot and a half since I been gone. What you feedin' him? Fertilizer?"

Barrett laughed and dragged a knuckle under her eyes. She turned to the woman who stood self-consciously at Wes's side, smiling at Adam with a tender look in her eyes.

"Rose, it's so good to meet you." Barrett gave her a hug, trying not to revert to her old pat-pat, kiss-kiss method.

Rose stiffened, then gave her a halfhearted hug in return.

"It's good to meet me, Miss Elizabeth? You've known me near all your life."

Barrett's smile froze on her face and her eyes slid, first to Chase, who quirked a brow at her, and then to Wes.

Wes handed Adam back to her, then curled his arm around his new wife's shoulders.

"She's just teasin' you, Rosie. Ain't you, brat?"

Barrett smiled with relief and nodded. "Sorry. Sometimes my jokes have bad timing. Are you tired?" Barrett hooked her free arm in Rose's without waiting for an answer. "Let's get something to eat, then we'll help you unload. Did Wes tell you I want to be called Barrett now?"

Chase grabbed one end of a huge leather trunk and heaved while Wes lifted the other end. They crab-walked it toward Wes's cottage as Bo tried his best to get tangled in their feet.

"You and the brat worked things out, did ya?" Wes asked as he stepped over Bo.

Chase glanced up at his brother, fighting a smile. "Does it show that much?"

Wes snorted and shook his head, then stepped onto the tiny porch.

"Thought you was ready to drag her off to the bedroom during dinner when she started laughin' at Adam."

Chase fought the physical reaction conjured up by the mere memory. Her laugh had sounded like distant music on a summer breeze, and when her playful, twinkling eyes had turned to his, he had indeed wanted to take her off and turn her musical laughter into sighs of passion.

"Things are good, Wes." Chase kicked open the front door and they threaded their way into the tiny parlor, setting the massive trunk down in the center of the room with a thud. "She's not the same woman I married. In fact, she's a completely different person."

Wes headed back out to the wagon, dusting his hands on the seat of his britches, his boots crunching over the still frozen ground. Chase followed a few steps behind him.

"So, you've forgiven her for being with Aidan?"

Chase's stomach lurched at the plainspoken reminder. He'd tried to wipe that memory from his mind.

"Yes. At least I'm trying to forgive her. I know with time and good memories behind us, I will. For now, I just try not to think about it."

Chase hefted a wooden box onto his shoulder, then tossed a large canvas bundle to Wes.

"I guess that's all anyone could ask," Wes ruminated on his way back to the cottage. "A body doesn't forgive something like that overnight."

Chase was relieved to get off that subject. The sound of a jingling harness and the *clip-clop* of a single horse pulling a light carriage heralded company. He and Wes tossed their burdens onto the cottage porch and turned to watch Carrie Davis jostle to a stop.

"Wes! My soul, I didn't know you were home. Welcome back. Did you bring a wife back with you?"

Wes nodded and pointed his chin toward the larger house.

"Rose is with Barrett, spoilin' the little heir rotten."

"Well, I'll just have to go meet her and see if she's good enough for you," Carrie teased. "Chase, could you help me down?"

Chase wiped his palms against his denim-clad thighs and swung Carrie down from her perch. When he released her, her hands stayed on his shoulders as she stumbled, then righted herself. He grabbed her around the waist again and steadied her.

"Are you all right?" he asked, wondering if something was indeed wrong. She'd been by to visit nearly every day since the snow had melted, and it seemed she was forever tripping or stumbling into him. He'd lost count of how many times he'd had to steady her. He wondered if she could be developing some sort of condition that affected her coordination.

"Oh, I'm fine. I've just been clumsy lately. Tom tells me I need to pay more attention."

The back door to the house slammed, and Barrett and Rose made their way across the yard to the little group, already looking like best friends. Bo ran out to meet them, circling Barrett, watching as Adam surveyed his surroundings over his mother's shoulder. Carrie immediately scurried to the two women, and Barrett automatically transferred Adam into her outstretched arms.

Barrett had mentioned to Chase, one night as she lay curled against him in bed, how desperate Carrie was to have a baby. He'd seen it. The single-minded attention. The almost frantic need to hold Adam. The yearning sadness in her eyes.

"My soul, Barrett," Carrie chirped, "it's nice to see you in a dress again. I'd feared you'd given them up permanently for denim trousers and flannel shirts."

Barrett laughed and shook out her skirts. "I was thinking of changing. Give me a comfortable pair of jeans over a twenty-pound dress any day. You should try it."

"Heavens, my Tom would never hear of it," Carrie declared, nuzzling the feathery down of Adam's head.

Wes swiveled to face Chase, his amused blue eyes narrowed in question. Chase simply smiled and shrugged. "I *told* you she wasn't the same person."

The sound of several horses thundering past the house jarred Barrett from a deep sleep. Chase leaped out of bed and listened as the rumble faded, then died. The muffled, distant crash of glass breaking had him ramming his legs into his trousers before the sound died in the air. The thundering hooves started again, coming back past the house before fading completely into the night air.

"That was at the cottage. Stay here while I check on Wes and Rose."

Sliding a heavy jacket on over his bare chest, Chase shoved his feet into his boots, then pounded out the back door, Bo a furry streak behind him.

"I don't think so," Barrett mumbled to herself as she scrambled for one of the pairs of Chase's jeans that Rose had helped her alter. She slipped them on under the homely nightgown, pulled on her boots and a cloak, then wrapped Adam in an extra quilt before dashing out the door with him just seconds behind Chase.

A dim light in the cottage illuminated the jagged shards of glass left to frame the parlor window. As Barrett burst through the front door, Chase and Wes spun, leveling a rifle and a shotgun directly at her heart.

"Barrett!" Chase roared, then shoved his gun into Wes's hand. "I might have killed you! I told you to stay put!" He crossed to her, grabbing her shoulders and shaking them, then wrapping her in his arms, crushing her to his chest. She could hear his heart pounding against his rib cage.

"I'm sorry," she barely managed to squeak, so shaken at the sight of those barrels pointed at her and Adam that her knees rattled against each other. She sank down on the sofa. "What happened? Is it the same troublemakers?"

Within a week after arriving home with Rose, Wes had begun to be harassed in one form or another. Graffiti on the barn telling him and his wife to get out of town, rotten meat tossed on the front porch, hate letters appearing during the night—a couple of them pinned in place with knives. All of this, no doubt, done by the same faceless troublemakers who had threatened Wes when he first arrived. But those threats had died down after a while.

"Now they've sunk to breaking windows?" Barrett jeered. "These people are acting like cowardly little boys."

"It's not just a broken window. This was tied to the rock." Chase handed her a dirty sheet of crumpled paper, the scrawl in black ink barely legible.

We dont want yer kind in are town. Git yer black ass and yer black wife back where you come from, or stay here and die.

Barrett's stomach rolled at the threat. She handed the note back to Chase.

"Do you think they're serious? Do you think it's the Klan?"

Chase took the note, smoothing out the coal-black spikes of hair as he plowed his fingers from forehead to crown.

"I *know* they're serious. But I don't think they're the Klan."

Rose appeared with a broom and began silently sweeping up the winking slivers of glass. Barrett laid her hand on Rose's arm.

"Are you all right?"

Rose stopped her sweeping and smiled at Barrett.

"I'm fine. These people are just mean-spirited cusses. Most of the folks here have been downright neighborly. I ain't worried with Chase and my Wes around."

Wes agreed. "I think this is just a handful of soreheads, brat. Troublesome, but not dangerous."

Barrett and her twentieth-century mind couldn't trivialize the sense of danger. But she didn't want to alarm Rose, and she knew that Chase and Wes had already formed their own opinions that wouldn't be swayed. Instead of arguing, she propped Adam in a chair by the fire and grabbed a broom, helping to sweep up while Chase and Wes covered the hole in the window.

On their more sedate return trip to the house after cleaning up, Barrett gazed up at the stars, breathing in the crisp night air as Chase draped his arm over her shoulders. She snuggled her head against his chest and studied the heavens.

More than once she'd admired the clarity of the night sky. She'd never seen so many stars in her time as she did right now, with the heavens looking as if someone had spilled a truckload of silver glitter across a black-velvet floor. The very air seemed to glisten. Surely the lack of automobile exhaust and factory fumes had a lot to do with that. And the quiet was exquisite. No cars or trucks roaring down the road, no horns blaring. No radios cranked up so deafeningly loud you could feel the bass thumping even when you couldn't hear the music.

Granted, she missed the music. Not the pounding bass of a teenager's passing car, but the ability to slide in a CD and immerse herself in anything from Bach to Billy Joel to Garth Brooks. And she missed telephones. Instant answers to questions. Instant help in a crisis. Instant remedy for loneliness.

But she hadn't been lonely since arriving in this time, and that was a new and foreign experience for her. She glanced up at Chase, this ready-made husband of hers, and her heart swelled when he dropped his gaze to hers, a shaft of moonlight illuminating his piercing eyes.

As one, they stepped up to the back door.

He dipped his head and she lifted her lips to meet his, savoring the bolt of lightning that always seared her to the core whenever their lips met. She cherished the sense of belonging to this man, tucked under one of his arms as she was, their son dwarfed in the other.

When she shivered he opened his coat and pulled her into its warmth. Her senses reeled as the heat of his body rose up to meet her. Her fingertips tingled when she touched his hard, bare chest.

"Umm," she hummed, then trailed soft, teasing kisses across its downy surface. Chase leaned against the door, his head back, a low moan rumbling in his throat when Barrett inched kisses up the center of his chest.

"I think I like this," she murmured against his skin as she began to explore with her hands. "Adam in one arm, me in the other . . . I have you at my mercy."

Her hands wandered at their leisure, skimming over bare skin, then denim. Dipping into his waistband, feeling his stomach tense into hard ridges at her touch.

Chase stood there, his head back, his eyes closed, letting her have her way with him. Finally he lowered his head and opened his eyes into dark golden slits. Finding her mouth with his, he reached behind him and opened the door. Barrett giggled as he backed in, dangling the carrot of his kiss to get her inside.

"I hope you're ready to pay off on all that teasing, Mrs. Alston," he whispered, his lips still on hers.

"Ready, willing, and able, Chaser," she answered, then proved it with more than words . . . proved it until the sun crept over the eastern horizon.

Chapter 12

BARRETT DRESSED FOR church, cramming herself into a corset, wishing she could show up in her
jeans without sending ladies into a swoon left and
right. She hardly ever wore a dress anymore around the
house. Even Rose had cut down a pair of Wes's jeans
and wore them to garden or do laundry. And Wes had
taken to good-naturedly grumbling about what a bad
influence the brat was.

Chase came up behind her and lassoed her waist with
his arms.

"Need some help with those buttons?"

Barrett smiled and craned her neck to receive a peck
on the cheek.

"I'll need *more* if I let *you* help." She laughed as she
slapped his hands away from undoing the buttons on
her bodice. The sound of Rose and Wes coming
through the back door halted the playful wrestling
match.

"Later," Chase growled in her ear, then marched into
the parlor, yanking on the cuffs of his shirt.

"Get Adam for me, will you?" Barrett called behind him. She finished buttoning her gown, grabbed her cloak, and met the others at the wagon.

When they pulled up in front of the church, assorted members of the congregation hailed them. Several came over to introduce themselves to Rose and welcome Wes back. When Barrett caught sight of Margaret Keller, she excused herself from the group and caught up with Margaret before she entered the church.

"Margaret, how have you been?" Barrett fell in beside the woman. A fresh bruise bloomed at the corner of the timid woman's mouth. Barrett shook her head in sympathy.

"It's not what you think," Margaret said, then winced at the movement.

"Well, I think you ran into another door, so if I'm wrong that must mean your husband beat the crap out of you again."

"The cow kicked me."

That left Barrett speechless for a moment. "The cow . . . ?"

"Yes, when I was milking her."

Barrett stood for a moment, as if she were about to accept the idea. "That's pretty original. Can't say I've ever heard that one before. Of course, there weren't a lot of cows near the shelter then."

Margaret apologized with her sad, lifeless eyes. "I have to go in now. Ann's waiting for me." She turned to go, but Barrett held her arm to stop her, letting go when the fragile woman flinched.

"I'm sorry," Barrett sympathized. "I see she kicked you in the arm, too." Margaret simply stared straight ahead, blinking furiously and biting her lower lip. "For the love of God, Margaret, talk to me when you get tired of putting up with this. If not for yourself, then for Ann. Do you want her to think this is what marriage is all about?" Margaret swallowed hard and glanced at Barrett before looking away. Barrett took her hand, but only after making sure there were no bruises on it. "I can help you, but you have to take the first step."

When Barrett released her hand, Margaret scurried into the sanctuary, looking back over her shoulder once before disappearing through the door.

"Sometimes you can't tell people what's best for them. They have to find out for themselves." Mr. Gideon came up to stand beside Barrett, and she turned to take his hand.

For the first time she looked at him as he truly was, a celestial creature, created by God to be an angel, not a man with human failings, and not the meddling fool she'd thought him to be, and it intimidated her for a second. He still wore the guise of the little old minister, but Barrett remembered the breathtaking image he'd revealed to her.

She smiled, knowing his words held a double meaning. "Yeah, some people have to have what's best for them shoved down their throats, don't they?"

He popped his empty pipe between his lips and smiled around the stem.

"Glad to know the hatchet's been buried somewhere other than between my wings."

Barrett dropped her head and grinned. "You were right all along. I needed to learn to love and be loved. But I guess you already knew that."

He nodded sagely, cupping the bowl of the pipe in his palm, puffing on imaginary smoke.

"Do you want the locket back? I know now I could never leave Chase and Adam." She fumbled at her collar, pulling the necklace from beneath her bodice.

"No, no. The offer is still open, and you still have doubts." She started to protest, but he silenced her with a raised hand. "Besides, your learning isn't over, and neither is Chase's."

"What do you mean? We're getting along fine."

"I mean there are some bumps in the road ahead of you. For both of you."

"What kind of—"

"I'm sorry, child. That's all I can say."

Chase came up behind her then, with Rose and Wes and Adam. Mr. Gideon ushered them through the door and they took their seats, leaving Barrett to wonder throughout the service exactly what kind of bumps she had to look forward to.

After church Carrie bustled up to their little family, surprising Barrett by asking if she would finish teaching her how to smock.

"Smock?" Barrett repeated stupidly, trying to figure out what the heck smocking was and how one went about it.

"Yes. You said you'd finish teaching me after Adam was born, if I didn't learn it all before you had him. Is today inconvenient?"

Barrett blinked and pursed her lips. This was an interesting dilemma. She couldn't even fake her way out of this one—she had no idea what it was to begin with.

"Well," she stalled, trying to come up with a plausible excuse, since everyone was listening. "I'd like to, but . . ." Her mind went blank. Where was her creative thinking when she needed it?

"Rose can teach you," Wes volunteered, and Barrett could have kissed him. "She ain't busy this afternoon after lunch. Why don't you come over then if Barrett's busy."

Carrie agreed while Wes threw a brotherly wink toward Barrett. After her obligatory fussing over Adam, Carrie darted off to meet Tom.

Barrett mouthed a thank-you to Wes as Chase helped her into the wagon.

After lunch, when Barrett saw Carrie's carriage pulling up the drive, she made sure she stayed busy so there'd be no question of her having to teach Carrie this smocking stuff. When Carrie left, she didn't stop in at the house, but dallied outside, talking to Chase, then followed him into the barn. Relieved to be off the hook, Barrett turned back to the kitchen, wishing fervently that she had a microwave and a freezer full of frozen dinners.

Barrett rolled over and snuggled closer to Chase, wondering what had awakened her. It couldn't be much past midnight. She tried to sink back into the sleep that still held the edges of her consciousness, but something wasn't right. The night sounds were all wrong. In fact, there weren't any.

She opened her eyes and looked around. A faint orange glow flickered outside the bedroom curtains.

"Chase!" Barrett flew to the window and dragged

back the curtain as Chase shot upright in bed. "There are men with torches outside the cottage!"

Chase slid into his pants and boots almost before Barrett finished speaking. He was halfway out the bedroom door when he stopped and looked back.

"Stay here, Barrett. I mean it. Stay here." The back door slammed behind him just seconds later.

Barrett shoved her feet into a pair of slippers, checked on Adam, then left him sleeping in his cradle while she went in search of a gun. Chase must have grabbed the rifle—it was missing from its post by the front door. She ran to the pantry and yanked the shotgun off its rack, then slipped out the front and edged her way around the house.

Half a dozen torches cast weird, dancing shadows over the frightening scene at Wes's cottage. Barrett's breath caught in her throat as she watched a handful of men with kerchiefs over their faces form a semicircle around Wes and Chase. The leader's voice, obviously disguised, carried clearly in the frigid night air.

"Lay your rifle down, Alston. This is between us and the nigger."

The rifle never wavered as Chase stepped closer to Wes and held his ground.

"Throw it down! Now! Or I'll blow his head off." The other man's gun rose to point at Wes's head.

Chase hesitated, then tossed his rifle to the ground. Barrett could see Rose on the front porch, standing tall, her tightly clasped hands her only sign of fear.

"Now get out of here, Alston. Like I said, this don't concern you."

Chase's feet stayed planted. "I'm not going anywhere." His voice sounded deceptively casual. "Get off my land now and I won't be forced to hunt you down and kill you."

The leader moved in and swung the gun down to land the tip of the barrel on Wes's chest.

"I said git. Or watch your half-breed brother die instead of get run out of town back to where he come from. We let him stay when it was just him, but he ain't bringin' no wife in here and fillin' our town with their kind. Let one into town, an' first thing you know, they're all over. It ain't gonna happen here. Now git or I'll shoot."

With lightning speed Chase grabbed the barrel of the rifle, centering the tip against his own chest.

"Then shoot."

Barrett gasped, slapping her hand over her mouth, nearly dropping the shotgun. What was he doing? He was going to get himself killed! She fought the urge to run to him. What should she do? How could she help him?

The leader struggled to pull the gun away, but Chase kept an iron grip with the barrel pressed against the bare skin over his heart.

"You want to kill my brother, or even run him out of town, you're going to have to kill me first."

A low murmur started among the group.

"My brother's a man, just like all of you. He bleeds red, just like all of you. You hate him because his skin's darker than yours? That's a reason to kill a man? What happens if someone decides they don't like the color of *your* skin? Or maybe they decide to kill everyone who doesn't have blond hair? Or blue eyes? If you want to kill him because of his skin color, you're going to kill me first. And then go home and explain to your wives and family how you killed a man because he didn't look like you."

The murmuring grew, then one man stepped up and threw his torch down. "Killin' a nigger's one thing, but I don't plan to hang for killin' a neighbor." That said, he walked out of the ring of light. One by one, the torches hit the ground until only the man whose gun pressed to Chase's chest remained. The man looked around him, his courage visibly draining when he realized he stood alone.

"You sonofabitch," he growled loud enough for Barrett to hear. "This ain't over."

Chase flung the gun barrel away from his chest.

"Any time," he said, his head cocked in challenge.

The lone man's puffy raisin eyes narrowed with hate between his bandanna and the brim of his hat. He backed away, out of the glow of the dying torches, and disappeared into the shadows of the night.

It wasn't until Chase and Wes stood alone in the yard that Barrett breathed again and her knees threatened to buckle. She dropped the forgotten shotgun and raced toward Chase, torn between covering him with kisses and killing him herself.

After Chase finished mucking out the stalls and putting down fresh straw, he peeled off his shirt and poured a dipper of cool water over his head. The mid-March day had turned balmy—one of those rare times in late winter that teases with the promise of summer. He hung the dipper on the lip of the bucket, then picked up the currycomb and headed for Old Sam's stall.

A feminine shadow fell across his path from the open barn door where the late-afternoon sun spilled an elongated shaft of light.

"Well, you weren't gone long," he said, squinting at Barrett's silhouette. "I figured you and Rosie would spend the day shopping."

He opened his arms for a welcoming kiss, then blinked and let his hands fall to his sides when he realized his visitor was Carrie.

"Oh, Carrie, I'm sorry. I thought you were Barrett. She's not here. She and Rose took Adam in the wagon over to the general store for supplies. I'm not sure when she'll be back. Can I help you with something?"

Carrie hesitated for a moment, then moved into the barn.

"Yes, you can help me, Chase. If you will."

A nervous smile played on her lips. Her gaze dipped to scan the length of Chase's bare chest. He turned to find his shirt and saw it hanging on a nail next to the water bucket at the end of the barn.

"Let me get dressed, then I'll help you with whatever you need."

He headed for his shirt, but Carrie caught up with him just as he lifted it from the nail, shocking him speechless when she yanked it out of his hand, threw it to the dirt floor, then slid her hands from his stomach to his shoulders, resting her head against his chest.

"Help me, Chase," she said. "Please help me."

Alarmed, he grabbed her shoulders and pushed her away from him.

"Whatever you need, Carrie. What's wrong? Is it Tom?" He couldn't imagine what might have happened to cause her to behave this way. "Tell me. What is it?"

Carrie looked him in the eye as she reached up and began unhooking the front of her bodice.

"You can help me, Chase. No one needs to know."

Stunned, Chase could only stand there, watching, wondering if he'd dozed off and slipped into a bizarre dream. Not until she slid out of her bodice and began working on her skirts did he snap out of his shock.

"Carrie!" He grabbed the hands busily working at the hooks of her skirt. "Stop it! What are you doing?"

"Chase," she choked, lifting her hands to caress his chest. "Give me a baby. Give me what Tom can't. No one has to know. You got Elizabeth with child right away. You can help me. I need a baby, Chase. I don't think I can live without a baby."

She wrapped her arms around his neck and pulled his head down to meet her lips before he knew what she was doing. Just as he reached to grab her hands and push her away, he lifted his gaze to meet the shocked eyes of his wife as she stepped into the barn.

Barrett slowly walked toward them, her head cocked, two deep lines forming creases between her brows.

He shoved Carrie away as she struggled to keep her lips on his.

"Chase, make love to me," she begged as she threw herself at him again.

"Barrett, this isn't what it looks like."

Barrett stopped as Carrie whirled around with a gasp, crossing her hands over her chemise in a belated act of modesty.

Barrett's voice was controlled, calm, with a hint of tightly held rage sharpening the edges.

"It looks like her lips were clamped on yours. It looks like you're both half naked, and it *sounded* like she was begging you to make love to her."

Chase snatched up his shirt and shoved his arms into it.

"Yes, but—"

She spun on her heel and marched out of the barn. He charged after her, casting a disgusted look back at Carrie before barreling out the door. He caught up with Barrett on the back stoop, grabbing her arm and pulling her toward him.

"Barrett, let me explain."

With a flick of her wrist, she freed her arm, leaving Chase with a throbbing thumb and an empty hand. How had she done that?

"Barrett!" he called to her back as she slammed into the house. He caught up with her again in the parlor.

Rose jumped to her feet from her seat by Adam's basket, her startled gaze bouncing back and forth between the two of them.

"Rose, would you mind giving us some time alone?" Chase asked, trying to keep his voice calm. Trying not to bellow.

"Rose doesn't have to leave, but *you do*!" Barrett yelled, then picked up a pillow from the sofa and threw it at his head. Chase caught it and dropped it to the chair. Rose mumbled something, scooped up Adam, then scurried out the front door with him.

"I'm not going anywhere," he informed his wife. "I'm going to explain this, and you're going to listen."

Barrett crossed her arms over her chest and glared at him.

"Explain away."

Chase stepped toward her but stopped when she took a step back.

"I wasn't kissing Carrie. She was kissing *me*." Barrett rolled her eyes. "I'd taken my shirt off to work before she came in. I thought she was looking for you. But she asked me to help her, and she was acting so strange I thought something might have happened to Tom."

Barrett shifted her weight and continued to glare.

"For God's sake, Barrett, she's insane! She asked me to give her a baby. Said Tom couldn't give her one. She started taking her clothes off and promising no one would know."

Surprisingly, the anger in Barrett's face softened somewhat. She dropped her arms, then crossed them again.

"Then what?"

"Then you walked in. She threw herself at me and I was trying to push her off when you walked in. I was as shocked as you were."

The back door creaked open, then closed with a click. They both swung around to see Carrie, fully dressed, standing just inside the kitchen, her head bowed, wringing her hands at her waist. She walked meekly into the parlor, then raised her eyes to meet Barrett's.

"I'm sorry," she whispered. "It's all my fault. Chase wanted nothing to do with me."

Barrett unfolded her arms but didn't move from her spot.

"Why, Carrie?"

Carrie's eyes filled with tears. "I want a baby so badly. Tom and I have tried for years. You had to have gotten pregnant almost on your wedding night. I knew Chase could get me pregnant, where Tom couldn't."

Hot bile roiled in Chase's stomach. He had no proof that he could get a woman pregnant any more than Tom Davis could. He shoved the thought from his mind, tried to bury it in a grave twelve feet deep.

Carrie covered her face with her hands and sobbed, deep, soul-jarring sobs. She stood there, a lonely, pitiful sight, until Barrett went to her and guided her to the sofa. For the first time since this started, Chase felt the stirrings of sympathy for her.

"What makes you so sure the problem is with Tom?" Barrett asked as she sank to the cushion beside Carrie.

"Because if it's not Tom, that means it's my fault, and I couldn't bear that. I couldn't bear the thought of never having a chance to have children."

Barrett let out a long sigh and leaned back into the sofa. She stared at the ceiling for several seconds, as if searching her mind for answers to a question Chase hadn't heard. Then, as if making up her mind about something, she got up, disappeared into their bedroom, then returned seconds later with Dr. Logan's thermometer.

"Are your periods . . . your monthly courses regular?" she asked Carrie, whose face immediately flamed to the color of a ripe tomato. She shot a glance at Chase, then cast her gaze to her lap and kept it there.

"No," she answered in a weak, whispery voice.

Chase couldn't understand why Barrett had asked that question, and in front of him, unless she just didn't care right now whether she embarrassed Carrie or not.

"How often do you have one?"

Carrie's face, if possible, turned an even deeper red. Chase knew he should leave, but he was beginning to wonder about Barrett's sanity as well as Carrie's.

"I never know. Sometimes a month. Sometimes two. Sometimes five or six weeks," she said in a barely audible whisper.

Barrett pulled the thermometer out of its case and handed it to her.

"I don't know how accurate this thing is, but it's better than nothing. Every morning at the same time—and this is important—at the same time and before you get out of bed, I want you to take your temperature. Put the thermometer under your tongue. See these little marks? These are tenths of degrees. I want you to chart your temperature, literally make a chart. You know how to do that, don't you?"

Carrie nodded, her eyes darting up long enough to assure Barrett.

"Okay. Make a chart and log your temperature on it, right down to the tenth of a degree. Every morning. Do you understand?"

Again, Carrie nodded.

"All right. Now, the morning your temperature drops a few tenths of a degree, then you and Tom need to make love that day. And for several days after that."

Carrie's face, which had begun to regain its normal

hue, flared again to near burgundy. She swallowed and blinked at her lap, but never once looked up.

Chase didn't know whether to stop this conversation or not. Was Barrett manufacturing these wild ideas to fill Carrie with false hope? What possible connection could one's temperature have with conceiving?

As if reading his mind, Barrett spoke.

"Studies . . . I've read about . . . have proven that a woman's body temperature drops slightly just prior to ovulation, then rises several tenths of a degree and stays there until her period . . . monthly courses start, usually about two weeks later."

Carrie finally raised her eyes, the predicted hope clearly there.

"What's ovulation?"

"That's when a woman's ovary releases an egg. If the egg is fertilized by a man, then she's pregnant. The only time a woman can get pregnant is during ovulation, when the egg is ready to be fertilized. The egg only survives a few days if it isn't fertilized. If you know when you're ovulating, you'll know when to make love. Oh, yeah, don't get up right away after making love. Tuck a pillow under your bottom to elevate your pelvis."

Chase had heard more than he would ever have wanted to hear of this conversation in mixed company. He wouldn't have been surprised to find his face rivaling Carrie's in shades of burgundy.

He escaped outside and was met by Bo, who trotted up to him with a stick in his mouth, then dropped it at Chase's feet as if it were a golden offering to the god he worshiped.

Chase rubbed the perky ears, picked up the slobbery

stick, and tossed it for Bo to fetch, relieved to be doing something normal, something masculine.

He still couldn't credit what Carrie had done, and her actions upset him all the more when she explained herself. When Barrett decided she wanted another baby, would he be able to give her one? If he couldn't, would she turn to someone else to get her pregnant? Would she turn to Aidan?

Barrett swiped at her hair and shivered in the chilly breeze, even though clouds of steam rolled up at her from the washtub. A cold front had moved in during the night, pushing the balmy, false summer of the day before somewhere south, and replacing it with a damp cold and a gray sky.

She returned to scrubbing the mountain of diapers while Rose finished rinsing the other clothes and hanging them out to dry. There were at least another dozen diapers left to scrub when Ann Keller came around the corner of the house.

The spirited teenager Barrett first met had lost some of her exuberance. The sparkling life had died in her eyes, replaced with a sadness someone her age shouldn't know.

She could kill Miller Keller.

She dried her hands on her jeans and went to meet Ann. The girl smiled up at her weakly.

"How nice to see you again, Ann." She hugged the girl around the shoulders and walked with her over to Rose.

"You met my sister-in-law, Rose, at church, didn't you?"

Ann's eyes widened and she glanced back and forth

between the women before nodding. "Yes, ma'am. It's nice to meet you again." The girl turned her wide, innocent eyes back to Barrett, a glimmer of the old curiosity there.

"Does Mr. Alston allow you to wear trousers like that?" She flicked a glance at Rose. "And you, too, Miss Rose. Don't your husbands get angry?"

Barrett smiled, but her hands itched to circle Miller's throat and squeeze.

"Of course not. We're grown women. We have the right to decide what we'll wear and what we won't wear." The thought briefly crossed her mind that in 1887 there might be one of those go-figure laws that gave a man rein over his wife's wardrobe, but she ignored the possibility. "Besides, we only dress like this around the house. So what brings you out on such a gloomy day?"

The glimmer in Ann's eyes died at Barrett's words.

"Mother wanted me to ask you to come by and see her."

So Margaret might be ready to take the first step.

"Did she mention when?"

"Today, if it's not inconvenient."

"You tell her I'll be there as soon as I get this laundry on the line."

When Ann left, Barrett finished with the last of the diapers, even though Rose offered to do them. She did, however, take Rose up on her offer to keep Adam while Barrett talked with Margaret.

Adam decided he was hungry, so Barrett took the time to nurse him, which was probably for the best. At least now she wouldn't have to worry about her milk letting down and soaking her clothes before she could get home.

When she went in to change, dreading the thought of dragging around those skirts, a mischievous voice in her head suggested she wear her jeans in an act of defiance.

She didn't need a lot of encouraging. She also decided to forgo the wagon, sliding a saddle over Old Sam's back and swinging astride.

"I don't know how long I'll be gone," she told Rose outside the barn. "Will you tell Chase when he gets back, if I don't beat him home?" The men had gone to break up a beaver dam at one of the streams on the property.

"Don't worry about Chase. And I'll fix supper if you don't get back."

That in itself was enough to inspire Barrett to linger at the Keller house.

She kicked Sam into a trot, then downshifted to a canter and pointed him east.

The sterile dark-green door swung inward and Margaret ushered Barrett into the house before she even had a chance to knock.

"Miller will kill me if he sees you dressed like that!"

Barrett gasped at the sight of Margaret's face. An emotionally dead blue eye peered out through a slit in the swollen dark-purple lid. Her lower lip mushroomed on one side in a rainbow of purple, yellow, red, and black, and a painful-looking split had just barely begun to heal.

"Oh, Margaret," Barrett moaned, guiding her into the

spotless parlor, gently pulling her onto the sofa. "What has he done to you?"

Margaret's good eye glistened, but she blinked away the moisture.

"What can I do to stop him? I have to live, for Ann's sake. I don't want her to grow up without a mother."

Margaret's tone implied that if it weren't for Ann, she would gladly lie down and let her husband beat her to death, to put her out of her misery. Barrett tamped down her rage at Miller. She dredged up all the professional cool that she had laid aside since arriving here.

"What was his excuse this time?"

Margaret stared at her lap and swallowed.

"I made green beans instead of pinto beans for supper last night."

Oh, for the love of . . .

"Do you think you deserved what he did to you because you cooked the wrong beans?"

Margaret continued to study her lap, clearly unsure of the answer. A classic portrait of an abused woman, beaten into believing she deserved every blow landed.

"If you asked Miller to wear your favorite shirt, and he mistakenly put on the green one instead of the blue, would he deserve what he did to you?"

Margaret stared, then her gaze slowly rose to Barrett's, with the first glimmer of possibility that she might not deserve what she got.

"No," she answered, a little uncertainly.

"Of course not. And neither do you. No one deserves to be beaten, unless it's for beating on someone else undeservedly. Then he needs a taste of his own medicine."

Margaret still looked unsure. Convincing these women who'd been brainwashed by a loved one was a slow process. Barrett just hoped she could reach Margaret before he killed her.

"How do I stop him? What can I do?"

The first words to leap to Barrett's tongue were "Get counseling," but she swallowed them. Abuse counselors in 1887? Experts on domestic violence in this day and age? And all she had to offer were her required psych courses from college and a couple of summers volunteering in a shelter.

"The first thing you have to do is get out, so he can't hurt you anymore. You and Ann both. Do you have somewhere you can go?"

Margaret nodded reluctantly. "My sister lives across the river."

"Good. Plan on staying with her for a while. Next, Miller has to be confronted with what he's doing. I'm not suggesting you confront him alone," she hastened to add when Margaret gave her a terrified look. "No, we need some men to do it." She chewed on her lower lip and twirled a strand of hair while she thought. Would Chase pull his nineteenth-century male head out of the sand long enough to confront Miller about his married life? His helping out with Adam and not grousing because she liked to wear pants was one thing, but interfering in another man's business might be too twentieth century to hope for.

"I'll have Chase bring Reverend Gideon to talk to him," she volunteered, and prayed she wasn't promising more than she could deliver. "But Margaret" —Barrett took the woman's small, work-roughened hands in hers— "you may have to leave him. If he refuses help, if he denies he has a problem, he'll kill you if you stay."

She could almost hear the denials going on in Margaret's mind, hear the excuses and the refusal to leave her husband. But the woman had more strength than Barrett had given her credit for. After a long minute of silent deliberation, Margaret raised her head and nodded.

"All right, then. Let's go pack some things for you and Ann, then we'll go to our house and arrange for Chase to take you to your sister's."

It didn't take long to pack a trunk and a couple of valises, but when they'd dragged the things down the stairs, Barrett remembered she hadn't brought the wagon.

"We'll leave them here and Chase can pick them up on the way. Where's Ann?"

"She walked to Maeva Bickford's house."

"Where do the Bickfords live?"

Margaret cocked her head at her, and Barrett knew Elizabeth would have known that.

"They live two farms down the road from you."

"Okay, we'll pick her up on the way home. Let's go." Barrett chose to ignore her apparent lapse in memory.

Before they took a step, the front door flew open and Miller Keller barged in.

"Whose nag is that . . ." His gaze fell on Barrett, then raked her from head to toe, taking in the flannel shirt, the cut-down jeans, the loose curls she'd left down, framing her face.

Margaret flinched, as if already fending off blows.

Miller stared at Barrett, his distaste so apparent she thought he might spit on her. Then his eyes fell on the trunks and valises.

"What's this?" he boomed, and Margaret cringed even more.

Barrett allowed only a couple of seconds for Margaret to answer, and when she didn't, Barrett supplied the information.

"Margaret and Ann are going . . . away for a while."

"Going away? Where the hell do you think you're going?" he bellowed, standing there as intimidating as a grizzly on its hind legs.

"Just away," Barrett offered when Margaret finally opened her mouth to answer.

"Like hell you are. Drag that stuff back upstairs, woman, then get me my supper."

A stagnant cloud of whiskey fumes blasted across Barrett's face. She blatantly waved her hand in front of her face in an attempt to dilute the noxious air.

The man jerked his head back, as if slapped, then hate glittered in his sharp black eyes. He'd been drinking, yes, but he certainly wasn't drunk. He slid his gaze to his wife, who was cringing beside Barrett.

"I said get your sorry ass upstairs and then get me some supper, or when I get through with you, you won't be able to get up."

"Miller, you can't keep hitting me," Margaret spoke for the first time, her voice quivering so that she could barely be understood.

"I can do anything I damn well please. Now haul this stuff upstairs. And you, Miss High-and-Mighty Alston, can get your britches-wearing ass back to your own house where you belong, instead of meddling in mine."

Barrett stepped in front of Margaret and glared up at the Neanderthal towering over her. Her heart drum-rolled against her ribs, fear lodged in her throat and dried out her mouth like a wad of cotton. If they backed down now, Margaret would be dead before morning.

"Get your valise, Margaret," she instructed calmly, surprised that her voice betrayed none of her paralyz-ing fear. "We're leaving now."

When Barrett bent to pick up one of the valises, Miller roared, "You ain't going nowhere!" then back-handed Barrett on the side of the head, knocking her out of the way and sending pinpoints of light swim-ming across her vision.

Barrett shook off her stupor in time to see Margaret hit the ground like a rag doll.

Instinctively, all the self-defense she'd ever learned kicked in. In the space of a heartbeat Barrett lunged at the bastard's throat, her thumbs sinking into the soft tissue above his collarbone as she yelled, "Noooo," loud and deep, fueling her adrenaline, giving her more strength. Miller choked, gasping for air, his hands clawing at hers. But her attack had hit home and the pounds of pressure behind her thumbs weakened him immediately. Holding on like a leech as he fell to the floor, she landed sprawled across him with her knee be-tween his legs. Instinct, again, made her straighten her leg behind her, then bring it plowing into his crotch with every ounce of strength she had, shoving him a good foot across the floor. She continued to yell, land-

ing another knee in the family jewels, when suddenly
hands were on her, pulling her away, breaking her hold
on his throat, lifting her off of him.

"Barrett! Barrett, stop! I'm here now. Stop it!"

Chase's voice penetrated her screaming mind—and
her screaming voice. She stopped struggling, then
threw herself at Chase, wrapping her arms around him,
burying her head in the wool of his shirt.

"Oh, Chase! Oh, Chase!" was all she could manage
to stammer.

He held her tight, one hand against her back, the
other cupping the back of her head.

"Shhh. Shh. Calm down now. Calm down," he said,
his words as gentle as if he were quieting Adam. His
lips brushed the top of her head. He held her while
Miller gasped and choked and moaned at their feet. Finally Chase tilted her chin with his knuckle and she
looked up into his precious, knight-in-shining-armor
face.

"Can you tell me what happened here?"

Barrett nodded, and then she remembered Margaret.
She darted around Chase, relieved to see Margaret
leaning against the wall, with another black eye to
match the first one, but alive and apparently all right.
At the sight of her, Chase cursed, but Margaret looked
up at him with a reassuring nod.

"Miller's going to kill her, Chase, if we don't get her
out of here. We were leaving when he came in, and
when I bent to pick up the bag, he hit me and then
started in on Margaret."

Chase, whose body had gone rigid when he'd seen

Margaret's face, now turned stiffly to the man rolling on the floor, retching and holding his crotch.

"What are you doing here, anyway?" Barrett asked as her husband glared down at the pitiful excuse for a man.

"Rose told me Margaret sent for you," he answered without ever taking his eyes off Miller. "I had a feeling there'd be trouble, but I never expected to find you beating up on Margaret's husband." A touch of humor teased his words, but then he turned to her, all traces of humor gone. "Are you all right? Did he hurt you?"

His hands traced over her skull, not waiting for her to answer. He stopped when she winced under his touch.

"You've got a lump the size of an egg here. Is that where he hit you?"

Barrett nodded, gingerly feeling for herself.

Miller groaned and rolled to his knees as Chase hurried to help Margaret struggle to stand.

"I'll fetch Dr. Logan as soon as we leave," Chase told her, but Margaret shook her head.

"I don't need a doctor. I've been fixing myself for years now." She gave Chase a sad, heartbreaking smile that begged him not to drag any more witnesses into this.

"As you wish," he conceded. "But you and Ann are going home with us."

"They ain't going nowhere." Miller staggered to his feet and grabbed the rifle propped behind the front door. Still bent nearly double, he pointed the weapon at Chase, then rubbed his throat and swung it toward Barrett. "You're going to take this troublemakin' slut and get off my property. And I don't ever want to see her and her britches back here again." The barrel wavered back to Chase's chest.

Chase looked at the gun barrel, just inches away. Then, with what seemed to Barrett like casual disinterest, he lifted his hand and plugged the tip of the barrel with his index finger.

"You know, Miller," Chase said conversationally, as if he chanced getting his hand blown off every day, "when a man stares down the length of a gun barrel for very long, he never really forgets what it looks like." Miller's eyes shifted uneasily, and he no longer seemed quite so sure of himself. "And somehow I'm not all that surprised to find myself already acquainted with your rifle here, considering we met just a few nights ago."

Chase yanked the firearm out of Miller's grasp, emptied the bullets, then tossed it to the floor in the parlor.

Miller stood there, the blood draining from his face, his skin turning to parchment.

"Now," Chase continued calmly as he pushed up his sleeves, "this . . ." —he landed a solid left into Miller's eye, bouncing him off the door frame— ". . . is for ever laying a hand on your wife. And this . . ."—blood spurted from Miller's nose when Chase's fist made contact—"is for the lump on my wife's head. This"—Miller flew through the door and landed with a thud on the porch when Chase nailed him on the jaw—"is for what you did to my brother and his wife. And this"—Chase strolled out to the porch, yanked Miller up by his shirtfront, then plowed an uppercut under his chin—"is for calling my wife a slut."

The man landed in the dirt by the porch steps, unconscious. Chase stepped back inside, balanced the trunk on his shoulder and picked up both valises. He stepped over Miller on his way to the wagon he'd brought. Barrett gave the man a wide berth. Margaret, however, walked up to him and kicked him in the ribs on her way past.

Chapter 13

CHASE HAD LEFT two days ago to take Margaret and Ann across the river to Margaret's sister, and since around noon yesterday Barrett averaged looking down the road in search of him about every five minutes. She had no idea when to expect him back, but he hadn't thought he'd be much more than three days.

She'd never dreamed she could miss someone this much. When she was in the house, she kept listening for him to come through the door, or to come up behind her and slide his arms around her waist. When she was outside, she kept listening for the sound of his ax against wood or the murmur of his and Wes's voices as they worked.

The nights, of course, were the worst. Even if she hadn't surprised herself with how she wanted him all the time. She missed curling against him to fall asleep, planting her cold feet on him somewhere to warm them. She missed having him rub his cheek against the top of her head and waking to find him touching her somewhere, always.

"I think I got everything." Rose's voice snapped Barrett out of her musings and brought her back to reality. "If I forgot something, I'll just send Wes to get it."

"That's fine," Barrett said as she picked up the bundle of baby things she and Rose had collected. "Are you sure you want to do this?"

Rose smiled. "I love this youngun like my own. Besides"—her smile turned all misty—"I'm going to need the practice."

"Rose!" Barrett squealed, then wrapped her arms around her and danced her around the room. "A baby! A playmate for Adam! His cousin! My nephew!" Barrett babbled on and Rose glowed like the flower she was named after. "This is wonderful! But do you feel up to keeping him all afternoon?"

Rose just shook her head and lifted Adam from his cradle. "You don't worry none about me. This boy ain't big enough to cause much trouble. You just find somethin' nicer to do with your time than stare all moony-eyed down that road."

When Rose left with Adam, Barrett made a couple of circuits around the house, feeling lost with both of her men gone. Bo scratched at the back door and Barrett let him in, glad for his company.

"I was wrong, boy, wasn't I? Not *all* my men have deserted me."

Bored and lonely within minutes, she decided to take a long, uninterrupted bath. But after heating the water and filling the tub, once she sank into the scented bath, all she could think of was when Chase had walked in on her, then made love to her for the first time. So much for the long bath. She washed, dried off, then wandered into the bedroom to dress.

Instead of pulling on her jeans, which, she had to admit, she was getting sick of, she decided to rummage through the armoire and see if she'd missed anything enticing to wear.

A flash of blue caught her eye immediately, and she pulled the forgotten dress from the back of the wardrobe.

Elizabeth's wedding dress.

Not the traditional lacy gown. Rather, an exquisite dress tailored finely enough to be special but functional enough to wear more than once.

On impulse, Barrett shimmied, laced, and hooked herself into all the layers of underthings, then settled the skirts around her waist before slipping on the bodice. She felt like a little girl playing dress-up. All she needed were some empty teacups and some imaginary cake.

The bodice hooked, Barrett turned and looked at herself in the mirror. She had to admit that Elizabeth had had an unfailing eye for style and color—before she'd gone into her matronly mud stage. The blue of the gown certainly complimented her own coloring—the dark, almost black hair, the porcelain skin, the gray eyes.

Barrett blinked and looked closer, then blinked again. She pulled the mirror nearer to the window and shoved her face so close that her nose almost touched the glass.

Her eyes—or rather Elizabeth's eyes—were changing color! The dark, stormy gray of a few months ago was now ringed with dark brown, and flecks of the same color threatened to overtake what was left of the gray in her iris.

This *couldn't* be related to childbirth. She'd been willing to accept that sometimes hair darkens after a woman gives birth, and sometimes the natural curl relaxes. But she'd never heard anyone even *wonder* if their eyes would change color.

Could she be making Elizabeth's body her own, bringing some of her own physical characteristics to the fore? The idea pleased her somehow. No longer did she feel like this body was a borrowed dress. Suddenly she felt as if the dress had turned into a precious gift someone had given her to keep.

With this new peace of mind, she wandered back into the kitchen, where Bo whined to be let out. She pushed open the door and followed him, realizing the day had grown mild since her last look down the road.

Still no sign of him.

Bo trotted into the barn, then seconds later streaked out, yelping with a spitting, hissing ball of stand-up fur on his heels.

"You just had to go check out the new litter, didn't you, nosy?" She giggled, watching the barn cat make her indignant way back to her family, tail twitching in the air.

Barrett strolled into the barn, checking the stalls for the baby kittens. She found them in the last stall, mewing, wobbling on shaky legs, blindly searching for dinner.

"Ahhh." She knelt and guided one errant kitten back toward its mother, then watched as it found her and greedily started to nurse. The little family entertained her for quite a while. Finally she rose, shook out her skirts, then turned to leave.

Chase stood outside the stall, watching her, a crooked smile curving his lips.

"Oh!" she breathed. "I didn't hear you come in!"

He looked wonderful in a new suit and shirt. He'd combed his hair back, a different look than his usual casually tousled hair. She slipped her arms around his neck and whispered how she'd missed him, pressing the full length of her body against his, feeling the proof that he'd missed her as well.

She brushed her lips across his teasingly, and the amber of his eyes nearly scorched her with their heat.

The mischievous, wanton imp in her backed away, luring him into a clean stall, her fingers slowly, tantalizingly unhooking her bodice as she went.

His eyebrows shot up and a broad, sensuous smile spread across his face. He followed her in, peeling off his jacket and yanking loose his tie.

She slipped out of her bodice, dangling it for a moment from her fingertips, then tossed it atop his jacket. Then she reached up and unbuttoned his stiff new shirt, fighting the urge to rip the buttons off as she had done on that other day. As she worked on his shirt, he busied himself with the hooks on her corset. He stopped only long enough to allow her to slide one arm from a sleeve, then pulled her down atop him, onto a fresh mound of hay. The back of his fingers slowly brushing her skin above the corset burned a slow, hot trail.

Her hands fumbled at his waistband and she rolled to his side for better access.

"I've missed you so much," she breathed into his mouth. Missed him so much, even the scent of him was different.

"And I've missed you, Elizabeth," he whispered back, nibbling on her lip.

Barrett froze at the name.

"Barrett, I'm home! Where are you? Whose carriage is this—"

She shot upright and stared at her husband beside her, then jerked her gaze to the man standing in the doorway of the stall.

Chase!

Oh, my God! Oh, my God!

She scrambled to her feet, furiously trying to ram her arms into her bodice.

"Chase! This isn't what it looks like! I didn't—"

Chase's jaw flexed and a vein pumped at his temple.

"It looks like you're both half-naked. It looks like you had your mouth clamped onto his."

"Chase, I thought it was you! I didn't know he was your twin! I didn't know you *had* a twin!"

She ran to him, tried to hold his face in her hands and explain, but he shoved her away so hard she nearly fell to the ground. She whirled to the man still lounging half dressed on the hay.

"Tell him, Aidan! You *are* Aidan, aren't you? Tell him I thought you were Chase!"

Aidan simply looked at his brother and shrugged.

Chase spun on his heel and stormed out of the barn. Barrett turned to Aidan, still reclining, as if he expected to pick up where they had left off.

"You bastard!" she hissed, then raced out of the stall, struggling to hook her bodice as she stumbled across the yard.

Chase kicked his way out the back door just as she

reached the stoop, his arms laden with dozens of dresses. He nearly knocked her down again as he flung the garments onto the ground.

"What are you doing? Those are my clothes!" She tried to grab his arm. She had to make him listen. "This is all a mistake. You've got to believe me!"

He yanked his arm free and when she would have followed him into the house he turned and pointed a rigid, trembling index finger in her face.

"Don't," he said with more loathing than Barrett could have imagined possible. "Don't ever consider coming back into this house."

His tone, the disgust in his eyes, ripped at her heart like a dull, jagged blade.

"Chase, you've got to listen." She tried to keep her voice calm.

He slammed back into the house.

She caught up with him in the parlor and snatched at his shirt.

"You've got to believe me! I love you! I thought Aidan—"

He grabbed the front of her bodice and dragged her to the back door. With one mighty shove she went shooting into the yard.

"You come back in and I'll kill you," he said, his voice so deadly calm that Barrett believed him. His gaze raked her unevenly hooked bodice. "Keller was right, after all," he spat, hurting her more than a backhand to the cheek.

Seconds later he returned with another armful of clothes and threw them near the first as he marched across the yard.

Aidan strolled out of the barn, fully dressed now, yanking at his cuffs in a manner just like Chase.

Barrett wanted to kill him.

Chase strode up to Aidan and slammed a fist into his face, knocking his brother flat on his back in the dirt.

He grabbed Aidan's lapels and yanked him to his feet, then shoved him toward the carriage waiting by the barn.

"You take her, and you get her out of here," he said, his low voice still deceptively calm. "And I'd better never lay eyes on either one of you again."

"You can't mean that!" Barrett cried. She couldn't believe him! She loved him. He was her world. Her life. Her very breath.

He walked past her like she wasn't even there.

When he got to the door he stopped, and without turning he warned, "Don't go to the cottage. Don't see Adam. Just get out of my sight."

Barrett grabbed his arm and shoved herself between him and the door.

"Chase, you've jumped to conclusions. If we all sit down and talk, I can explain this thing. It's just a stupid mistake!"

He flung her away from him, as if she were a poisonous snake ready to strike.

"If I ever get the urge to listen to you," he said with a sneer, "I'll take a knife and stab *myself* in the back and save you the trouble."

Barrett gasped and choked on unshed tears at the hate in his eyes and the venom in his voice. How could he throw away what they had without even listening?

"Then you'd better aim for your heart," she said, straightening her shoulders and throwing back her head, "because there's nothing there to hit. You wouldn't even bleed."

He didn't so much as flick an eyelash as he stared her down.

She had to try one last time.

"Chase, if you make me leave, if we don't talk this over and make it right, when you hit rock bottom and you cry out for someone, all you'll hear back is the echo of your own loneliness. I know what I'm talking about."

He dragged his gaze down the length of her body, returned it to her eyes, then slammed the door in her face.

Nausea roiled in Chase's stomach, inching its way up his throat for the hundredth time that day. And for the hundredth time he closed his eyes and swallowed it, but the vision of his half-naked wife and brother rolling in the hay had imprinted itself on the back of his eyelids.

He opened his eyes to the dark, lonely bedroom, lit only by the parlor fire. With a vicious curse he flung himself out of bed and rammed his fingers through his hair as he paced the floor, trying to put the terrible memory at least a step or two behind him.

His anger, his overwhelming rage, had come and gone several times throughout the day, but the piercing pain of hurt and betrayal remained constant, his companion both waking and sleeping. The pain was like a blister on his heart, rubbed raw by the simple act of breathing.

He paced the bedroom, working his way into the parlor and then into the kitchen.

The tub sat by the stove, still filled from her bath. His pacing stirred enough of a breeze that the delicate scent lifted from the water and perfumed the air, conjuring memories of the first time they'd made love after Adam was born.

The rage returned like a wave crashing over him. With a string of curses he grabbed the edge of the tub, dragged it across the floor, then shoved it out the back door. He upended the copper tub, sending a perfumed waterfall spilling into the winter grass and swirling into inky puddles in the moonlight.

He left the tub as it lay and went back inside.

He could handle hate. He could handle rage. Hell, he could handle jealousy at being cuckolded by his brother. But he couldn't handle the raw, gnawing hurt and the empty, cavernous void caused by the woman he had forgiven once, the woman he'd allowed himself to fall in love with, the woman who'd given him reason to live.

He felt as if something ugly, something spawned from within the depths of hell, had sprung to life inside him and was now trying to claw its way out, ripping at his insides, shredding his soul with saber-sharp talons.

His mind, against all of his most determined efforts, kept replaying the scene he'd walked in on, torturing him with every vivid detail.

He'd rushed into the barn after checking the house, anxious to see his wife, aching to have her in his arms again, and hoping whoever was visiting wouldn't stay long.

When he rounded the door to the stall, his heart nearly stopped beating. He wanted to kill. He wanted to cry. He wanted to vomit. Had he been a lesser man, he would have done all three, but sheer force of will kept him from it, and now that will kept him breathing, one breath at a time.

He might have given her a chance to talk, to explain, if she hadn't said she hadn't known he had a twin. Hell! What had she thought to accomplish by making such an outrageous claim?

He dropped into the rocker by the stove, leaned his head back, and tried to make his mind as blank as his stare.

He didn't know how long he'd been there, had no idea what time it was, when a sound at the back door yanked him awake.

If she was coming back to try and talk to him, he'd . . . he'd . . .

The door swung inward and Wes stepped into the kitchen, looking first toward the parlor, then seeing Chase.

"How's Adam?" Chase grumbled, already knowing he was in the best of hands with Rose.

"Keepin' his lungs exercised," Wes answered. "But Rosie's lovin' every minute of it."

He walked on in, flipped a kitchen chair around and straddled it, facing Chase. He reached into a deep pocket of his overalls, pulled out a bottle of whiskey, then slammed it onto the table.

"Let's get drunk."

Chase felt his lips pull into a half grin.

Wes. If Aidan had been half the brother Wes was, Chase's life would have been perfect. He might even still be living at Woodchase.

He reached over and grabbed the bottle, pulled the cork out with his teeth, spit it across the room, then poured at least three shots of liquor down his throat before passing the bottle to Wes.

The whiskey burned a path to his stomach, where it curled into a warm ball and seeped into his senses immediately. He coughed a wheezing, breath-catching cough and blinked away the fire. He'd never been a drinker, and he hadn't eaten since breakfast. It wouldn't take him long to get drunk.

Wes downed as much as Chase, screwed up his face when it hit, then wiped at his tearing eyes.

"Hooey, little brother. That's smooth."

They sat by the stove, drinking in silence, listening to crickets chirp, an occasional bullfrog croak, hoots from the barn owl.

Though the liquor swirled in his brain and made his knotted muscles relax, it never came close to blurring the edges of his pain.

"What you gonna do, Chaser?" Wes finally voiced the question Chase knew had been on his mind since that afternoon.

Chase allowed his head to thump back against the rocker, and he stared at the ceiling.

"I don't know."

Wes nodded slowly in agreement, as if those words had been precious pearls of wisdom.

"She tried to tell me she didn't know Aidan was my twin. My God, knowing Aidan, I might have believed her, if not for that."

Wes continued to nod, then stopped and struggled to focus on Chase.

"You know, li'l brother," he slurred, "she tol' me one time she din't rememer nothin' before Adam was born. Said it was like she jus' woke up here, with no mem'ry of the past. She even had to as' me where the attic door was. Maybe she's tellin' the truth."

Chase sliced his gaze to his brother without bothering to move his head.

"Yeah, Wes. And maybe you're not drunk. And maybe I'm not going to have a hell of a hangover in the morning." The only thing Chase regretted about his imminent hangover was that the process of getting it hadn't dulled his wrenching sense of betrayal.

"She said I wouldn't bleed," he said, more to himself than to Wes. "She said I didn't have a heart. Hell, no. Not after she got through yanking it out of my chest and stomping it in the dirt."

Wes offered him the bottle again and Chase took another gulp. He wiped his mouth with the back of his hand. The liquor seemed to be doing the opposite of what it should. His mind became more alert, his memories of her vivid, tumbling over each other as they raced through his mind.

"I loved her, Wes," he said, then raised his gaze to his brother's. "I fell so hard and fast, I didn't have time to think about it. I started loving her again when she cursed like a sailor while she was having Adam. And every day after that, no matter how hard I tried, I fell farther, until I finally gave in to it. I'd wanted a companion to come here with me and start a new life, so I convinced myself I loved her. But I found out what love really is, Wes, when she let her hair down and stopped doing penance for betraying me. And when she looked at me I thought I'd died and gone to heaven." He leaned his head back again and stared at the ceiling. "Now it feels like I've

died and gone to hell. I loved her, Wes. And, God help
me, I love her still."

Barrett woke to the sway of the moving train. The train
to Richmond. The train taking her away from Chase and
Adam.

She rolled onto her back. Her rock-hard breasts ached
like a toothache. The headache that had started the day
before throbbed to life. Her eyes felt like swollen slits in
her face. Her throat ached from crying. Though she
couldn't possibly have any tears left, one traced its way
from her eye down into her hair, cutting a moist path to
the pillow.

Barrett still couldn't believe the last twenty-four hours.
She couldn't believe Chase had kicked her out. She'd
stood there in the middle of the yard, frozen with disbelief, until Aidan tossed all her clothes into a heap in his
carriage, then tried to guide her into the seat.

She'd balled up her fist and blindsided him, giving
him a bruise on his temple to match the one Chase had
given him on his jaw.

"Damn, Elizabeth. I was only trying to help," he'd
yelped when he disentangled himself from the carriage
wheel.

"I don't need your kind of help," she'd hissed. "And
my name is *Barrett*!"

He'd merely grinned at her with a patronizing smile.

In the end, she'd gone with him. She didn't dare go to
the cottage. Not with Chase literally ready to kill her.
She'd decided to get away from the property, give Chase
time to cool off, then go back and talk to him.

But Wes, bless him, had come looking for her and

found her at the hotel. He hadn't asked any questions. He'd just told her to get on the train and go stay with her mother—Elizabeth's mother. He'd said as long as she was close by, Chase would continue to fuel his hate.

Barrett trusted Wes. He knew Chase better than anyone, so she'd gotten on the train, informing Aidan that he would pay every cent of her expenses as well as see her to her mother's door, and he was not to speak a word to her in the meantime.

She rose in stages from the hard, narrow berth, feeling a hundred years old and probably looking it. Her breasts swelled even more, and just the act of breathing caused excruciating pain.

The porter had already come in with a full pitcher of water, so she freshened up, cringing at the sight of the swollen face and bloodshot eyes looking back at her from the mirror. After washing, she expressed as much milk as she could into the basin, trying to relieve some of the terrible pressure in her breasts. That done, she pulled on the first wrinkled dress her hand fell on in the new trunk Aidan had bought, ran a brush through her hair, shoved her feet into a pair of slippers, then left her compartment for the dining car.

Halfway through a breakfast of dry toast and coffee—which was all she thought her stomach could handle—Aidan slid into the seat beside her, blocking any escape route other than crawling under the table.

"Good morning," he said as he whipped a napkin into his lap.

She wanted to slap his cheerful greeting back down his throat. But she ignored him, as if the seat were still empty. She didn't have the will for a confrontation right now. She didn't even have the will to shove the toast between her lips and chew.

"How did you sleep?"

She ignored him.

"Is that all you're having for breakfast?"

She studied the peaks and valleys of the passing landscape.

"Are you going to hold this against me forever?"

At that, Barrett's swollen eyes widened and she slowly turned her head to pin him with her gaze.

"Have you no conscience, you bastard? Do you not care that your actions have torn apart two people who love each other?"

The steward walked up then, and Aidan ordered a breakfast big enough to feed the whole dining car. Then he turned back to her.

"If I remember right, *you* approached *me*. And *you* were the one who began disrobing."

"I thought you were Chase!" she yelled, and several heads turned to stare at her.

"An understandable mistake, though I'm better-looking. But if you wanted him to believe that, why did you tell him you didn't know we were twins?"

Barrett opened her mouth to answer, then realized the truth would be equally unbelievable, no matter how much she diluted it.

"I was upset. I didn't know what I was saying. For Pete's sake, my husband had just caught me with the man who'd taken his wife's virginity." That much she knew for certain from carefully worded conversations with Rose.

"An unfortunate choice of defense on your part, I

must admit. But Chase will get over it. The fair-haired son of Woodchase is too honorable to divorce you."

"Divorce me?" Barrett nearly choked on the words. "So just staying married should be satisfactory, even though he hates me for something I didn't do?"

Aidan merely shrugged. *"C'est la vie."*

"That's life?" Could the man be that jaded? "What were you doing there anyway?"

"Just stopping in to visit my beloved twin after a business trip. I'd been to Lexington to purchase horses. And of course I wanted to meet my new nephew. Pity I never got to see him."

It didn't escape Barrett that Aidan didn't hesitate to call Adam his nephew. There'd been no leering insinuation that the baby might his son. Had Chase been mistaken about the two of them having sex just days before the wedding? But Aidan hadn't denied her claim that he was the man who had taken Elizabeth's virginity.

Barrett's head throbbed even harder.

"Why do you hate Chase so that you would sleep with his wife, and now this? You *know* I thought you were Chase."

"I can't say that I hate my brother. If I'm truthful— and I'm *always* truthful, if nothing else—I would say I'm jealous."

Barrett watched him through narrowed eyes and waited for him to continue.

"I may have been born first, but all that got me was an inheritance. I'm very good at inheriting money. I do that very well."

"But your parents are still alive."

He leveled a condescending look on her.

"You know as well as I, I'm referring to Grandmother Alston's family money. And since you and Chase left, Grandfather Tyler kicked his toes up and left me as his heir. He never did agree with the golden boy leaving Woodchase. An expensive mistake on Chase's part. But then, Chase never needed money to make him happy."

Barrett shook her head. Had she missed something in this conversation?

"If you've got all the money, and the approval of the family, why are you jealous?"

Aidan's jaw clenched and unclenched, so much like Chase that it tore at Barrett's heart.

"Because he's got you." The simple words, tossed off like they meant nothing, stole Barrett's breath. Aidan's gaze swung around to meet hers. Behind the cynical facade of a misanthrope, was there a man suffering from unrequited love?

Chase swung the ax into the top of the stump and left it there. He had enough firewood to last him ten years.

He stacked the last few pieces of split wood onto the enormous pile that had grown up over the past three weeks, then yanked the ax out of the stump and headed for the cottage.

Rose greeted him from the swing on the tiny porch. A chubby Adam sprawled across her lap like the king of the castle, gulping at his bottle. His wide, gold-flecked eyes followed Chase, and a milky smile curved around the odd-shaped nipple at the sight of his father peering down at him.

"How's my boy today? Huh? Have you been good for Aunt Rosie?"

"Like an angel," Rose answered for him. "I got your dinner on the table. Wes will sit with you while you eat. You're later than usual today."

Chase nodded and kept his mind blank. Since the day he'd kicked Barrett out, he'd worked from sunup to sundown, stopping only to eat and to check on Rose and Adam. If he didn't allow himself to stop moving, he wouldn't have time to think of Barrett.

"I'll be taking Adam home with me tonight," he said as a tiny hand wrapped around his index finger. He'd missed the baby more than he had ever imagined he could, and it was time to start being a father to him again.

"I think that's a good idea, though I don't mind if you want to wait a spell longer."

"No. It's past time," Chase said, then wandered into the house to wash up and eat.

Rose said good-bye to Adam as if Chase were taking him across the ocean instead of across the yard.

"Now, Rosie," Wes said, "it won't be long before you have your hands full all over again."

Chase forced a grin, but inside his stomach rolled and his heart tightened into a hard ball in his chest. Suddenly a crushing, smothering blanket of loneliness settled over him and his mind cried out for Barrett, against all his best efforts to stop it.

"You be sure and check his milk when you heat it," Rose ordered.

Chase saluted, waved Adam's hand at the couple on the porch, then walked across the yard. He balanced Adam in one arm and a flour sack filled with a multitude of baby things in the other.

As they approached the door, Adam's face screwed up and turned red moments before a muffled rumble sounded from within his diaper. A very recognizable odor instantly intermingled with the breeze.

Chase rolled his eyes heavenward. He hoped this wasn't an omen of things to come.

Once inside the house, Chase dispensed with the offending diaper and worked at cleaning up the mess on Adam's bottom.

"Not a good way for the prodigal son to come home," Chase informed the gurgling infant. Adam cooed at him and Chase thought he could forgive this child anything. With the worst of the mess cleaned up, Chase rummaged in the flour sack for a clean diaper. Adam entertained himself by staring at his hands, then he focused on his chubby foot waving in front of his face. With wide-eyed concentration, he reached up and grabbed his foot, then pulled it down to his face and stuck his toe in his mouth.

Chase watched the whole process with awe. The baby had actually reached out and grabbed something.

"Barrett, come and see what Adam—"

His words died in the air. For one brief, wonderful moment, he'd forgotten. And now the huge, gaping void filled with nothing but loneliness seemed larger than ever.

What had Barrett said on that last day? *When you hit rock bottom and you cry out for someone, all you'll hear back is the echo of your own loneliness.*

Had that been a curse or a prophecy?

Barrett sat at a worktable, mechanically cutting out yards and yards of snowy white silk, while Adele Grant, Elizabeth's mother, sat across from her, stitching the pieces together.

Someone's wedding gown. Barrett couldn't remember the girl's name. Whoever she was, Barrett wished her better luck in *her* marriage. Strange, she had never gone through a wedding ceremony, never promised to love and honor Chase until death, but he was her husband as surely as if they'd been married by the pope. And she would love him until the day she died.

"Don't you want to talk about it now, Elizabeth? It's been almost a month. You might feel better for it." Adele removed her tiny wire-rimmed glasses and looked at Barrett. "Heaven knows, you haven't been yourself. Imagine saying you wouldn't know which end of a needle to use, when I've taught you everything I know. You've just not been yourself since you came home, sweetheart, and you've got me more than worried."

Barrett raised her gaze to the woman across from her. It had been hard to call this woman "Mother" for the first time, knowing that either she would never see her own mother again or she would never see Chase again. And she'd wondered if the woman would sense that the person inside her daughter's body was not Elizabeth. But if Adele had any doubts, she had yet to voice them.

She hadn't insisted that Elizabeth's mother call her Barrett. Try as she might, she couldn't come up with a reasonable explanation for the request, and the sweet little woman deserved at least that much. After all, the true Elizabeth was dead, and Barrett considered opening the locket and returning to 1997 more and more seriously each day. Surely she'd learned whatever she needed to send her home. She'd almost given up on hearing from Chase. He must truly hate her.

"Tell me what happened, dear. Tell your mother. You can't keep it locked inside of you forever."

Barrett laid aside the scissors, unconsciously rubbing the blister on her thumb. Maybe it would help to talk about it.

Slowly, like someone laying down a fragile, heavy burden, she told Adele Grant what had happened that day. Saying the words were like reliving it all over again, and several times Barrett had to stop and breathe deeply in order to go on.

"So, Aidan told you he loves you, and now he's done this to you twice," Adele said, shaking her head. "Someday that boy's going to get his comeuppance. But I'm surprised at you, Elizabeth, for being so gullible. You know as well as I that Aidan loves only himself and whatever Chase has. He's always been like that."

"What do you mean twice?"

"Why, this time, and the time before you got married. I wish now I hadn't told you not to tell Chase. You should have told him right away that Aidan came calling, pretending to be him. I don't condone what you were about to do for one minute, but thank heavens you saw the dueling scar on his shoulder and pushed him off. If only he hadn't managed to . . ."—Twin spots of crimson flamed on Adele's cheeks and she looked away. ". . . to break your maidenhead. But at least you know little Adam is Chase's, since you pushed him off before he could . . . that is to say, Aidan didn't . . ."

Aidan had deceived Elizabeth? And she'd never told Chase the truth. No wonder he'd been so livid. He obviously knew Aidan had taken Elizabeth's virginity. But just barely, from what Barrett could gather.

"I'm sorry, dear. I should have told you to tell him the truth, but I was afraid he'd never believe his own brother would do something so unspeakable. I feared he would think you had returned Aidan's favors. And at the time, you weren't sure if he'd broken your . . . well, your . . ." Adele fluttered her hands and kept her eyes averted. ". . . there was always the chance that Chase would never know."

This explained so much. So many of the pieces fell into place now. Chase's initial attitude toward her and Adam. Why Elizabeth never explained. Why Chase had fought loving her and why he'd kicked her out.

Dear Lord, she'd told him she didn't know he was Aidan's twin. No wonder he wouldn't listen.

But what now? What good did this information do her? She had no proof. If she went to Chase, he would think she was making it all up.

No, he would have to come to her. She knew him well enough to know that. He would have to absolve her actions in his mind and be willing to forgive her. Did he love her enough to do that? Did he love her enough to eventually give her the benefit of the doubt?

Chase stared past his reflection on the inky black of the windowpane. Another night of trying to sleep, trying to put Barrett from his mind. But instead of time easing the pain and dulling his anger, he found himself thinking of her more. And he found himself thinking of what Wes had said about her not remembering anything before Adam was born.

If it were true, if something happened to her during childbirth, it would explain so much. Her sometimes oddly worded language. Her transformation from an excellent cook to one who could burn water. Her metamorphosis from a spotless housekeeper to one who declared that dust should be a table ornament. The list was long indeed.

It would certainly explain why she'd gone from that hated knot of hair and those drab clothes to being all soft and feminine and full of color. And she'd definitely changed from the cold, stiff woman of their wedding night.

He turned and caught sight of one of his shirts peeking out from beneath the bed where it must have fallen behind the headboard. He bent and snatched it up, shook it out, then tossed it over the rocker. The essence of Barrett, the scent that was hers alone, swirled around him like a fine mist, nearly bringing him to his knees with waves of memories and an ache to feel the touch of her hand again.

She'd changed so much. She wasn't the same person. He'd thought that so many times.

A tingle started in his spine and crept like a spider up the back of his neck.

She wasn't the same woman. Could it be true? Could she have wiped the past from her memory and not known Aidan was his twin? Could the stricken look on her face in the stables have been shock instead of guilt?

"Chase!" Adele Grant glanced upstairs before swinging the front door open wide. "It's high time you got here. Time to take your wife home."

"I came for answers first, Adele."

Chase had started having second thoughts on the train. Twice he'd nearly gotten off to catch the next train home. What if he got to Richmond and she'd taken up with Aidan? What if she laughed in his face and told him she'd never loved him?

So be it, he thought. He had to know. If it would end, it would end now, with no questions left to haunt him.

"Is she here?"

Adele ushered him into the small parlor littered with knickknacks and doilies.

"Before you see her, I have something I want you to read." She opened a drawer in the secretary and pulled out a packet addressed to him. "I was going to mail this today. You read these before you see her. She wrote it all down. What Aidan did to her. Asking for my help. And it's my fault she never told you, but that's in there, too."

His mother-in-law left the room then, leaving him alone with his questions and the package.

He untied the twine and peeled away the paper to reveal a stack of letters addressed to Adele in Elizabeth's handwriting. He looked around, uneasy at reading someone else's mail. Finally, he opened the first letter, dated the day after their wedding, and sat back to read.

By the time he had finished the last one, written only days before Adam's birth, he was pacing the floor with clenched fists, wanting to knock a hole in the wall.

He dropped the last page onto the pile of opened letters, then charged out of the house, ignoring Adele's startled call. He had to find Aidan.

*　　*　　*

Barrett woke from her nap, rolled over and tried to go back to sleep. The only peace she got was during sleep. The only time she wasn't miserable was during that dreamless oblivion.

But more sleep eluded her, and she knew she would pay for this nap by being awake into the wee hours of the night. She rose and wandered over to the windowseat that overlooked the front of the house. New green leaves sprouted from the bare branches on the trees. Her gaze fell on the opened letter on the seat, and she sighed. Carrie had written, sweet and concerned, and she'd ended by saying that she thought she was pregnant. Barrett blinked her burning eyes and turned her gaze outside, dragging her thoughts from a place she'd learned to call home.

Tulips and daffodils splashed color over the green canvas of the lawn. Three little girls jumped rope at the home across the street. A mother scurried after a tiny toddler just learning to walk, until a handsome man scooped the boy up and dangled him in the air, generating high-pitched squeals of delight from the tot.

Barrett sank down on the windowseat and let her head fall back against the wall. That could have been her and Chase and Adam. How she missed her little Adam! Her arms ached to hold him as much as they ached for his father. But it had been a month since Barrett last saw Chase. Every day she approached the mail with mixed emotions—praying that she would hear from him, praying it wouldn't be divorce papers. And every day she walked away with less hope than the day before. Today she didn't even bother to check, and that was when she realized she'd lost all hope.

Her fingers wrapped around the heart-shaped pendant as she stared into her soul.

It was time to go.

Blinking back burning tears, she lifted the filigreed heart on its chain, took a deep, sad breath, then flipped the locket open before she could change her mind.

Nothing happened.

Then the wall beside her bed shimmered in a kaleido-scope of colors and a doorway formed in the wall. Through the door she could see herself in 1997, still wearing the slinky turquoise nightgown, lying curled on her side, as if she'd just fallen asleep.

Odd, how foreign that body looked to her now. Al-most like looking at a stranger. She rose from the win-dowseat and walked over to the shimmering wall. If she walked through the door, she'd be home. Would she re-member Chase and Adam and Wes? Or would she wake up and go about her business, working and eating and avoiding her family?

She swallowed back more scalding tears and stepped to the door.

"Good-bye, Chase," she whispered.

The bedroom door flew open and banged against the wall.

"Barrett!"

Chase stood there, framed by the doorway, a trickle of blood tracing a crimson line from a cut on his cheek, tiny scarlet patches blooming like flowers on his dirty white shirt.

He'd never looked better.

And this man *was* Chase. She could never again mis-take Aidan for him.

She spun around to see if her route to the future had closed. The wall still shimmered, beckoning her to step through the door and go home.

Chase showed no sign of seeing the manifestation.

"I know the truth, Barrett," he said as he staggered to her. "I know what happened before the wedding."

She just stared at him.

"Wes told me you couldn't remember anything after Adam was born. You didn't know it was Aidan. I believe you didn't know I had a twin."

She swallowed, speechless, shaking her head.

"But you were wrong." He came one step nearer, took her hand, then guided her fingers to his lips and pressed a kiss on them. From the split in his lip, a dark-red drop of blood coated her fingers.

"I do bleed." His voice cracked with the words, and Barrett's soul reached out for his. "Since you left I've bled in a thousand different ways. I love you, Barrett. I'm sorry I doubted you, but I will never, ever doubt you again. Will you forgive me and come home?"

Barrett glanced back at the stranger on the bed. Her heart raced in her chest. She looked back at Chase and ached to caress his face. Instead, she held the locket in one hand and with the other she took his hand in hers.

In a voice not much more than a whisper, she asked, "Do you take this woman to be your lawfully wedded wife?"

His brow furrowed, then a relieved grin spread across his face.

"I do."

"Do you promise to honor and keep her, in sickness and in health, as long as she lives?"

"I do."

The shimmering wall slowly returned to normal. Barrett felt the locket fade to nothingness in her hand. She slid her hand up his chest and pressed her body to his, sending up a heartfelt thank-you to her guardian angel.

"Do you promise to love me for the rest of my life?" she whispered against his lips.

"No," he whispered back, holding her as though he would never let her go. "I promise to love you 'til the end of time."

Time Passages

_LOST YESTERDAY
Jenny Lykins   0-515-12013-8/$5.99
Marin Alexander has given up on romance. But when she awakens from a car accident 120 years before her time, she must get used to a different society and a new life—and the fact that she is falling in love...

_A DANCE THROUGH TIME
Lynn Kurland   0-515-11927-X/$5.99
A romance writer falls asleep in Gramercy Park, and wakes up in 14th century Scotland—in the arms of the man of her dreams...

_REMEMBER LOVE
Susan Plunkett   0-515-11980-6/$5.99
A bolt of lightning transports the soul of a scientist to 1866 Alaska, where she is married to a maddeningly arrogant and irresistibly seductive man...

_THIS TIME TOGETHER
Susan Leslie Liepitz   0-515-11981-4/$5.99
An entertainment lawyer dreams of a simpler life—and finds herself in an 1890s cabin, with a handsome mountain man...

_SILVER TOMORROWS
Susan Plunkett   0-515-12047-2/$5.99
Colorado, 1996. A wealthy socialite, Emily Fergeson never felt like she fit in. But when an earthquake thrust her back in time, she knew she'd landed right where she belonged...

_ECHOES OF TOMORROW
Jenny Lykins   0-515-12079-0/$5.99
A woman follows her true love 150 years into the past—and has to win his love all over again...

VISIT THE PUTNAM BERKLEY BOOKSTORE CAFÉ ON THE INTERNET:
http://www.berkley.com

Payable in U.S. funds. No cash accepted. Postage & handling: $1.75 for one book, 75¢ for each additional. Maximum postage $5.50. Prices, postage and handling charges may change without notice. Visa, Amex, MasterCard call 1-800-788-6262, ext. 1, or fax 1-201-933-2316; refer to ad # 680

Or, check above books	Bill my: ☐ Visa ☐ MasterCard ☐ Amex _____ (expires)
and send this order form to:	

The Berkley Publishing Group   Card#_____

P.O. Box 12289, Dept. B   Daytime Phone #_____ ($10 minimum)

Newark, NJ 07101-5289   Signature_____

Please allow 4-6 weeks for delivery.   **Or enclosed is my:** ☐ check ☐ money order

Foreign and Canadian delivery 8-12 weeks.

Ship to:

Name_____	Book Total	$_____
Address_____	Applicable Sales Tax	$_____
	(NY, NJ, PA, CA, GST Can.)	
City_____	Postage & Handling	$_____
State/ZIP_____	Total Amount Due	$_____

Bill to: Name_____

Address_____City_____

State/ZIP_____

ROMANCE FROM THE HEART OF AMERICA
Homespun Romance

__A CHERISHED REWARD   0-515-11897-4/$5.99
    by Rachelle Nelson
__TUMBLEWEED HEART   0-515-11944-X/$5.99
    by Tess Farraday
__TOWN SOCIAL   0-515-11971-7/$5.99
    by Trana Mae Simmons
__LADY'S CHOICE   0-515-11959-8/$5.99
    by Karen Lockwood
__HOME TO STAY   0-515-11986-5/$5.99
    by Linda Shertzer
__MEG'S GARDEN   0-515-12004-9/$5.99
    by Teresa Warfield
__COUNTY FAIR   0-515-12021-9/$5.99
    by Ginny Aiken
__HEARTBOUND   0-515-12034-0/$5.99
    by Rachelle Nelson
__COURTING KATE   0-515-12048-0/$5.99
    by Mary Lou Rich
__SPRING DREAMS   0-515-12068-5/$5.99
    by Lydia Browne
__TENNESSE WALTZ   0-515-12135-5/$5.99
    by Trana Mae Simmons
__FARM GIRL   0-515-12106-1/$5.99
    by Linda Shertzer
__SWEET CHARITY   0-515-12134-7/$5.99
    by Rachel Wilson
__BLACKBERRY WINTER   0-515-12146-0/$5.99
    by Sherrie Eddington (9/97)